Lo Fi

LIZ RIGGS

RIVERHEAD BOOKS

NEW YORK

2024

RIVERHEAD BOOKS
An imprint of Penguin Random House LLC
penguinrandomhouse.com

Library of Congress Cataloging-in-Publication Data

Names: Riggs, Liz, author.
Title: Lo fi / Liz Riggs.
Description: New York : Riverhead Books, 2024.
Identifiers: LCCN 2023034956 (print) | LCCN 2023034957 (ebook) | ISBN 9780593714577 (hardcover) | ISBN 9780593714591 (ebook)
Subjects: LCGFT: Novels. | Autobiographical fiction.
Classification: LCC PS3618.I3955 L64 2024 (print) | LCC PS3618.I3955 (ebook) | DDC 813/.6—dc23/eng/20231102
LC record available at https://lccn.loc.gov/2023034956
LC ebook record available at https://lccn.loc.gov/2023034957

Printed in the United States of America
1st Printing

Book design by Alexis Farabaugh

To all my favorite bands

I said, "A line will take us hours maybe;
Yet if it does not seem a moment's thought,
Our stitching and unstitching has been naught."

WILLIAM BUTLER YEATS, "ADAM'S CURSE"

Sometimes when sailors are sailing
They think twice about where they're anchoring
And I think I could make better use of my time on land.

THE FORMAT, "IF WORK PERMITS"

Lo Fi

Side One

1.

I stamp hands at The Venue, off Eighth. I like asking for people's wrists—the spot where the forearm fades into the joint, where the skin is always smooth, like the reed of a woodwind instrument before it's been used. Watch the ink sink in there: the familiar shape of a curled-up cat, ruddy red and orange—the color of rust.

I prefer the early part of the week, the open-mic nights on Mondays, the bright-eyed undergrads with long hair and surprisingly sharp vocals, the indie bands with too many members and sleepy refrains who look bored by their own beats, playing to a petered-out crowd on a drizzling Tuesday. No one talks about the kind of grit it takes to play to a mostly empty room, especially here in Nashville, the way the sound reverberates off the corners of the space like it weighs something. I tried it—once. Onstage, playing my own songs. Don't ask.

But even the bad people who play here are good, making the kind of music you hold your breath to, where you don't even realize you aren't breathing until the song ends and you're suddenly coming up for air.

The rain won't relent tonight. It falls on the sidewalk in waves, muffling all other sound: heels on concrete, cab doors slamming shut, voices of early arrivers huddling under the overhang outside the doors. A rhythmic, frenzied torrent.

It's a Saturday in May and I'm working the door with Julien, the skinny guy who's always sitting somewhere reading. Julien has worked here since before I started. His black hair, normally straight, is slightly wavy from the weather. Black jeans and a dark gray T-shirt with just one sleeve rolled up, as if the other had come undone while we were prepping the doors. His red Chucks squeak on the linoleum. Tonight he's quiet, drinking tap water out of a plastic cup, thumbing through the *Nashville Scene,* which is mostly ads for dry-cleaning places and two-for-one bar specials. He carries the same ratty messenger bag every night, as though we're the kind of workplace that requires work *things*—a computer or notebooks or files. Tonight there's a book sticking out of it, one I've never heard of.

—If I wanted to work in silence, I tell him, I would have become a writer.

—Didn't you study poetry? So, technically speaking, aren't you? he asks, glancing up, long hair in his eyes. A writer, I mean.

A slight chill pricks at the base of my neck.

—Or a librarian, I say.

His eyes fall on me and then back to the page, his irises the color of leaves lingering between summer and fall. He flips a page in the magazine, shifts the stool between his legs. When did I tell him I studied poetry? It's a fact I mostly don't bring up, because it's as useless in conversation as the degree itself—especially when I'm doing absolutely nothing with it.

Outside, the night is black and wet. Hazy, hell-colored brake lights blur in the parking lot; a cluster of guys in pastel polos stub out cigarettes on the patio railing. Upstairs, a last-minute sound check, the lead singer trying to get his guitar in tune for a Barenaked Ladies cover.

Doors are opening soon. A local nineties cover band, the kind that sells out every single time, because people are suckers for nostalgia, for the VH1 days, for getting drunk with a purpose on an otherwise dreary night. The faces tonight will be familiar—some of them, at least—even though Julien says this band brings out the kind of people who don't normally go to shows. We'll still see the usuals too—leather jackets and fresh tattoos, sometimes still freshly cling-wrapped. I've only been working here a few months, but I'm getting better at guessing: which arms will be inked with Bible verses, ex-girlfriends' names, which will sport expensive custom line work. Blurs of people wait for us to open the door: drummers in pearl button-downs, guitarists with fingers scarred from years of breaking and changing strings, men with long, wiry beards so thick they could house entire melodies. People who are already fucked up, people who are alone, people who are meeting someone, waiting on someone, trying to forget someone.

—You never showed me the song you wrote, Julien says now.

It comes to me briefly, the two of us on his porch on Music Row the week before, one of the few times I've hung out with him after a show. Muted golden starlight, like looking through a screen. A chill in the spring air—too cold, really, one of those nights where you try to bend the weather to your will but you can't. I'd never seen Julien's basement apartment, or the porch up above, scattered with ashtrays and guitar picks and a rocking chair as large as a medieval throne, probably left behind by a previous owner who couldn't be bothered to move it. It was late and I'd had a few, and in my haze I had the nerve to mention a song I'd written in college, back when I was actually coming up with melodies instead of just lyrics. We sat on the porch and climbed into the chair and he played a few chords and we had a few beers, but then his friend Colin showed up and told us a long and offensive story about a date he'd just been on, and the mood or the vibe or the moment—if there'd even been one—dissolved like a bit of dust.

—What song? I say, and ask him for a cigarette.

He shakes his head. It's after nine—we're late. The clock in the corner quietly ticks, keeping the rhythm like I can't.

I'm wary of people who show up at the club right on time. Usually it's because they don't go to many shows, or maybe someone told them a Very Precise Set Time, which leaves them standing outside, tapping their feet, looking at their phones and waiting. Or perhaps they're somebody's parents, the idea of which always sends a small pang across my chest—not because I so rarely talk to mine, but because if I were performing my poems to a sparse crowd of bored strangers (can they be called songs if you don't have any melodies?), my parents are the last people on earth I'd want to see in the crowd. The early arrivers don't know that our schedules are never tight, even on nights when Andy, the owner, swears they will be. Even when the weather is perfect, when cabs aren't stalled and restless outside.

Julien opens the door and the boys outside shake off the rain like dogs. When somebody asks for a coat check, Julien laughs and then tries to rearrange his face into something more polite, into his usual straight lips and unreadable eyes, eyelashes black black black. He says no, his voice familiar in a way I still can't place, some uncanny valley of friendship, though we barely qualify as friends.

Flushed cheeks, a stack of tickets damp from the rain, so wet the paper is like cotton. I take their palms, the cold dew on the skin of their wrists, and stamp each one with a rusty cat. Veins, scars, regrettable ink, bequeathed jewelry and young skin, wristbands from other venues, creases where their wrists meet their palms. I hear every type of voice, some saying hello, some talking on a cell phone or into a Bluetooth, others talking among themselves.

Girls in cowboy boots come spilling out of cabs. An assistant at CAA, an intern at Vector—the kind of industry people who are at every show. House music seeping down from upstairs, rain on concrete, on steel, on rubber, on concrete again. A news alert hums through someone's phone: a flash flood warning. Julien's reviewing the guest list, written on a bookmark from a bookstore I haven't heard of. Outside, a line forms beneath our sign. Flickering into the black night, the red lights of The Venue: a bit of Nashville history, I've learned. Jane's Addiction and Katy Perry and Leonard Cohen, just to name a few former headliners. Independently owned since the eighties, capacity around three hundred. Tonight we'll max it out.

I see his birthday on his ID before I see his face. Leap Day, 1984. It's not that he's the only man ever born on February 29, but that tiny face beneath my thumb—tan, no smile—

My arms stretch out from my body like they belong to someone else, shoving him back into the line while my cheeks flame hot. Nick. Long hair, slick from the rain, a shadow of scruff. A T-shirt, perfectly wrinkled. For a second so brief I can barely even pause inside it, I think he's here to surprise me, to visit—but then I'm back with my feet on the ground, a stamp in my hand that I wish was a drink, and I realize that his appearance here is an accident. His stupid grin, open with whiskey; I can smell the Jameson on him more than the rain. Gray eyes like a winter day; they shouldn't even be pretty, but that stupid fucking ring of blue around the outer edge. Like someone has circled his iris in cerulean crayon.

—Holy shit, he says. Alison Hunter. What the hell are you doing here?

—Don't call me that, I say. Nobody calls me that.

Julien glances over at the two of us and mouths *Al-i-son* to me.

But already Nick's reaching to pull me into him, the space between us closing, quieting: a vacuum of sound. His hands are at my cheeks now, like he's here on purpose. Cool and damp, his left fingertips rough, callused.

—Seriously? I *live* here. Which I'm pretty sure you know. What are *you* doing here?

His hands are still at my cheeks, his gray eyes on mine. He leans in like he's going to kiss me with his Jameson breath. Instead, he says quietly into my ear:

—I promise I was going to text you.

—I thought you were on tour.

My arms are crossed, but the muscles are loosening, heat already spreading out across my chest, up between my legs. Over Nick's shoulder, Julien's eyes meet mine for a second, a question in the corner of his gaze and then—back to the line.

—I am, Nick says.

A freckle on his upper lip, a memory of a rainy night in Ann Arbor, cheap beer and cheaper weed, the dim light of a Michigan alley. Nick's hands in mine, his music still shimmering on the soundtrack of the memory. He steps back and tries to explain: he's just in town for the day, his band had a song they needed to record. Nick—in my city, wandering around just miles away, without me even knowing it. I don't recognize any of the guys he comes in with, but that's probably because Nick and I have never existed in a realm where we shared friends, where I've known anyone else in his life beyond the two other guys in his band.

—I'm here, he says softly, directly into my ear. His breath hot, his lips grazing the ring of cartilage. He's a little drunk, my favorite version of Nick.

—You're full of shit, I say.

—I'm in your city, he says now.

Behind him, the line is antsy. Expectant eyes and wet hair and hands on hips. I try to will myself out of his touch and take the stamp to his wrist.

—Don't be mad, he says, and I look past him over to Julien, who's waiting for an older couple to unfold their printed tickets. He's not paying attention anymore.

—I'm here, Nick says again into my ear.

The timbre of his voice, rich and familiar and melodic, is already edging its way into my memory. I'm always filing Nick away somewhere into the past, where, for nearly a full year now, he has existed.

If I don't hear Mr. Jones tonight, I'm gonna lose it. Just a vodka tonic. Oh whatever, sure, make it a double. Colt, where are all the goddamn polishing rags? Someone threw up on the balcony. On it, not over it. I think that guy's doing lights on the Animal Collective tour. No, they got dropped. You want a bump? Don't text him back. Don't do it. Where's the A2 guy? Can you hold my drink? There isn't a nice way to say this so I'm just going to say it. I sat next to him on a flight back from LA. They gave us a buyout. He knows I live here. Do you know how much money those Christian singers make? It's criminal. I'm talking about Crush, not Crash. He has an actual perfect penis. Everybody's "in town recording." Yeah, of course they're in a band.

I wasn't supposed to meet him, really. I wasn't even supposed to be there that night at the pool bar below the Blind Pig in Ann Arbor. It wasn't really an undergrad spot, but I was looking for a place where I wouldn't run into anyone. Where the news that my parents weren't coming back to the states for Christmas could be quietly drowned in tasteless beer. Where I could be depressed and alone. That night Wilco was playing overhead, and Nick sat down next to me. The hair alone told me he wasn't a student. The voice that sounded like slipping under sheets, like the moment before you come. He asked me if I was going to the show at the Blind Pig and I said no. When I asked him who was playing tonight, I knew the answer before he responded.

—I am, he said.

2.

Who was that? Julien asks, pouring me a Yuengling into a nondescript paper cup.

The bottle is the color of his eyes, which give away nothing. He asks the question like he's asking if I want to order pizza—we pick up food around this time most nights. The lag: most of the early crowd has arrived, but the band isn't on yet. It's still raining.

—He didn't even tell me he was in town, I say, mostly to myself.

People are arriving in the parking lot, oblivious and wet. Upstairs, voices shit-talking, shouting, ordering drinks, getting phone numbers, asking when the set starts, opening tabs. Sonic dissonance slightly muffled by the rain. For a moment I want to explain Nick to Julien, but something stops me. Julien's looking back at a copy of the local weekly. A song of Nick's hums in the back corner of my head, clashing with the opening notes to a Replacements deep cut over the house music.

—Not cool, Julien says, but I can't tell if it's a delayed response to Nick or if he's scolding a girl who's just tossed her umbrella into the parking lot.

The waves of rain swallow all the sound for a moment as we await the late, the already drunk, the question marks, the cool kids.

—Psalms or Sailor Jerry? I ask, nodding to a group of guys approaching from the parking lot. I'll buy you a highball if you guess first.

The guys are drenched, they split instinctively, the first two to me, the latter three to Julien. *Bible verse*, I mouth to him.

Jacket sleeves up on the first, I press the stamp in. Philippians 4:6–8, inked onto the inner wrist. A passage I had to memorize as a kid. I try not to laugh—it was too easy. When the guys are out of sight, I glance over to Julien:

—Philippians, not Psalms. Does that still count?

—How do I know you're not lying?

—Lying about Bible verses is pretty messed up. Cutthroat, even.

Julien laughs, shakes his head. The faintest blush of peach appears by his temples, maybe, or maybe I'm just having a bit of synesthesia, assigning colors to the slivers of our friendship. He looks back down at the magazine. A new song comes on, one that was number one for a million weeks when I was thirteen, a melody that's impossible to forget.

It's close to ten when the cool kids start filtering in. My aunt Izzy is one of them, cooler at forty than I am at twenty-three. She comes through the door shimmery, happy, dressed like Stevie Nicks in a long black velvet dress, a short man on one arm, a beautiful woman her age on the other. The woman looks like Izzy in that way that friends and couples do, when you can tell that certain people are together based on their style, their age. Their hair is the same dishwater blond, their chins small, pointed, slightly lifted. Their eyes warm.

—Anthony, Clem, meet my niece.

Clem drops Izzy's arm to hug me. The three of them are perfectly dry, as though someone has ushered them in under an umbrella. Izzy hugs me: steak, expensive liquor.

—Look at you, hard at work, she says as I stamp her hand.

She says it earnestly, like she's legitimately proud of this *barelyajob*

job. She smears the ink on her left wrist with her thumb, presses a finger to my nose. Her finger is cold but my body warms.

—You look beautiful, Izzy says. You'll come see me tomorrow? I have to be on set for a shoot in the morning, but come by in the afternoon.

Before I can even nod or introduce her to Julien, she floats up the stairs with Anthony and Clem like an apparition.

A text from Nick: What time do u get off?

It's like this with us. Him living in my pocket, but not in my life. I start to respond, but when I glance up, my roommate, Sloane, is in the doorway, tipsy and gorgeous, bitching about the rain.

—Oh my *lord*, nobody knows how to drive in this city. I was like: I am not about to die driving past a discount liquor store because some guy from Murfreesboro doesn't know how to steer through a *puddle*. That was absurd. Drivers here would never make it in—

—You're here, I say, reaching out to squeeze her hand. We do not hug—we're around each other too much for that. She waves away my outstretched hand.

—Barely, she says. That guy almost *killed* me. Like, there should be a phone number I can call. It's supposed to be a *black car service*, not some sketchy airport cab company.

—You need a drink, I say.

—What a mess, Sloane says. Do you need my ID? Here here, even if you don't. I just got a new pic anyway, let's test it out.

I take her ID, turn it over in my hand. Of course the photo is gorgeous. It's Sloane. She's lightly tanned, her left eye hazel and her right a piercing blue, so that you're constantly glancing back and forth, taking in their beautiful discrepancy. Everyone is always commenting on Sloane's chimeric eyes and her cheekbones, the beautiful razor's edge of her jawline. She doesn't need a ticket because she works at the radio station in town, so she's on the list for everything.

—I have our mix too, she says, holding a loose CD out to me. Please take this off my hands.

—You actually burned it?

She's grinning but rolling her eyes at the same time.

—Like it was 2004, baby. But this is the last one I burn. You are the only person in the world who still has a CD player.

I laugh and twirl the CD around my index finger.

I wonder if Julien's noticing her insanely symmetrical face, her eyes, that bone structure, those flushed cheeks. Barely any makeup, her hair dark and straight, framing her face in a bob. I have the urge to tell her about Nick showing up, but behind her a line has started to form again, people squinting through the rain, tapping their feet.

—Do you have to let these children in? she asks, widening her eyes and nodding to the crowd behind her, a trio of girls looking like they're at their Very First Nashville Show. Cowboy boots and styled curls, everything ruined by the rain.

—I'll meet you up there in a bit, I say. Go get drunk.

She scurries up the stairs.

More rain, more faces. A few minutes after Sloane, in comes a girl I don't recognize: jet-black hair, in a tight leather miniskirt and black boots, a vintage T-shirt, gold hoops. Red lips, her hair curly: wild and thick and endless, the kind that would defy any attempt to straighten. She reapplies her lipstick, lets the line pass her by as she shakes off the rain. Instinctively, I touch my finger to my lips.

Julien's nodding in conversation with one of the sound guys and the girl approaches and hugs them. The boys' faces lighten at the sight of her, lips quickly settling into smiles. She does looks familiar, I realize now—from some after-party, most likely, or other shows around town. Could be an A&R assistant, an intern, maybe just a barfly. Julien crosses her name off his list and smiles, teeth and all.

The girl runs a hand through her hair and laughs—far too loud—at something he says, then loosens a curl caught in her earring and heads upstairs. I can see the hair follicles on her pale calves, the outline of tight muscle as she walks up the stairs.

Two drunk scenesters—ripped jeans and greasy hair—approach; I stamp their hands. After they leave:

—Was she on the list? I ask.

Julien glances over. He briefly holds his cup between his teeth as he flips through the local weekly.

—Yeah, I added her late.

—What's her name? I ask, scanning the list.

—You've never met?

—Would I be asking if we had?

Julien raises his eyebrows at me.

—Jess, he says.

—She's hot, I say.

He shoots me an unreadable look: lips set straight, like he's tempted to smile but won't.

—With a *k*, he says.

—What?

—Jessika with a *k*.

I want to roll my eyes but don't.

—Are you in love?

Julien laughs quietly then—no teeth—and says:

—You're absurd.

Before the band goes on, the house music plays LCD Soundsystem, Miike Snow. Without the headliner on yet, people are antsy, the collective level of drunk teetering over a delicate edge. My eyes scan the room for Nick and I run a hand through my hair. My whole body is buzzing. I want one of Colt's benzos.

Like he is every Saturday, Colt's behind the bar, short blond hair—he should let it go longer—and a white bar rag over his shoulder. He's wiry, like a disheveled professional rock climber. So pretty, so fun to look at—even with Nick somewhere in the room. But with Colt there's no real intrigue; it's all right there on the surface, even if the surface is pretty good. Getting to him is the tricky part now, all the elbows and ponytails and shoulders between me and the bar, my free-ish drink. He catches my eye with his—steely blue—always looking like he wants to fuck while I try to decide how much I want to indulge the fantasy, how free I want my extra drinks to be.

The crowd is dense and drunk already and I snake through it. Strangers' sweat collects on my elbows, forearms, hip bones, my T-shirt riding up. Cigarettes and store-brand deodorant, astringent perfume, coconut shampoo—then at last: whiskey. I reach for the bar like it's a lifeboat.

—Christ, they're vultures, Colt says, pressing his palms against the lip of the bar, leaning toward me. But not you. What do you want?

I hold up my beer. He wipes a bit of sweat off his face with his forearm, sinewy and damp with rain. His flannel is open, a vintage Doors shirt hanging loose from his frame underneath.

—That's it? They can wait, he says, looking down at the dozens of people waiting along the thirty-foot bar that stretches toward the stage. Jessika is at the opposite end, tapping her credit card on the bar to get someone's attention. She's tall, or maybe she's just got great posture and high heels. Either way she stands out, even from the opposite end of the bar.

I feel somebody pressing up against me, and I use my elbow to shove them off. Colt turns around, reaching up for a bottle of Four Roses. Around his waist a serpent tattoo curls as he turns back around and pours two shots, passing one to me. We take them and my throat catches fire.

—Do you have any—

A barback I don't recognize—he must be filling in for our usual guy—whispers something into Colt's ear, and he turns away. I reach behind the bar and grab a beer. Jessika catches my eye from down the bar and flashes me a friendly smile, impressed. A girl next to me stares. I look at her like *What?* and push my way back out of the crowd. Onstage, the opening band's guitarist is thumbing through a major scale.

Nick is at the mirror in the men's room when I walk in. I bypassed the line next door. My beer is flat. I swallow half of it as he looks up from the sink, wiping his hands on a paper towel. Gray eyes looking me over, a song of his in my head. *I put your bag up on a shelf that I can't reach / I can't reach you anymore.* The confidence I had when I walked in is disappearing quickly. I take a breath, try to shore it up.

—Man, Al, you didn't have to follow me into the bathroom.

He smiles, tosses the paper towel in the trash.

—You didn't have to follow me to my city, I say, sliding past him.

I say this like that isn't exactly what I've wanted him to do for the past year, like I haven't imagined him here dozens of times, checked his tour dates, drafted and deleted who knows how many emails and texts to that effect.

I let myself into a stall and sit down. The back of the door is peppered with promos: a Matt Pond PA show coming up in July, a study on gut health that needs volunteers at Vanderbilt, a new two-for-one beer night at the Beer Sellar downtown. Oh, and an old ad for an open mic last month. *The* open mic, the one I need to forget. I peel that one down and stand back up. I can't pee while Nick's out there listening.

—You're not really gonna stay mad, are you? I'm here now, he says. We're in the same place. Can't we just hang out?

I open the door and step out of the stall. The lights are way too bright. I should talk to Andy about putting in something less garish.

—You didn't come here to hang out with me, I say.

—That's not true. Listen, we were supposed to go straight to Cincinnati from Atlanta, but Timmy got a last-minute session with a producer in town we've been trying to book time with, so we stopped last-minute. I've only been here for, like, six hours.

—We've been talking about you coming here for almost a year. Like you didn't know I worked here?

—Okay, yeah, that's on me.

—No shit.

He reaches an arm out for me now, his fingers slightly tugging at one of my belt loops. My feet are planted but weak; I'm a loose seed ready to be pulled. A snare drum in the main space taps out eighth notes—the band is out. A discordant series of cheers, distorted bass.

—At least come out with us after.

The door opens, a guy walks in. Nick's hand slackens from my belt loop. The guy grabs a paper towel and leaves.

—I'm not crashing the band's night.

—I'm not with the band, he says. I'm with Garret and Matt.

—You just said you were with Timmy.

—He's still at the studio.

—I don't know who Garret and Matt are.

—Really? Garret plays with—

—I don't care who Garret plays with. And I'm not going to watch you guys do karaoke in Printers Alley.

Now he smiles. Like someone's taking a photograph, like if he just keeps smiling I'll forgive him. The problem is that I will, I already have, I will again.

—So take us somewhere better.

I like bad music.

I know enough about music theory to be dangerous, to recognize what makes a melody work or how to transpose a song from C to Am or why a perfect fourth sounds, well, perfect. But at the end of the day, I listen to the same old shit. Check my playlists, the records I wear down, all the pop singers and the one-hit wonders and the bubblegum sounds I can't seem to shake. So on nights like tonight, when the whole purpose is to play music that was never all that great to begin with? Well, I'm just charmed by it all.

Once the band is on, though, you have to resist the urge to seem too into it. It's a prerequisite for going to hear live music in Nashville: a little bit of you has to believe you could be doing anything the people onstage are doing, and doing it a little bit better.

—How do you and Jess-with-a-*k* know each other? I ask Julien down at the door.

I'm waiting to get cut for the night; I honestly can't believe I'm still working.

—She manages Denim, he says. My friend Johnny's band.

The name produces an immediate palpitation in my throat: Denim's keyboardist was at the open mic—the one Sloane talked me into doing, the one I keep trying to forget.

—Do you know them? Julien asks.

Everybody in town knows Denim right now, I say, pulling my mind out of my memory.

—So she's, like, a friend-ager or a real manager? I ask.

—Real one. She works for Red Light.

I wonder how she got a job at an actual management company at her age, how she's already managing a band that's opening for Fleet Foxes and Feist.

—Is she older than us? I ask. With that job, I'm surprised—

—I think we're the same age, he says. Me and Jess.

—Wait, how old are you? I ask.

He glances at me, a look like *I've told you this before.*

—Twenty-five, Julien says.

It's just a couple of years, but for a moment, still, I feel like a child.

—Are you two dating? I ask.

I haven't worked here very long, but I know that Julien doesn't usually "add people late" to the list. He's strict about it. A pain in the ass, really. He looks over at me and lets the question hang there for a moment. He shrugs.

—We've gone on dates, yes, Julien says, and the door swings open: a rush of pounding rain and pretty faces and damp skin and the smell of smoke and burnt rubber.

I stop working before Julien officially tells me I can. I haven't eaten, but I'm not hungry. I just want a drink, want to slip away into the night.

Eddie, the annoying new Belmont student we're supposed to be training, keeps pestering me about his upcoming jazz gig. He pulls up a video of last week's show, tries to shove it in my face while I'm waiting for my drink.

—I think Julien needs help at the door, I say, turning away.

Nick, then, on my other side.

—What do you want? he says into my ear.

—You really don't need to buy me anything. I get—

—Jameson?

I should stay sober, stay mad, but I'm losing time with him, minutes and hours already slipping away into the rainy night. Our time has always been like this: an hour or two before a show or after, a sliver of an afternoon once he's finished with sound check. I can't waste any more of it.

—Four Roses, I say.

We weren't supposed to keep up with each other after his Ann Arbor residency. He wasn't supposed to get signed to Rough Trade, then Sub Pop. I was supposed to settle into my new city, to move on. I was definitely not supposed to fall—

The band is on, and everyone knows every song. Counting Crows and Third Eye Blind and *Is this Spin Doctors or Lit or Deep Blue Something?* Nick, singing into my face, his breath rye whiskey and ash. Is it too soon to ask about the other girl in his life? To shout her name above the music? When I start to, because I am a masochist, he just shakes his head, points at his ears. He's got earplugs in, and he wouldn't be able to hear me even if he didn't.

The drums are simple but pounding, the energy of the front man is electric, his voice howling but familiar, the kind of timbre that can slip in and out of any imitation—in other words, perfect for a cover band. The crowd: swimmy, sweaty, everyone singing along, because everyone's been listening to these songs since middle school, first on the radio in somebody else's car and now in the white-noise background of pharmacies and supermarkets, and it's a relief to hear them repurposed like this, as they were intended: for hordes of twentysomethings to shriek along to.

Even drunk, I can't help but think about how our brains are wired to connect more deeply with the music of our youth, how a song you love fires off dopamine in your brain and hormones like you're taking a drug—science, really, all that nostalgia for the bands we loved when we were seventeen.

For me it's the songs from when I was twenty-one, only a couple of years ago—so many that remind me of Nick that I've stopped keeping track, stopped making mixes and jotting down lyrics, because it doesn't really matter anymore. Even though every time I think of him, every time I see him, I want to ask: Aren't there any songs that remind you of me?

Songs that remind me of Nick, in no particular order:

"Heavy Metal Drummer" (Wilco)
"Knocked Up" (Kings of Leon)
"All I Need" (Radiohead)
"Tugboat" (Galaxie 500)
"Disarm" (Smashing Pumpkins)
"Ziggy Stardust" (Bowie)
"Little Red Corvette" (Prince)

And one more Wilco, for posterity: "Jesus, Etc."

When the show ends, the rain hasn't stopped. Headlights shining from the cabs at the curb, chaos as drunk people splash to their rides. Julien takes off his red Chucks and puts on galoshes. He's talking to Jessika beneath her umbrella, but he stops to ask me if I'm okay to drive. I tell him I'm not driving. Damp cotton socks, wet cement, wet leather, wet vinyl—

I drag Nick away from his friends and pull him into a cab, a tug on his jacket instead of his hand. The rain soaks us on the short sprint to the car, drenching my hair, my eyelashes, the back of my shirt. He reaches over and squeezes my thigh, asks how I am, a gesture right on the line of friendly and flirtatious. Though *line* is hardly the word, because the line is more like air between us—invisible but necessary, fluid but functional.

He pulls out his earplugs and says:

—Tell me about your new life. Is this what you do every night?

—More or less, I say, waving around the humid back of the cab, the squatty buildings of the Gulch obscured in the rain behind us. Nick looks around the back seat, as though this is where I live, as though this cab is my home.

He rubs at the foggy windows with his sleeve and leans back, tapping his long fingernails against the vinyl to a song I don't recognize. With that expression on his face he looks drugged, which after two beers and three shots I suppose he is.

Out the window, a brewery under construction on Eighth; Bondi Blue neon, lighting up the hat store. I give the cabbie directions to a dive bar over on Twenty-First, ask Nick if he's fine to smell like cigarette smoke in the morning. He says he already does—he can't believe you can still smoke in bars here. On the way there, just ahead of us by the music school, a Toyota hydroplanes in the standing water, then skids to a stop, barely saving itself.

—How's Allison? I ask, still dumbfounded that he's been seeing someone in Chicago who has my name.

—Can you turn it up? Nick asks the driver as the song changes. I can't tell if he heard me, but I can't bring myself to repeat the question.

3.

In the morning, the city has flooded but my lips are dry. The sun is buried behind shelves of gray, the clouds a shadow over the city. Down on Tenth, cars run the stop sign by the corner store; a neighbor next door is playing a kick drum. It's still raining. Water rushing down the curbs in an endless stream, cars spraying fountains onto the sidewalks as they drive over toward Twelfth. Sloane's dog, Lou Reed, refuses to walk for days. Nick is gone.

I pee, brush my teeth, masturbate in the shower. I think of him, and even though it's been less than twenty-four hours, he still appears in my head like a carbon copy—like I'm remembering a version of him from years ago, rather than the version I've just seen. My joint smolders as I smoke in front of the mirror, clouding myself out. My clit is like a fist, still pulsing. I reach between my legs—I'm still wet there—and take another hit.

Midday at The Venue, later that week. Light cracks through the windows alongside the stage. The bridge of one of Nick's songs is stuck in my head. I haven't heard from him since the weekend of the flood. Five days. Anytime we've come too close he tries to put space between us, as if five hundred miles up I-65 isn't enough.

From the back room at The Venue—all pool tables and black

booths—you can still see the flooding and the remnants of the storm downtown. Swaths of First Street have been submerged and the Cumberland is slowly receding, a mass of brown brackish water stretching over to Germantown. Thirteen inches of rain in thirty-six hours. A small tornado apparently touched down just outside town. The whole ground floor of the Grand Ole Opry was briefly underwater. The roof of a studio over on the east side blown off—a handful of musicians scrambling inside while rain pounded down, trying to save their master recordings. A whole pile of instruments destroyed at Soundcheck, where every musician has stored their gear at some point. And like the assholes that we are, Sloane and I spent most of the past week in the pool at her friend Abby's place, in the beautiful clear days after the storm.

It's odd, being at The Venue in daylight. We usually close only one night a week. Mondays, sometimes. More often Sundays. The posters stuck to the beams and the office door are garish, mottled with weathered pieces of paper, splitting strips of tape, and rogue band stickers melted into the wood. The Shins, Local Natives, Justin Wilson, the Wild Loose. Even though half of the posters advertise shows from months ago, I've never felt the need to take them down until Andy says something, until there's no space for a show that's actually coming up. The Justin Wilson one is a custom screen print, and it seems redundant, having it both on the door downstairs and on a beam upstairs. I carefully remove it, peeling back the tape so I can leave the corners intact. I've always liked trying to preserve things that were never meant to be permanent anyway.

I run my fingertips along the bar, as though I'm expecting dust. As though this place has ever sat empty more than forty-eight hours. I flick on the overhead fans and fingers of light stretch over from the windows on the opposite wall. The space was first an old flour mill, a million years ago, and eventually a cannery; now it's a shell of exposed brick and wood beams, restored but still rustic. Sometimes I swear the venues in this town are the only places people seem to care about preserving.

Andy's guitar is one of those three-quarter-size ones usually marketed to kids and teenagers learning chords for the first time. I can't even look at my own guitar at home now. It's been nearly a month since the Incident, as Sloane and I have taken to calling it, but the memory is like an earworm, a song you're trying desperately to forget. It's a distracting daymare anytime I pick up the guitar, anytime someone mentions a songwriter's round or an open mic. Sloane keeps telling me it wasn't so bad, but she wasn't the one up there, the one *trying* to play. She doesn't know.

What comes to my hands first is the little run of chords from "Norwegian Wood." I've always liked the sound of that simple opening E, checking the tuning of the instrument with the reverberation of the bass E string. Someone's been playing it in drop D, though, and I tune it back to standard by ear.

Jesus, Sloane said that night. *It wasn't even that bad! I mean, like, are you really the only person to knock over a mic? Have you ever seen Steven Tyler perform? Dude can't even remember the words to "Crazy," and I'm pretty sure everyone under the age of fifty knows them.* As if knocking over a mic was the only thing that went wrong that night.

Andy's left a couple of joints in the center drawer of his desk. I crack the window and take a few hits. Damp spring air rushes in. I do have pages and pages of lyrics—verses I wrote about Nick after he left, couplets I can't stop thinking about, bits of alliteration that belong with a tune. But for months—closer to a year, really—I haven't been able to come up with any kind of melody that sticks.

The weed is mellow, my head pleasantly swimmy as I try to match a melody with the chords, stringing the couplets about Nick back-to-back. But the tune gets lost, my voice gets tired. I try a different chord progression, struggling to chase the tune down, but the notes disperse until I'm just losing it, losing it, losing it.

~~*You keep saying to play it / I remind you I hate it*~~

A door creaks, then quiet. I sit up, my spine tense, and the moment is gone. I slide the guitar back into its case, set it on the couch next to me. The last latch has barely snapped shut when the door to the office opens and Julien appears in the doorway.

Standing there he seems awkwardly far away, as though he's waiting at the threshold of my bedroom. Dark jeans, a faint white line where the fabric has faded in the outline of his shitty old Nokia phone. A carabiner of keys hangs from his belt loop and he flicks it open and shut with his thumb. His T-shirt is thin, a drab weathered yellow that looks like he's either had it since childhood or got it at Goodwill last week.

—Were you playing? he asks, stepping out of the doorway, amber light rushing in behind him. He looks at me so intently that I instinctively put my hand to my lips, worried I have something on my mouth.

—No, I say.

—It kind of looks like you were playing.

—Barely, I say.

—Do you play out ever?

—No, I say. Definitely not.

He nods, his eyes still focused. My face is very warm.

—Stop looking at me like that, I say.

His head cocks just slightly to the side.

—Like what? That's just the way I look.

A door opens somewhere downstairs, the sound of hinges swinging, air coming in. A voice yells up from the atrium, a girl calling Julien's name. He glances at the time on his phone and then over his shoulder.

—It's nice when it's quiet, he says, finally looking back at me.

—It's weird, I say.

Melodies I thought I came up with but realized later they were somebody else's songs:

"The Wind" (Cat Stevens)
"Nothing Else Matters" (Metallica)
"I Will Play My Game Beneath the Spin Light" (Brand New)
"I've Just Seen a Face" (the Beatles)
"Sugarcane" (Michael Ford, Jr. & the Apache Relay)
"Since U Been Gone" (Kelly Clarkson)
"Broadripple Is Burning" (Margot & the Nuclear So and So's)
"Close to You" (the Carpenters)
"Money Making Nashville" (Evan P. Donohue)
"Just Stay" (Kevin Devine)
"Brakeman" (Nathaniel Rateliff)
"Timshel" (Mumford & Sons)

Some days, it's hard to believe I haven't always lived here. My family moved a lot when I was a kid, mostly across mediocre Midwestern suburbs while my parents planted churches—Kansas City and Cincinnati and then back to Michigan, where I was born. Then, as soon as I was off to college, my parents moved to South Korea. Missionaries, though I tell everyone they're in foreign aid. Sometimes, when I'm not thinking of them but know I'm supposed to be, I feel guilty about how freeing it was to not have them around. There were times where I pretended they were no longer with us. Not dead, exactly—just *gone.*

I have no ties to the Midwest now, and when I graduated from

Michigan, sad and aimless, Aunt Izzy told me to come visit Nashville over Christmas. I'd been living in Ann Arbor and working at the Blind Pig, but mostly I was getting drunk, five or six nights a week, and Izzy had just moved back from LA, to a spot outside Nashville. So I went. Izzy is a stylist in the music industry and she said she could find me some work, plus let me crash with her for a few months until I found my own spot. She thought I'd like the town—it's creative and young and "up and coming"—but mostly I liked the boys.

The baristas who always had a day's worth of scruff and Saturday nights free, the skinny guys in leather jackets drinking two-for-one beers at the dive bar down the street, the songwriters with vintage instruments who weren't famous themselves but wrote songs for people who were, the drummers with sleepy eyes and callused palms, the guitarists with front-man energy and long fingers, the lead singers with full lips and perfect voices and charm in overdrive. Even the law students drinking at the bars on Division and staying until last call with their flavored vodka and low-calorie beers, the bartenders who actually played the drums, played the drums for a friend, played the cello, played the piano, played the fiddle, played the session fiddle, played the harp, played the upright bass, played the banjo, played pedal steel. I loved them all.

None of them had real jobs, but they all had good hair.

I don't know what I was expecting, back in January, when I came in to interview for the job. I'd never really had a proper job interview in my life, babysitting my way through high school and college. Back in Ann Arbor, the guys who'd hired me at the Blind Pig were just desperate. Anybody would have gotten the job.

It was freezing the afternoon I went to interview at The Venue. Was I supposed to dress up? Dress *down*? I remember texting Nick, but he was in the middle of a radio interview somewhere in Boston, and even if he'd responded, how would he have known? Like a lot of people I knew, he'd never had a real job in his life. I did enough googling to find out that Andy was the owner and the talent buyer, meaning he had his hands on every band that stepped onstage here. Izzy said to dress *somewhere in the middle.* What she meant: *Be cool.* I landed on a fake leather jacket, with black jeans faded into a feathery dark gray.

—Tell me why you're interested in this role, Andy had said. Sitting at the bar, a club soda in his hand, my hands enormous and empty.

This *role*. How fancy that sounded.

—Well, I've always loved music, I said. I minored in, uh, popular music studies, so, you know, I've had this interest. I majored in, well, never mind. But yeah.

As if my degrees meant anything within these walls. As if studying for something qualified you for anything. Thankfully, one of our sound guys, who I'd meet that weekend, started ringing out the sound system right as I trailed off. We waited for the feedback to quiet and then Andy apologized.

—Do you play? he asked then.

—Not like that, no, I said.

—Like what?

—I don't know. Professionally. Live. In public, I said.

—Do you write? he asked.

—Not really, I said.

—I need someone who can do four or five shifts a week, he said. The shifts can be long. You won't be in the audience too, remember. You'll be at the door.

—Yeah, I'm fine with that. I know.

—Working, he said.

I nodded.

—You'll report to me, but you'll work mostly with Julien. I think you'll get along. You'll probably take home a hundred, hundred and fifty bucks a shift.

My rent at Sloane's—I'd just moved in—was $350.

—Okay, I said. I can make that work.

—Come up to the show on Saturday night. If you can get here for sound check at four p.m. that'd be great. We'll do a trial night. See how the fit is.

—Okay, I said, and stepped down from the barstool.

The whole thing seemed almost like an accident. I could have gone to any club in town, really, but somehow I ended up here.

How did I actually feel, when I first pulled into town? Hour nine of the drive from Michigan, past the shiny new restaurants in the Gulch and the police parked outside the projects on Edgehill, the kids filtering over from the fringes of the Belmont and Vandy campuses. When I got to the neighborhood Izzy told me I'd love, on Twelfth, I'd expected something more like a city block in Chicago: crowded storefronts and bars packed next to each other, pedestrians and bikers and parallel parking. But the street was quiet. A pizza place with a sprawling patio, a beer bar with globe lights strung above its tables, a wine store that didn't look open. A couple of coffeehouses and a Christian bookseller, a Popsicle shop before the park. It was walkable, but nobody was walking. Was it disappointment I felt, expecting the facade of a New York city block and seeing this sleepy stretch of neighborhood spots? Or was it relief?

Relief, I think—to have put several states between me and Nick, a geographic barrier I was foolish enough to think would serve as a buffer. Relief to be surrounded by so many people with so many dreams, or rather so many people with the same dream, but so many different talents? Or maybe I was just relieved by the noise, relieved to have music playing—from somewhere, by someone—all the time, every day, no matter what. Even if it wasn't mine.

On my night off, I get stoned while Sloane picks up pizza, falling deep down a rabbit hole on social media. I click through Nick's socials—pages where I've spent many hours over the past year. I know this already but I still have to confirm: there's no photographic evidence of us there, none whatsoever. I'm embarrassed at the messages I've left on his pages over the past year, wanting to delete them but worried he'll be notified if I do; I don't know how any of this works. So instead I click through his photos again, just to make sure I didn't miss anything. But I know I'm not there, because we've never taken a photo together.

As for his pictures, they range from reckless and stupid to sexy and vaguely staged. I click out of his page and search for Julien. We're not friends yet, I realize, and I add him without overthinking it, annoyed that his profile is both private and minimal, just a photo of him with his back to the camera, standing somewhere in a field. It's blurry—totally useless. I wouldn't even know it was him if not for the name. I search for Jessika; I have an odd desire to confirm her birthday, to look at hers and Julien's side by side, to calculate the exact difference in age between us. But I can't, not now. Her profile is private too. When I type Colt's name, nothing comes up at all.

My computer dings with a notification: Julien accepting my friend request. He must be online now. I navigate back to his profile, ready to click through his photos. As I hear Sloane's keys rattle against the door, a message pops up in the bottom right of my screen: Nick.

I was just thinking about you, it says.

4.

A dream: backstage, my hands running through Colt's hair, over Nick's hips. A finger slipped inside me, ice cold, but it's not enough. Hands tugging at my hair, so hard I'm sure chunks of it are falling out, but it doesn't hurt. I can't see myself, but my hair is darker, my lips are red, my curls are thicker, maybe. Andy walks in: we pull apart. Nick's dick is in my hand, Andy is gone, we're alone again. Not at The Venue, but in a room I don't recognize. Lemony lights and a peeling poster of a lead singer—ZZ Top or Iggy Pop or someone else. Julien's voice, asking me a question. Our clothes are off—Nick? Julien?—and our faces are blurry. Sloane's voice carries from somewhere in the living room. I run a hand through my hair and it's mine again, ragged blond tangles, just waves. I'm alone.

When I pull into The Venue a few weeks later, before sound check, cars have appeared in the parking lot, like doors are already open—like *we're* already open. The parking lot is dotted with them: an old Honda Civic, a black Mercedes Sprinter van, Julien's Explorer, the color of a sad winter day. I run my fingertips along the bumper and over a tiny, peeling sticker: Belle and Sebastian. Something he clearly tried to take off in recent years—*Belle and Seb,* it reads now—but he gave up, the plastic practically fused to the plastic.

—What are they doing here already? I ask Julien upstairs, pointing out the office window to the band. The Wild Loose, an indie band who's playing tomorrow night, is unloading some instruments from the van.

—They wanted to meet Danny, Julien says. I think they're in town a night early, recording or something. I told them they could come up before tonight's sound check.

Danny still isn't here, though. He works as a studio sound engineer by day—mostly alt-country with spiritually leaning content, like a Christian Dave Cobb—and when he's here he usually spends his time consulting with the bands back at the sound booth or working in the larger office downstairs, big headphones on, eyes squinting at his computer. He has an A2 guy, Simon, with long dreadlocks and a sweet grin; he does all the monitor mixing and mic work for the bands, but he isn't here either. The band is still lingering by the van. All eight of them, which is way too many people for a band.

—Do you think the lead singer is the one on the phone? With the concave ribs? Or the guy with the long curly hair?

The skyline behind the band, over on Broadway, is dotted with construction cranes—behind the convention center, at the traffic circle on Eighth. Julien's next to me now, the sleeve of his shirt grazing my shoulder.

—Neither, he says, pointing to the guy who's sprawled on the hood of the van now, doing little snow-angel movements with his arms and legs.

—You win, I say. Definitely a lead singer.

He nods.

—Cute bumper sticker, by the way. Always loved Belle and Seb.

—It really just will not come off, he says, a half smile spreading across his face.

—Did you ever see them live? I ask. I think they're playing War Memorial next month.

—Oh yeah, I think Jess told me about that. One of her bands is opening.

—You might end up losing the whole bumper if you keep trying to get the sticker off, I say. Or you could just say fuck it. Introduce the world to Belle and Seb.

He laughs and then his face settles into that intense look again, eyes studying me, like I've said something much more serious than I have.

—Glad to meet another Seb fan, he says.

My laughter is instinctive, high-strung, waiting for something to break on his end. I'm about to tell him I'm messing with him, looking down briefly at his feet to spare myself his stare, but when I look up, he finally breaks—laughing, eyes squinty, head shaking, like it's all just a way to fuck with me.

It's the lead singers you have to watch out for. That magnetism, especially onstage, that you need to make a band work. Presence. Some combination of ego and delusions of grandeur, enough to propel the band but not so much that they implode. The kind of personality that takes up space in a room but then makes you feel like you're the only other person in it. People offer to pay for their drinks at bars, ask them for advice when making small talk, ask them for directions, for restaurant recommendations. People ask who they are: if they're a surfer, a drummer, a carpenter, a professional athlete. A model, an actor, a musician.

—Don't guess, Andy had told me the first weekend I worked, a sold-out show with a guest list longer than normal.

—Okay, I said. No guessing.

—Not with the list, not with the IDs.

—I can do that.

—We always ID. And when someone tells you they're on the list, wait for them to say their name or ask it. Don't guess it. Even if you're certain you know who they are. Even if they say they're Julien's girlfriend or my kid or, I don't know. Just don't guess.

It seemed simple enough in theory, but in practice it was an act of restraint. Because I knew which girls were Mollys, Kates, which guys were Trevors or Jeremiahs or Jesses. Which people were fucking the lead singer, the guitarist, the drummer, the bass player. And which people wanted to be.

Sloane's car pulls into the lot; she parks across two spots to the left of the entrance and leaves her windows down. My phone buzzes in my pocket. A text from Nick, with a link to a song from a Detroit folk band that I can't get to open. When I look out the window again, Sloane is somehow already talking to the band, a cigarette in her hand, her head leaning back in a cascade of laughter.

—Iggy Pop played here? she asks, as she steps into the office upstairs a few minutes later, eyeing the posters on the back wall.

—Metallica too, I say.

—Aw. My little metalhead, Sloane says.

—Did you guys know that Che Guevara was rhythm-deaf?

This comes from Eddie, who's sitting on the couch with a slice of pizza in his hand. He's dressed in overly stylized Western garb, rust-colored corduroy flares and a brown button-down that's too small, fabric stretched across his chest, pearl snaps wanting to pop. I'm sure he's just in from an intro-level stats class at Belmont, but he looks like he's on his way to Dolly Parton's birthday party.

—Why is everybody here? Julien asks. We're not even open yet.

Jessika is here too, like she works here, like she's one of us—half of her hair tied back, curls fanning out from her head. She briefly rests her head on Julien's shoulder as he leans over a clipboard. He's actually trying to work when nobody else is, though something in his face softens a bit.

—I gotta talk to you about the Denim slot, Jess says to Julien. Let's say four-week residency. Believe me, in a few years when these guys are full-blown superstars, you don't want to be the guy who refused to book them.

She's pushy but convincing, her confidence laced with flirtation—a seductive blend. But Julien somehow doesn't bite.

—Talk to Andy, he says. You know it's still his call for now.

—*I'm* probably rhythm-deaf, I say to Eddie.

—Impressive, Jess says to me.

She has a mild accent I can't place, a Southern drawl that's slightly smothered.

—I could see that, Eddie says, and even though I asked for it, I can feel the irritation heating up my chest.

—No you're not, Julien says, looking at me with his eyes narrowed.

—There're these videos of Che, Eddie goes on, dancing a mambo when everyone else is dancing a tango. But you want to see real dancing, come with me to Motown Monday later. Who's in? My buddy's bartending.

Julien and I share a quick glance—*no.*

Jess turns around and leaves the office; I hear the door to the bathroom open and close. Colt comes in, looking pale, but somehow still good.

—I thought you were off, Julien says to Colt. He looks frustrated—too many people in the space when he'd obviously planned on being alone.

—Delivery, Colt says. Our distributor had to come today instead of tomorrow. I didn't realize the whole Scooby Doo gang was here.

He tries to make eyes at me, but I look over to Sloane.

—Let's roll, she says to me.

—To where? Colt asks.

—Third Man, I say. We can walk. It's basically across the street. Literally point-two miles.

Sloane has supposedly gotten us on the list for a record release there this afternoon.

—*You* can walk, Sloane says. I'm driving.

My phone. Another text from Nick, about the song he sent. Made me think of you. He always does this: just as the space between us seems permanent and I'm starting to put him behind me, starting to run off into the distance, miles and miles and miles away, he zips the space back up with an offhand text, an email, a late-night Gchat just asking how I am. And then the zipper's stuck and I'm alone and I can't get out of the fucking dress.

Eddie finishes his slice of pizza and puts his feet up. He's settled in, like he's at a friend's house and doesn't plan on leaving for days. Julien's trying to do something on his computer, but his face is all twisted up in frustration. Jess comes back and sits down next to him, nuzzling his shoulder like a kitten. He keeps his eyes on his computer. Everyone seems slightly annoyed to be here, and yet everyone has chosen to come up hours before they're needed. Colt leaves the office. A few moments later, we hear the sound of a bottle being opened down in the main space.

—Ready? I ask Sloane. You guys have fun on your big afternoon off.

A train is stalled on the tracks between The Venue and Third Man Records. A mural of an American flag outside the Rescue Mission—we take pictures in front of it to put online later, mellowed by a sepia filter, oblivious to the backdrop of urban blight. A Kings of Leon song blasts from Sloane's speakers, something about kissing the stars, making us feel completely unique even though the album's sold millions of copies. Even though everybody everywhere is listening to it, playing it over and over until it loses all resonance. The song changing, the sound of a bottle cracking against the concrete.

As it turns out, Sloane has not, in fact, gotten us on the list. Though there is a list, there is only *one* list—as in, the release is a completely private event. You cannot buy tickets, and you can't even really just wait around. It is, as Sloane frames it to me on the way there, *invite only*. She just failed to mention that we haven't exactly been invited.

I assumed that Sloane's radio cred meant we'd have actual access to the show, which is starting at the oddly early hour of five p.m. Eddie's covering my shift at the door. The streets back here are full of dilapidated warehouses and strip clubs. You can get turned around even if you're staring directly at the map on your phone. The Venue is really only a block or two away, but not the kind of block or two you should walk, even though I suggested we try. A highway overpass, antique shops that never appear open, boarded-up storefronts. But then, planted right in the middle of it all, Third Man Records: Jack White's studio, store, venue, his own little music factory. All shiny and black and yellow and new. Sloane parallel parks on Seventh by the train tracks, so studiously that she doesn't even look over her back shoulder after initially eyeing the spot.

—I saw him last week, she says. Mr. White, Prince of Nashville. Just getting himself a piece of pie.

I ask where and she mentions the restaurant down the block on Eighth.

—The Willy Wonka of the music world. Out in the wild, I say.

Sloane laughs, a loud, sharp cackle. In her rearview mirror, she ties her short hair back into a tight ponytail and changes the song on her phone.

—You're going to be obsessed with this, she says, nodding to the dash.

—Turn it up, I say.

—Your Warped Tour buddy was there too, she says.

—Who?

—Door guy. Dark hair kind of in his eyes?

—Julien?

—Julien, yeah. Jujubean. He's cute. A little emo, but cute.

—He is, I say, and then immediately ask: With Jack White?

That laugh, again: like a pint glass shattering at an after-party.

—Jesus, no. Alone.

—That makes more sense, I say.

—Reading *Spider-Man*, Sloane says. Actually, that girl was there too. The tall one? Pretty hot?

—Jessika, I say.

—Are they dating? Sloane asks.

—With a *k*, I say.

Sloane lays on her horn for a friend she recognizes crossing the street, and our conversation is drowned out by the piercing F.

At the door, Sloane does her sweet-talking thing. She looks effortlessly hot: a white ribbed tank top, cutoff shorts, an expensive watch, and no makeup (or, more likely: just enough to make her even more effortlessly beautiful, not so much to be noticeable). I take a picture of the line we're in—a string of skinny hipsters waiting in a gravel alley along a chain-link fence—and text it to Nick. It looks like nothing, but the black-and-yellow backdrop of Third Man will let him know where we are. My service is spotty and I can't tell if the text has gone through, but when I look up, Sloane is waving me toward an irritated redhead with vampiric skin and bloodshot eyes who holds out a wristband for me, asking in a monotone: ID?

Inside, it takes several disorienting seconds for my eyes to adjust to the darkness. Low indigo light, faint wisps of fog curling up at people's feet. We're in a spherical room, the infinity walls curving up toward the ceiling. Everybody else apparently agreed in advance to dress in all black.

The nice cocktail spot on Division is catering the drinks, a kind of curated open bar. A few spaces ahead of me in line, a tall guy in a yellow shirt bounces on his toes, his keys clipped to the belt loop of his jeans, red sneakers. Julien? Did he say he was coming to the show? Then he turns and it's someone much older, a face I've never seen, an expensive camera on his shoulder. Sloane and I move with the line.

My eyes have adjusted and I'm scoping the inky space for more familiar faces. The same people tend to show up at all the shows around town: underemployed recent Belmont grads who are recording their alt-country debuts down at Welcome to 1979, tour managers home for a week before hitting the road again, sound engineers on break from marathon recording sessions at Bomb Shelter, unrecognizable songwriters, now and then an actual famous musician—Ben Folds or Hayley Williams or even Robert Plant. I recognize a few Belmont guys over by the front of the stage, another guy who works the door down at Robert's, a bartender from the Villager. Faces I've grown familiar with, names I can't quite recall.

Jessika is there too, across the room, talking with a few guys whose backs are to me. She has a big camera slung over her shoulder now, a pass sticking out of her pocket. The kind of person who's actually on the list, who wears lipstick and manages bands and pursues her own art in her free time. I can hear her laugh even above all the buzz—that bracing cackle from across the room. She's standing with the drummer from Denim, a ragged waif of a guy who looks like a walking hangover. They're talking with a handful of older men, the kind you can tell are music execs just by their age and their designer jeans.

Drinks appear. Sloane and I find a little bit of space just to the left of the makeshift bar, where I can watch a bartender with nice eyelashes make expensive drinks for people who don't have enough cash on them to tip him.

My phone vibrates: Nick.

Jealous of your life, it says in response to the picture I texted him from the line outside.

Sloane glances at his name on my screen and shakes her head at me.

No you're not, I almost type back, but instead I turn my phone off, slide it back into my pocket. Look up at Sloane like: *See? I'm not thinking about him. I don't think about him. I don't even think about thinking about him.*

But even with my phone off, I'm wondering: Do his bandmates ever lean over his shoulder, ask him who he's talking to? Do they give him a look like Sloane just gave me? I've met them all at their shows before, but now I wonder: Did they think I was just some fan?

A hand on a shoulder, the sound of ice shaking into plastic. Overeager laughter. The flash of an iPhone. The twang of an unplugged guitar being tuned, the chatter of a girl flirting and failing. The brief sensation of being completely alone, silent, lost in the pulsing crowd. The smell of weed and then sage and then weed again.

The thing about Nashville: everybody here knows someone who knows someone. Either you're in the music industry or you're industry-proximal or you're proximal to the people who are proximal to the industry. And this town is small. Every week I see Andy dropping his girls off at the elementary school on Tenth; Colt catching a cab downtown; Julien on his front porch on Music Row; our sound guy, Danny, walking through the littered streets of Midtown after an open mic. Jessika now, everywhere, it seems. Even Eddie, as I duck my head in avoidance, chatting up the baristas at the coffee shop across from the Belmont campus, hanging flyers for his jazz nights on the bulletin boards by the bathrooms. Your eyes are always open for someone you might recognize. It isn't a city for hiding in plain sight, for slipping away into anonymity. It's the kind of place you come to be known—whatever that means to you.

Sloane disappears off to the bathroom and a pair of hands squeezes my shoulders. I turn around to find Colt, short hair wet, smelling like whiskey. Color has returned to his cheeks. He's standing too close, and he plucks an eyelash off my cheek.

—Make a wish, he says.

—No, I say.

He laughs, blows the black comma off his fingertip and into the air.

—How'd you get in? he asks.

—I have my ways, I say. I thought you were waiting on a delivery.

It's always a little out of context, seeing him outside The Venue, no bar mop over his shoulder or case of beer in his hands.

—Not anymore, he says.

—Do you have any Xanax? I ask. All these texts from Nick have made me jittery.

—Find me later, he says. Or come by tomorrow. We can play.

—I'll come by, I say. But I don't want to play.

—Even better, he says.

He leans in close to me and kisses my jawline. He punches his number into my phone and slides it into the back pocket of my shorts. His hand briefly cups my ass. I want to roll my eyes, shove him off, but I can't defuse my own desire. He looks too good. And then, it's extinguished. His hand out of my pocket, reaching into his own, pulling out a toothpick that he slides between his teeth.

—I'll be back, he says, and turns around, a shape disappearing into the crowd.

Now I'm wet and I hate it. Fuck Colt and his pretty fucking face.

Songs to listen to when you're trying unsuccessfully to forget someone:

"Mr. Brightside" (the Killers, obviously)
"Into Dust" (Mazzy Star)
"Tennessee Rose" (the Deep Vibration)
"Transatlanticism" (Death Cab for Cutie)
"Lost Cause" (Beck)
"The District Sleeps Alone Tonight" (the Postal Service)
"New Hampshire" (Matt Pond PA)
"Saints and Sailors" (Dashboard Confessional)
"Mix Tape" (Brand New)
"This God Damn House" (the Low Anthem)
"Land Locked Blues" (Bright Eyes)
"Chasing a Ghost" (The Head and the Heart)

I slink into a spot where I still have a decent view of the stage. Sloane's taking forever, probably talking to strangers in line for the bathroom. Her dad manages some massive, storied seventies band; she's known about town without even trying. At first I thought it was just because she works at the station, but she'd only been doing that for a few months when I met her, and already she knew everyone. Once I called her Almost Famous and she took a sip of a tequila soda and looked me straight in the eye and said: *Fame adjacent.*

The overhead lights go down. For a moment the whole room is swallowed in midnight black, until the stage lights go up in a foggy opal, the crowd a field of dim silhouettes. Then: a hand grabbing at my forearm. Sloane, pulling me into a pocket of privacy near the back. The lights are low and my body is light and Alison Mosshart is crawling across the stage in clothes that look like they've been smoked and shredded, the rest of the band settling in around her like she's the sacrifice, the altar, all psych rock guitars and frantic rhythms, their instruments like weapons, like it's a danger to the room for them even to be holding them up there.

Trippy, loud, and when the drinks mellow me out, it's like we're in another place, another city, another decade completely, like we're all just floating through space listening to the music pulse and Alison Mosshart scream like she's being murdered. I watch, mesmerized, her wild, drunken comfort—the way she owns the stage, the way she has made it her own, made it her home.

—You could do this, Sloane says. You just need a bigger stage next time.

—God no, I say. And anyways. She's drunk.

—No way, Sloane says. She's just *in it.*

Onstage, Mosshart looks wasted but somehow still precise. I let the envy melt over me, let the reality solidify around me: I will never step on a stage like that again. I finish my drink and order another.

Damp lips against my nipples, Nick's melody ringing in my ears. The white skin of Colt's waistline as I run a fingertip along his pubic bone. An index finger between my legs, lukewarm beer, the back of Colt's teeth. Tousled hair, shirt unbuttoned. We push our tongues across each other's and share a joint. He runs a finger up my forearm, his fingertips hot. There are several attempts at light conversation, but quickly I realize that's not at all what we're here for. Colt is not a conversationalist. Colt is unreasonable abs and a sultry voice, almost as good as Nick's. He is free drinks and distraction and light scruff and a strong jaw and when he pushes himself into me, all I can think of is how beautiful his face is but how ugly his dick is.

5.

Justin Wilson is missing. The news breaks days before he's supposed to play at The Venue. He posted something cryptic on social media—*going away away away, always better this way*—and then went dark. Nobody has heard from him in days. I'm in bed when I read the news, just a few lines posted on the *Nashville Scene*'s website, my feet bare, my lips chapped. At first, it sounds like overblown clickbait about a local musician. He's known for a lot of drinking, a lot of drugs, you could say, but with only a single post online and no other comments from family, nobody is doing much speculating, not yet. I don't like the feel of it, though. Especially not when paired with his frank—often dark—songs and his occasional dismal online musings.

I search around to see if his guitar player, Esther Wainwright, has said anything. They've had an on-again, off-again romantic entanglement for a while, but she hasn't commented. She's apparently been in Australia for a solo gig. I wonder if she even knows yet. Only local news seems to have picked up the story, and barely that. When I go to text Julien about it, I realize I somehow don't even have his phone number, just a work email. I send him a link to the story. Wilson's gig at The Venue this week was supposed to be a short set, not with Esther but with another local band—a local supergroup of sorts, with Wilson as lead, calling themselves How High We Go.

I wonder if he's dead, but then again I don't really know anything. I'm not a friend of his, I'm not family. I just work the door. I stamp hands. I'm not even a critic or a journalist, not a true insider. I'm not in a band. To even say I write songs wouldn't be fair, not in a town full of songwriters. If I'm anything at all here, I'm just a fan.

Julien responds to my email a couple of hours later, but all it says is: Whoa, no, didn't see this. Thx for sending.

—Good, you're here, Julien says.

It's the night Wilson is supposed to perform. The clock blinks: five after five. I pull out my headphones.

—I'm on time, I say. I was—

Sounds from an acoustic sound check seep into the office. I figured the show tonight would be canceled—postponed—when Wilson's disappearance was announced earlier this week, though I hadn't heard one way or the other from Julien or Andy.

—Set times are shifting, Julien says, handing me a sheet of paper. How High We Go is no longer on it.

Low Lights*—7:45*
Disaster Tourist*—9:00*

—Seriously? I ask.

—What? Julien looks up from his phone.

I wave the paper at him.

—You think I need a piece of paper to remember two show times? I know the bar isn't that high around here, but—

—Those aren't for you. I need you to hang them up back in the greenroom. Oh, and restock the water bottles too, he says.

He's inscrutable, glancing up at me and then back down at his phone, then over his shoulder to the main space.

—The openers are seriously still playing? I ask. Aren't they supposed to be friends of his? Hasn't anyone heard anything?

Julien passes me a roll of duct tape.

—Not my call, he says.

—Where's Andy? He's the one who booked this show, isn't he? Can't we at least postpone it? The guy is missing.

—Listen. I know. It's weird. But How High We Go wasn't the only band on the bill. And there are contracts involved. Promoters. Show guarantees. Plus, you're right, they *are* friends of his. And I think they want to play.

A case of beer crashes onto the wood floors outside. I hear Colt curse loudly.

—That doesn't mean they *should*, I tell Julien.

There are layers and layers of fame in Nashville, and you have to sift through them to understand anything. Izzy understands it inherently; Sloane is an expert at it. Recognizing the base of the pyramid and its fresh-faced wannabes: virtuoso guitarists, singer-songwriters staked out at every open mic, fiddle players and guitar players and banjo players standing on the street corners up and down Broadway. Then there are the people who aren't famous but think they deserve to be—and the ones who aren't famous but *think* they are, dressing up in wide-brimmed hats and Peter Nappi boots and dropping heavy credit cards on overpriced martinis at the Standard or Oak Bar. Then there are the local, regional, micro-famous, the people who sell out the Ryman three nights in a row every year, but don't always have national name recognition.

That is Justin Wilson. Still local, but always on the cusp of breaking out nationally. His first album, *Interlude, Key of J*, was sad acoustic sleep rock, with just the right amount of falsetto and flourish, angst and alternate guitar tunings, and it made some waves. He hasn't released anything since. Esther cowrote almost all his songs, but everybody always says it's Justin's voice—that *voice*—that carries the songs. They're not wrong. His voice is one of those haunting, once-in-a-lifetime howls, sadness just pouring through it. But I always wonder—would he have anything to sing at all if it weren't for her?

Sloane thinks the same thing. That maybe Esther deserves a little more credit, even if Wilson has the voice. *He's fucked without her*, she said, even though she doesn't actually know anything about their lives, how they write their songs, what their romantic relationship is like. But I've always thought of Esther as both muse and mistress, subject and songwriter. Maybe there isn't any him without her.

Esther tried to break out, solo, once. She released a few albums—critically regarded, commercially unsuccessful. I haven't really listened to any of them. It's Justin's career that gets all the attention. Whatever their dynamic is behind closed doors, though, it's impossible to ignore what happens onstage between them. Absolutely crackling. Energy and tension, full of intimacy: harmonies that braid together like bodies, breaths in between notes that sound like—

Everybody wants that kind of chemistry. And since the album that took off was technically *his*, he became the breakout success. That word—*breakout*. Like someone freeing themselves. Like they were in some kind of trap. Which is funny, because if anything in the music industry seems like a trap, it's the attention, the fame. The kind of thing you can really only break out of by disappearing.

Backstage: a sad cheese spread limp on the coffee table, a half-empty Miller Lite. Cold coffee in a white Styrofoam cup, teeth marks along the rim. Golden light garish as I tape the new set times to the wall next to the fridge, taking down the one with Wilson's name on it. Sloane's texts coming through in my pocket: Do you work tomorrow? Want to have taco night? I'm making margs. And getting beer. Yuengling right?

A slice into my finger, a straight line of red appearing along the outside of my pinkie, as if it's been drawn there. As thin as the high E string on the guitar.

Not having perfect pitch. Not knowing how to adjust the action on my guitar. Not having the finger strength to play a full song using only barre chords. Not being able to sing in front of people, even though I love to sing. Getting so much wrong at The Venue: not knowing where to put the recycling, not knowing how to fix the humidifier. Knowing I shouldn't sleep with the hot bartender but still wanting to sleep with the hot bartender. Giving my phone number out to singers that first month, so often that Andy starts to joke about it. Not taking myself seriously for so long that eventually I start to wonder if anyone else ever will.

Colt is sweaty and gaunt-eyed at the bar lineup, like he hasn't slept in days. He's cut his blond hair again. It's practically buzzed, which I hate. His face still looks beautiful, though I flinch remembering the rest of our night the week prior, its blurry edges, like taking a picture with your finger over the frame. Eddie's trying to show me the lyrics to a song he wrote, reaching across the space between us and shoving his phone toward me. As if this is the right time, as if I want to read his song lyrics in front of him while he reads over my shoulder, while I'm working. Julien is on the other side of me, shaking his head and laughing quietly, watching Eddie.

—We're eighty-six Yuengling, Colt says. Should be restocked tomorrow. I think that's the only thing we're out of. And try to avoid telling people about the pizza. It makes the whole place reek, and I don't know, this isn't a goddamn Papa Johns, y'know?

Technically, according to some ancient Tennessee liquor law, every bar has to sell a food item. We sell pizzas: frozen, microwaved, to be consumed in moments of drunkenness or desperation or both.

My eyes shift to Julien for a beat, my eyebrows lifted and his head shaking.

—And please remind the bands that the drink tickets we give them up front are the *only* drink tickets they get. No more tabs. These guys are gonna drink us fucking dry.

Eddie salutes Colt but he doesn't catch it. The smell of weed drifts over from somewhere backstage. Colt's palms are pressed against the lip of the bar, like he's about to start doing push-ups. Christ, we are a little Scooby Doo gang.

—Is that it? Julien asks Colt.

—You tell me, Colt says, a hint of irritation humming beneath the words.

—We should be out of here early tonight, Julien says.

—Al, you got a second? Colt asks.

I want to say it again—*because the goddamn headliner is missing*—but just then a delivery guy drops so many cases of PBR on the floor that the floorboards actually tremble. Everybody pauses for a moment, and then without any direction otherwise, the meeting disbands.

Julien heads for the stairs, calling back to me:

—I need you downstairs. Don't really have time for—

—For what? Colt asks.

The two of them stand there for a moment, their eyes fixed in a pissy little impasse.

—I'll be right down, I say.

In the office: Colt pushes me against the door, a firm hand tight around the back of my neck. No lead-up—just tongues across the slick surface of each other's lips, the rest of the day fading to black as I fumble with his belt buckle. It's all so unnecessary, loud, desperate. Like we can't wait, can't find anywhere else to go, can't control ourselves at all. And then the doorknob twists and I push him away quickly, running a hand through my hair, across my mouth.

Julien appears in the doorway. I exhale slowly, trying to stand up straighter. He looks from me to Colt and then back to me, his eyes squinted. Colt clears his throat and I take another step away from them both, like if I can back away far enough, I'll disappear completely.

—Doors, Julien says to me and then turns around.

Melodies that have been stuck in my head over the past five months instead of my own:

"Moth Eaters" (Justin Wilson)
"Play Crack the Sky" (Brand New)
"I Only Wear Blue" (Dr. Dog)
"Hush Now" (Justin Wilson)
"Fade into You" (Mazzy Star)
"Cathedrals" (Jump, Little Children)
"Wish You Were Here" (Ryan Adams)
"Paper Thin Walls" (Modest Mouse)

"Misery Business" (Paramore)
"Shanghai Cigarettes" (Caitlin Rose)
"Girls of Athens" (Pet Lions)

—Did you hang the new set times backstage? Julien asks later, down at the door.

—I managed.

He's sitting on one of the black stools, tearing wristbands apart. Doors aren't for half an hour, and the sun is setting in a lovely blurred blue out beyond Cummins Station. The wristbands split in quiet, rhythmic rips. Upstairs, a grungy bass line thumps away. Julien taps his foot to it.

—Do you play? I ask.

I want to talk about anything besides what he may or may not have just seen. He glances over, his foot stops keeping the beat.

—What?

—Do you play bass?

—No. I mean, not really. No—

Now his right foot is at an odd angle, like he's fighting the urge to twirl it. A nervous tic.

—Why?

—You look like a bass player, I say, shrugging.

For a few moments it's quiet in our little atrium. The bass line above us has stopped. Doors aren't open yet.

—Am I doing something . . . Are you pissed at me? Ever since I got here today—

Julien glances up and then looks down again. He looks good when he's frustrated, his irritation bubbling something up to the surface that I haven't seen before.

—No, he says.

—Sorry, I say. About earlier.

—I don't care what you do outside of work.

—I mean—

—At work, I care, but you're—he's—

He sighs.

—We're all adults. I just, I really just need you at the door when I tell you I need you at the door.

—Okay. That's it? I ask.

He nods, but he doesn't look at me. My face is warm, sweat beading at my hairline. I pluck several strands out and relish the quick pricks of pain.

He looks at me for a long time, then lets his eyes drift over to the door. The sun shifts behind a shelf of clouds, casting the front room in shadow.

—You're right, Julien says. It's kind of weird that we're still having the show.

Oh Jesus. I'm pretty sure she's wasted. Do you think he's dead? No fucking way. That's some Elliott Smith shit. Different Justin. He's not even famous. You smoke? Good, you shouldn't. Lost in the flood. He's producing now I think. No, insurance didn't cover it. I can't, I have the hiccups. Years ago, yeah, out by the lake. Nobody's looking. You can do it right now. If you go down on Sunday, during the day, the place is empty. Fifty Shades of Hay! *The bartender is fucking hot, yeah? It's been more than forty-eight hours. Yeah, man, he's probably dead.*

During the set, I lose track of Julien. I drink more than I should without realizing it, a thrum of energy starting in my chest and then short-circuiting in my stomach. I don't realize the nausea I've had until it's gone. Colt's feeding me gin and tonics and we're eye-fucking shamelessly—a look that always feels like a risk-free flirtation, though nothing really is.

I pass by the office on my way to the bathroom, surprised to find the door cracked. It's usually locked during shows, but now a sliver of light shoots through, like the single bow of a violin.

—Come on, what if it's not four weeks? a girl's voice says.

—It's Saturday nights, Julien says. I can't.

My palm was on the door, the cobalt paint flecked on my palm, but I pull it back, running it through my hair.

—Exactly, Jess says. It's Saturday night. That's the point.

Her voice, forceful and loud, is recognizable now.

—Maybe a Monday. Or Tuesday. I don't think they're there yet, Julien says. Not for a weekend slot.

—Bullshit, she says. First of all, they absolutely are. That's—I'm not even going to address that, because you know the kind of tours and late-night spots they're booking right now. You just don't like them.

—That's not true.

—You can't just book bands you personally like, she says.

—Why don't you just go talk to Benji over at the End? I know for a fact they have residency slots open.

—The End? No. no. You know they're bigger than that. These guys can bring in three, maybe four hundred on a night like this.

—Four weeks in a row? No way.

—They're local, she says.

Julien sighs.

—Listen to it, Jess says now.

There's a soft shuffling, a beat of silence in the conversation.

—I have, Julien says.

—No, not these. These are brand-new. They just recorded with Dave over in East. It's fucking good stuff, Jules.

I stand up slightly straighter.

—Fine, but no guarantees, Julien says.

It's quiet for a moment. I can hear the singer's drunken onstage chatter as she tunes her guitar, the crowd on edge and quiet.

—Julien, I say, pushing the door open with my palm.

What I didn't expect: the two of them wrapped in a hug, Julien's arms slung low around Jess's waist, Jess pressing her lips up into his neck. Julien catches my gaze over her shoulder.

—You really should come see this set, I say.

Jess doesn't let go, but Julien presses away from her, wipes his mouth with the back of his hand. Jess glances over at me. I wait for her to introduce herself, but she doesn't, and then we've missed the moment.

—Good or bad? Julien asks about the set.

—I honestly don't know yet, I say.

—I don't think we've officially met, Jess says. She unhooks herself from the hug and walks over to me, sticking her hand out. I'm Jess, she says.

—Al.

—You guys haven't met? Julien asks. I thought—

—With a *k*, I say.

She laughs. Hard to read her tone. But she's looking at me like she did from down the bar the night Nick was in town. A smile of familiarity, recognition.

—So good to put a face to a name, she says, like she's been waiting to meet me, like she's heard about me. Like I don't already know how to spell her fucking name.

—Okay, I'll leave you two to "work," she says, complete with air quotes.

—Nice to meet you, I say.

—Call me later? she asks Julien. I've got a showcase till eleven, but after that, okay?

Screeching feedback, slurred speech, the sound of feet on stairs, people trickling slowly out of the set. Resigned faces—the looks of people who want their money back but know they won't get it. Julien follows me in silence as we head down to the main space, the disjointed banter carrying quietly from the stage.

—Did you clock out? he finally asks, nodding to my drink.

—Colt gave it to me, I say, shrugging.

—I'm sure.

—You gave me a beer during my shift, like, three weeks ago. Don't be such a narc, Jules.

He laughs at this, an unexpected smile that springs across his face. Teeth: dainty and imperfect.

—*I* didn't call me that, he says.

I just look at him and shrug, taking a sip of my drink.

—Did you clock out? he asks again.

—I will, I say, indignant.

—Let's go see about this set, Alison.

The show is bizarre. The girl who opens, under her stage name, Low Lights, is fucked up, and she spends most of her set with her back to the audience. Her eyes can't seem to hold themselves steady, and when she does turn around she looks like a picture that's just slightly out of focus. She forgets the lyrics to her own songs, and at one point she sets her guitar down and walks offstage before coming back with a bottle of water and a disoriented, frightened look. When Disaster Tourist comes on, they try to do some kind of energy circle for Justin, but an amp goes haywire five seconds in, and a deafening shriek of feedback shatters the mood as Danny and Simon rush to do damage control.

Onstage, now, a busted amp; upstairs, a girl screaming obscenities on the balcony, drunk and sad. A blood-orange moon, my paper cut, still bleeding. Another text from Sloane: chicken tacos or beef? Simon messing up the monitors for the lead singers, Colt giving me miniature shots in secret by the back bar, his fingertips tracing my thigh anytime he walks past me. I'm clocked out though. Andy's gone. Julien's girlfriend is too. At the door, a cab driver hands us a cell phone of somebody he dropped off earlier. The smell of rain, but it's just humidity. Boredom dripping into heavy, mindless drinking. Julien—Jules—distracted and distant.

Whenever I watch the audio guys scrambling during a show like tonight, I can't help but think about how easy my job is. Sometimes it's just me and Julien, with Mazzy Star or Vampire Weekend or the Format playing overhead, as I flip through last week's *Nashville Scene*, mocking the best-of lists, asking Julien if Panera is really the best bakery we have. Other nights it's us and the whole city, the whole scene, an infinite line of people and names and faces. Melodies you want to hear over and over again, memories you're trying to crystallize but the drinks make it impossible.

You are a gatekeeper and a hostess, a face people might recognize or resent or never think about again. A film on repeat—night after night, ID, stamp, skin, next, ID, stamp, skin, next. Face after face. We don't even check bags. People could be carrying anything. Booze or weapons or glass bottles or coke or ketamine or whatever other drugs people do at shows. But mostly they carry nothing. Andy always says we can use our discretion: if someone looks way too wasted, or gives us shit, we can always turn them away. Julien does. But I still see myself as a conduit from the crowd to the artist, a benevolent figure at the gates of heaven. I don't turn anyone away.

—I thought we were eighty-six? I ask Julien upstairs.

He smiles, shrugs. He doesn't usually drink till the very end of his shift, by which point I'm on my second or third. But now he's halfway through a Yuengling, sitting on the couch, and I should be drunk but I feel dead sober.

—Band loaded out? I ask.

—Almost, he says. Simon's trying to get them done out back. You been at the bar?

Muffled house music, a drunken woman's voice carrying from the bar. A text from Colt asking me if I want a ride.

—I clocked out, I say. What a weird night.

—It's fine. That's not what I was trying to say.

My arm reaches out toward him, asking for a beer. The room is low-lit, the lip of the skyline a faint outline in the dark window. Over the house music, an unfamiliar song. A trash bag crashing into a bin. Julien passes me his beer and I take a sip.

—Oh, hey. Who was your friend? he asks. It's been a little while now, but I was meaning to ask you.

He stretches his arm up over his head, like he's working out a kink in his neck. The hem of his boxers is briefly visible, a line of silver against his pale hip bone.

—What friend? I ask.

—The guy. The night of the flood. The night I gave you a beer like a bad narc. He looked familiar.

I laugh.

—That was forever ago, I say. He's in that band Flirtation Device. They played here last year. Before I started?

This seemed like plenty of context, though I already wonder if I've said too much, tried to draw in too many details of Nick's life.

—I don't know them, Julien says. I just figured I'd seen him at another show.

—He's a—

—He's a what?

I narrow my eyes at him slightly, take a sip of the beer.

—Are we friends? I ask.

The sound of Colt's voice floats into the room as he closes out the lingering bar guests.

—Well, I'm letting you drink my beer, he says, as I pass the bottle back to him. So yes, I would say that we're friends.

It's all so formal, though—his tone, every syllable stiff and stilted.

—Jesus. You say it like this is some kind of deposition.

He laughs, erupting in a cough, a hand to his chest.

—It sounds like one, he says.

—You're so cagey.

—You think anyone who doesn't talk all the time is cagey.

—*I'm* not cagey.

—Well, you talk all the time.

That seems like a joke, but when I search his face for a smile, he lifts the beer to his mouth. There's a catch in my chest that I can't quite control, an accidental inhalation of smoke.

How exactly can I explain it—that Nick and I were one of those somethings that never actually was anything? Social media would have distilled us down into a simple *it's complicated*, but that would have hardly done it justice. And Julien doesn't need to know any of this. He's never even heard of Nick's band.

—Nothing, I say. He's nothing. Can I have my own beer?

Julien opens a mini fridge to the right of the couch, tucked behind the swung-open door. It's buried in show posters and press kits and guitar picks and tuners. He passes me a Yuengling.

—Okay, he says. Heard.

—Oh, come on. Don't you have someone like that? Someone from before you met Jess?

This time, I catch it: a small, thin smile—just for a second, like a frame in a cartoon that you only see for a flash. His eyes on me in that very focused way, enough that I have to look down. Someone tosses trash bags onto more trash bags outside the door, Simon says good night to Colt from the stairwell, Danny asks him if he needs a ride. My palms are warm. The bottle in my hand begins to sweat, a dribble of condensation down my forearm.

—Of course I do, Julien says.

Something in my chest clenches slightly; I want to ask who it is if not Jessika and does she live here and what happened and how much do you think of her, but instead I just say:

—So you know.

—I know, he says.

My beer isn't cold enough, but I'll drink every drop.

6.

Gasping for air, I come to. Six in the morning after the show, and my body pulses in a panic, as though I'm late for a flight, as though the SATs are already happening across town and I've missed them, fucking my whole fucking future. And then, milky dawn—daylight.

Tuesday, water. Last memories: The alley between Robert's and the Ryman, the stink of Second Avenue, the vomit of tourists. Shots of whiskey with Sloane at the back bar of Robert's, last call. Colt's hand up my shirt in the bathroom. Spinny city lights off Broadway and the cowboy boot stores and the arena and then the traffic lights in the wind on Twenty-First, screaming along to a late-nineties rock song on the radio.

A cheese quesadilla, all the water in the house, any liquid available. Sloane dancing in her underwear and an old Def Leppard T-shirt, drunk and delirious. I remember Julien too—something sunny there—but then the nausea nicks at the back of my throat and I peel myself from my pillow, fumble desperately in my nightstand drawer for one of Colt's benzos. Chew, swallow, cough, swallow. Lou Reed barks at nothing, my head pulses. In the bathroom I dry-heave and press my forehead against the toilet seat, waiting for the Xanax to kick in. When it does, I slide back into bed and touch myself, picturing Nick, picturing Colt, picturing Nick again, until I come.

What I know: It shouldn't take this long. It shouldn't be this hard. Half of this town is supposedly doing it, right? Most of Dylan's songs were only three chords, and there are only twelve tones in the chromatic scale. Even my favorite song of Nick's is just two chords over and over, the melody as simple as a schoolyard rhyme.

Could I trace the roots of my songwriting block back to somewhere useful? It started before the Incident, certainly. I've written lyrics—ones I like, even; some I love. The trouble is, none of these words have a tune, not these days. They just hang there silent, saved in my Notes app, staring at me mockingly. Now and then I pull one up, strum through a different chord progression, tack on a diminished seventh to see if it sparks any inspiration. But it just sounds like one of Nick's songs. I end up singing the opening lines of it instead.

The bar lights are up, baby it's last call. I wish I had a river. Justin Wilson's Disappearance: What We Know. Wilson Family Not Available for Comment. Flirtation Device Has a New Video for "Last Call" and It's Absolutely Perfect. Justin, We Know You're Out There. A Timeline of Justin Wilson and Esther Wainwright's Relationship. We clung on like barnacles on a boat / Even though the ship sinks you know you can't let go.

I'm avoiding Colt at The Venue, which means I have to talk to Eddie.

It's just as well, because ever since Colt and I actually hooked up, his interest has been steadily waning—the same old cliché. This is why I'm usually more careful. Not because I have some perfectly clear moral compass, but because everybody wants what they can't have. Everybody always wants something more, so long as you leave something more on the table. I'm nursing one of Julien's secret Yuenglings, swearing off Colt while Eddie rambles.

—I wouldn't touch a studio Gibson, Eddie says over my shoulder. I'm on Andy's computer, taking ten, looking at a guitar I can't afford. Trying to be alone before the second wave of people comes in.

—Overpriced, he continues. And I got a guy who works in the factory. *Hates* it, Eddie says. Bad brand. Bad instruments. But he can get you set up if you need it. Good guy.

—Are you even working tonight? I ask, shutting the computer and leaving the room.

Back down at the door, Julien's stamping the hand of a guy in bell-bottoms and sunglasses—even though it's dark out, even though we're inside.

—I'm going to push Eddie off the balcony, I say.

Julien lets out a short laugh, his whole face brightening for a moment.

—Let me know if you need a hand, he says. We share a long, conspiratorial look.

A few minutes later, the door swings open again.

—There you are, Sloane says, cutoff Tennessee football shirt barely reaching the waist of her jean shorts. Upstairs, Julien's already off dealing with a persistent promoter who's been waiting for his ear all night.

—Where else would I be? I ask.

Her evening looks well underway, her body pulsing with an undercurrent of energy—joy—that seems far removed from the night I'm having.

—I don't know, aren't you off yet? Who's on tonight? God, I just went to the most bizarre showcase.

She puckers her lips and I give her my cheek.

—Where at? I ask.

—Twelfth and Porter, she says. This guy was fucking wasted. He practically rolled off the stage during his set. And the head of Sony's A&R was there, literally just to see this guy play. I mean, he has a baby, a newborn, and he comes out on a Tuesday at nine p.m. to see this dude make a fool of himself. I was just going as a favor to Billy, because Lightning was putting it on, but holy shit. Do you have a cig?

She reaches up to tie her hair back and we go outside to smoke under the muted stars.

—The bartender felt bad for us I think, she says. He was just *feeding* us shots.

—Who's us?

—Billy, she says. Keep up. But he went home. To the baby. Ugh, I wish you'd been there. I ended up talking to that girl who manages Denim. Jesse? She's a badass. She's got, like, three bands getting a ton of buzz. Do you know those other guys, Kingston Lights? They're *hot.*

—I don't think so, I say.

—Wait, is her name Jesse or Jess? Whatever, Julien's girlfriend? Okay, when do you get off? Everyone's downtown, I'm on my way. Are you coming? Shit, we were overserved.

Car tires screech down on Eighth under the highway. Sloane's a little drunk, relishing the cig like it's going to be snatched out of her fingers. A few people from the audience start to slip out, car doors opening in the parking lot, headlights flicking on beneath the skyline glow.

—I'm supposed to be down at Robert's at eleven, Sloane says, looking at her phone. Just needed to tell someone about that showcase. I feel like I need to take a *shower.* Christ. What a mess. Can you call me a car?

I want to say no, she can call her own car—but she's too commanding, the kind of face and presence you just want to say yes to, even when she's being high-maintenance.

—You have a phone.

—It's dying, she says, waving a black screen at me. Please, she says.

She's whining but I don't care. I love her and she's made a pit stop in her evening just to tell me this story, just to share a cigarette.

—Come when you get off? she asks.

—Yeah yeah yeah.

Songs I listen to on repeat that night, trying to see if they will break anything loose:

"Interlude, Pt. 2" (Justin Wilson)
"Meet Me in the Bathroom" (the Strokes)
"Where Does the Good Go" (Tegan and Sara)
"Last Kiss" (Taylor Swift)
"Don't Look Back in Anger" (Oasis)
"Vera" (Pink Floyd)
"Dog Problems" (the Format)
"I Wish I Was Sober" (Frightened Rabbit)
"Perfect Day" (Lou Reed)
"Hero" (Regina Spektor)
"I Can Feel a Hot One" (Manchester Orchestra)
"Mona Lisas and Mad Hatters" (Elton John)

I pick Sloane up at Robert's later, after Julien cuts me around midnight, and drive us to the East Side, the lights of Broadway flickering a frantic neon in my rearview.

—Your bartender came through just as I was leaving.

—*My* bartender?

—Yeah, Colby or whoever.

—Colt. At Robert's?

—He is wild. He barely stayed five minutes, though. Kept offering me drugs I've never even heard of.

—Which ones did you do?

—Gross. I'm not getting drugs from a barback. Also, in case you weren't already aware: he wants to fuck you.

—Colt wants to fuck everyone, I say, though I decline to mention my personal experience in the matter.

There's traffic on the bridge and I slow to a stop. Sloane winds her window down and lights a cigarette, her long neck leaning out into the night.

—He is hot, though, she says. You should keep him in the orbit. Him and Jujubean. On the bench. Junior varsity. You know what I mean.

—Jujubean has a girlfriend, I say. You literally just hung out with her.

—Oh, yeah. She's sort of out of his league, don't you think? Doesn't she also sing backup for, like, Kesha too? I think I heard that from someone.

—I hope not, I say.

—But he's very emo-band, front-man cute, she says. Or maybe even like a bass player, you know, lurking in the shadows but still hot. Isn't that, like, exactly your type?

—He's also kind of evasive. I don't know, like, *reserved.*

—Just because he's not professing his love to you doesn't mean he's reserved.

—I don't think his girlfriend sings backup for Kesha, I say.

Sloane shrugs.

—Or maybe it was Katy Perry. I don't know. I don't know anything about Kesha.

—Colt told me he was a model. Said he was an extra for music videos.

—That's not a job, she says.

Sloane unplugs my aux cord and flicks on Lightning 100. We're at the stoplight just over the bridge when the song comes on: his high tenor recognizable before the song itself, peaking into harmonies even I can't hit. I have to reach out and touch Sloane's hand to keep her from plugging the aux cord back in, my heart producing disconcerting little triplets, the kind of rhythm I can never re-create.

—It's green, Sloane says, pointing up at the light.

Volume up, eyes vaguely on the road, head somewhere else: Ann Arbor, the Blind Pig, the alley off First Street. My right hand is still frozen above the dash, like a conductor holding an orchestra in the quiet. Sloane swats my hand away, but she's listening now too.

—Shit, I say.

—Oh my god. Is this him? I've never listened to them before. It's him, isn't it?

She turns it up. *Michigan midnights / where are you now / I'm seeing your face / all around town.* It's a song of his I've never heard before, and immediately I wonder why he never sent me the demo. Why I have to hear it for the first time on the fucking radio like the rest of the world. The traffic around us is claustrophobic as the song plays out. Then Sloane says very quietly:

—Wait, was that about you?

It's not until she says this that I stop looking at the road. Fragmented white moonlight, hazy fluorescent headlights streaming down Shelby, briefly blinding me. I glance over at Sloane in the passenger seat, her eyes wide and searching, her whole face dancing with expectant energy. Sure, it has occurred to me. It always occurred to me, with every song Nick had written since the night we met. How could it not? Even with that girl—partner? ex? girlfriend? the one whose name is also Alison, with an extra *l*—he had back in Chicago, we were still in touch, wrapped up in the sort of emotional entanglement that *I*'d been writing songs about, or at least lyrics. But how exactly do you voice that thought? The vanity required to assume a song is about you—well, there's a whole song about *that.*

And then, before I can go too far down that hypothetical rabbit hole: red and blue lights swirling in a blur in my mirror.

Nylon hot across my collarbone, air all swallowed up. Sticky, taunting leather. In the distance I glimpse a car door opening, hear the grunt of a motorcycle engine.

—Shit shit shit shit shit.

—Are you gonna pull over?

—Where the hell am I supposed to pull over?

Too many bars, not enough side streets. Sloane points to the right. I turn my blinker on and pull over, as if obeying the law now is going to make the difference.

Quiet. Drunk people walking down Woodland, cell phones glowing golden in their hands, hallucinatory lights from the bar on the corner. The officer's door closes behind him.

—You're fine, Sloane says quietly. You did nothing wrong. Be cool.

—I'm always cool, I say, which we both know isn't true.

She pinches the skin above my knee.

—License and registration please, the officer says, standing at my window.

—Officer, do you mind telling us why you pulled us over? Sloane asks, leaning across the console, practically in my lap, all wide-eyed and smiling. I want to put my hand over her mouth.

—Your taillight is out, he says.

He shines a small flashlight into the car, and immediately I'm aware of all of the detritus around us: a crushed Sprite can in the console, an empty beer bottle slipped into the pocket of the back seat, receipts from the pharmacy, the grocery, the liquor store.

—There was a song about Al on the radio, Sloane says. So we kind of lost our shit there for a second. Do you know Flirtation Device? She asks. I'd understand if not. They're sort of *up and coming*, but I get it, this is Music City.

—Have you two been—

A shrill whistle interrupts from a drunk woman on the corner. Denim button-down shirt, hair dry and bleached, roots exposed in the glow of a streetlight.

—License and registration, the cop says again.

My registration is buried—a stack of printed-off photos, looking a million years old, digital cameras already a clunky, antiquated memory. Three expired registration cards, a carton of colored pencils. A vinyl nylon case of emo-punk high school mix CDs. And finally, a valid registration card.

When the officer steps away, Sloane and I are both silent. The sidewalks in Five Points are full; it's midnight on a Friday. It's the hub of a low-key residential neighborhood—a mash-up of bungalows and body shops that bleed into an intersection of several dive bars. The kind of places you sink into to smoke and play foosball and get hit on by jaded old session musicians.

Beneath the streetlights: frat bros and third dates and early twenty-somethings drinking heavily, eyes unsubtle as they stare at us. Sloane starts to say something and I shake my head. Her exhalation is low, stretching down the block like a song.

He's back.

—How long have you lived here? he asks.

—A year.

—You'll need to update those Michigan plates, he says. And get that taillight fixed first thing, okay?

—Yes. I will. Yes.

Confusing John Hiatt with John Prine. Not knowing the tune to any John Prine songs. Not knowing enough about Dolly Parton. Not *worshipping* Dolly Parton, patron saint of Nashville. Not fully understanding diminished and augmented chords, even though I can play some of them. Losing my capo. Forgetting the chords to the first song I wrote. Saying I've heard of a band while not having any clue—*any* effing clue—who they are. Not recognizing a Merle Haggard song, an Emmylou Harris song, a Hank Williams song. Not being able to come up with my own melody for almost an entire year.

At some point, though it's hard to say when, I start feeling less like a fraud.

A few days later, the AC at The Venue is broken.

—Of course it never breaks in February, I say. Nobody's ever sitting at their house on the coldest day of the year saying, Holy shit, seems like the AC's broken.

Technically Colt's in the room, but it's like I'm speaking to no one. He's hungover in an obvious, dramatic kind of way: lying horizontal on the couch, eyes closed, his palms across his eyelids. I can't believe how good he still manages to look. Sweat drips down the small of my back as I sit at Andy's desktop, scrolling through more headlines about Justin Wilson: *Nashville Rocker Still Unaccounted For: Band and Family Tight-Lipped. Esther Wainwright: On Writing Behind the Scenes.*

I click on the link but it's just a piece from a few years back—Esther talking about her time as a hired-gun songwriter, nothing about her process with Wilson. I look to see if the story's gained national traction and I only see one headline, *Consequence of Sound,* echoing the original story. I wonder how famous you have to be for people beyond this town to care.

—You wanna come by tonight? Colt asks, without opening his eyes. We can—

It's the first time he's invited me over in a couple of weeks.

Just then Julien walks in, with something metallic sticking out of his flimsy messenger bag: the brassy bell of a trumpet. The instrument is loose, without a case, like he just picked it up while he was walking down Eighth. He looks at Colt and then at me and then at Colt again. Hot air presses down on me. Colt's right eye opens slowly, registers Julien, shuts again.

—Maybe, I say to Colt. Like I won't. Like I'm above a pretty face, an easy hookup.

Now Eddie is standing at the door, in loose Levi's and no shirt. A pearl-snap button-down is slung over his shoulder.

—Jesus, dude, Colt says, his eyes fully open now. Put on a fucking shirt.

—Too hot.

—Everyone else has their clothes on, I say.

—In a minute, he says. Need to cool off.

—Cool off somewhere else, Julien says.

—Anybody got any Advil? Colt asks.

—I might have something better.

—Or coffee.

—Put on your *clothes*.

—Fine, Eddie says, pulling his shirt off his shoulder.

—Or both, Colt says.

—You're early, Julien says. All of you.

—My AC was broken, I say. But apparently it's broken everywhere. Apparently nobody in this city has AC.

—I got a guy, Eddie says. He mostly does plumbing but he fucks with AC too. You can let him know Eddie sent—

—Someone's already coming, Julien says. Has Andy been by?

—Negative, Colt groans.

Julien turns around, steps out into the main space. I follow him. It's fractionally cooler out here, but the whole place is still sticky. My first summer in the South, and already I understand why things—time, people, traffic, melodies—move slower down here. It's hard to be urgent when it's ninety-five degrees and the humidity is pressing you back into the earth. Even Lou Reed is on a heat strike. For the past week, Sloane has had to carry him down to the curb every day to pee.

—Where are you going? I ask Julien.

—You don't have to come.

I try to ignore the shimmer of irritation in his voice. He glances back at the office, something he wants to say about Colt but doesn't. A distant car door slamming, the dull roar of a low brass instrument rehearsing at one of the studios on Cannery.

—I'm going to try to find the circuit breaker upstairs. And if that doesn't work I'm going to call our electrician, and if that doesn't work I'm going to call Andy and ask him what we need to do to cancel.

—You're gonna cancel a show because of no AC? We didn't even cancel a show when a guy went missing. Which, by the way, he still is.

—It's, like, a hundred degrees. People will be miserable.

—At least the whole band will be here, I say.

Julien shakes his head and turns up the stairs. His sneakers are light on the wood as his bag bounces against his hip, loose trumpet and all. In his hand he cradles the mouthpiece of the instrument.

—You're not gonna call Eddie's guy? I ask.

—God, Eddie always has to have a guy, doesn't he? Julien says.

I laugh lightly.

—I bet you're one of his guys and you don't even know it.

—Oh yeah? What would I be his guy for?

—His trumpet guy, I say. Why didn't I know you play the trumpet?

—Why didn't I know you were actually friends with Colt?

—You could be the phone guy. You seem like a guy who always answers his phone.

—Do I?

—Do *you* play live? I ask.

—No, he says.

—Will you play me "When the Saints Go Marching In"?

He shakes his head, looking at his feet, but there's a shadow of a smile.

—I don't know if it's true, I press on, but you do give off an *I answer my phone when people call* vibe, I say.

—How so? Like I'm always available?

—No, not that. Like you'd—I don't know. Like you'd pick up in case somebody needed you. Like you'd show up.

—You've never called me, though. How would you know?

—Well, I don't have your fucking phone number, I say.

He laughs, eyes going squinty, like it's actually unexpected, like somebody jumping an octave in a song. I follow him up the stairs.

—I saw your—I saw Flirtation Device on *Late Night* last night, he says at the top of the stairs, turning back toward me.

The sun is blocked by the buildings just south of downtown, and the hallway is suddenly dark, midday midnight shadows. He stops abruptly, looking at me. I'm too close to him. My body wants to tumble back to the next stair, but I reach out and steady myself against the wall.

—How'd they do? I ask, like it was a sport of some kind, like they could win or lose playing their new single on *Late Night*.

—You didn't watch? he asks.

I hate the thought of everyone else having all this access to Nick—everybody getting to see the same version of him on the screen that I do. Julien's face is still obscured in gray, and then: shards of light piercing through. He reaches to cover his eyes. I won't lie and say I didn't watch it; of course I did.

Julien takes a right, toward a door that leads to a large space we sometimes rent out for weddings. Instead, though, he turns in the opposite direction, unlocking a door to another hallway.

—Where are we?

He flicks on an overhead light. The heat is overwhelming up here, like I'm wearing it. Pricks of sweat on my wrists, between my fingers, the edges of my hip bones. I've never been in this part of the building.

—Trying to find the . . .

He trails off and turns on another light. We're in a tight hallway now, another door to our right, more exposed red brick at our backs. The air is still suffocating.

—They were good, Julien says now. I dig the song they played. I think it's on the album that's coming out in the fall?

He squats down in front of a steel circuit board that's set low on the wall. I pull out my phone and flick on the flashlight for him, holding it over his shoulder. Sweat trickles over my upper lip, my shoulder blades, my breastbone.

—How do you know them? Julien asks. Or I guess how do you know him?

In the low light it feels like we're underground, even though I know we're upstairs. A twinge of panic starts to creep up my sternum, like sound inching to the threshold of an amp's capacity, noise threatening to blow the boards.

—I met Nick at a show in Michigan. At the Blind Pig. I used to work there? I think I told you that. Shit, it's hot in here. Don't you—God, don't you feel like you're suffocating a little bit?

I run a hand up the back of my neck, then over my throat. It's dark, but I can see Julien's eyes narrowing at me.

—You okay? he asks.

—I'm fine—I just . . . You don't have any—is there any, uh, water? Is the air kind of thick up here, or is it me?

My head spins around, right and left. I'm disoriented, dizzy from the heat and the hallway and the rows and rows of brick stretching out down the dark corridor. Julien's keys clink together as he reaches to my right and unlocks a dark red door, swinging it open behind me.

I spill into the room as the door opens. Air rushes toward me. Not cold, but fresher, thinner—something much closer to oxygen. Julien is quiet beside me. The silence holds. What were we talking about?

—You good? he asks, looking at me as I stand up straight. A little claustrophobic?

His hand is light on my shoulder, and I'm not sure how long it's been there. As soon as I look at him, though, he drops it, slides it into his pocket. It's only then that I see where we actually are. The room is a little smaller than the main space downstairs—it would probably fit a hundred people or so—but it has the same wall of big windows facing south, the same gorgeous exposed brick. The ductwork above is more chaotic, and the ceiling is supported by ugly steel columns. The floor isn't fully finished. Cheap black chairs are stacked randomly throughout the space, covered with dust, like the scattered remains of a bar mitzvah ten years ago. Beams of sunlight illuminate flecks of dust in the air, like clouds of glitter. Maybe it's just that I can actually breathe now, that I'm no longer convinced I'm about to die standing in front of a circuit board with my coworker and his loose trumpet—but it really is a beautiful room.

—What is this? I ask.

Julien passes me his phone. *New Contact*, says the screen.

—Storage, he says, shrugging.

I type in my phone number.

Side Two

1.

My period is four days late.

I sit in the bathroom, tensing my lower abs, as if I could force my stomach to cramp, willing the blood to come. This has happened before—well, not this many days—but only when I was nineteen, before I'd even had sex, when I briefly convinced myself that I was experiencing an immaculate conception.

I have been careful, relatively speaking, with the exception of . . . I do the math, trying to count down to one specific, slightly sloppy night with Colt. Three weeks ago. After the blue room show. My stomach quickly sinks below the floorboards. I press the toilet paper to my crotch and my clit pulses through it. I analyze the pure white toilet paper for spots of blood, like it's a color you could miss. A text from Izzy buzzes on my phone, asking me if I'm still joining her for lunch today. Sloane's voice carries from the other room. She's getting ready, singing Taylor Swift loudly above her hair dryer.

She calls my name from the other room.

—Just a minute, I say, a cold edge to my voice.

I flush the toilet again.

—You good? Sloane asks when I come out of the bathroom.

—Hungover, I say.

—Oh no. Happy Monday. Are you pukey? she asks.

—No. I'm fine. You look good, I say.

—I always look good.

Her hair is pulled back into a tight bun and she's got on light coral lipstick. She's pouring coffee into a sleek-looking to-go tumbler.

—Dinner Saturday? she asks.

—I have to work, I say.

—Can't you get that annoying guy to cover? Or talk to Jujubean? Flirt with him, get him to give you the night off! Oh shit, I gotta run. Make me a new mix, will you?

—Julien and I don't flirt.

—Oh please. Make me a mix, make me a mix, make me a mix!

—What if I'm busy?

Sloane laughs loudly and just says:

—Yeah, okay.

Sometimes, in the middle of a show, when the lights are low and the energy is high, you can forget where you are. You can forget the club—yes, that comes and goes quickly—but you can also forget the city, the day, the night, your friends, your family. The guys you've loved, fucked, cried over, forgotten; the friends you've lost; the songs you've learned. All of it. You can be orphaned, right there in the middle of the room, and it doesn't even matter, because you live in the audience now.

—I swear to god that guy is fucking tone-deaf, says Eddie, his hands drumming on the metal railing.

Monday night, high moon, cigarette smoke wafting off the balcony as we stand outside. A handful of local bands are on, the closest thing The Venue has to an open mic. The crowd is thin and distracted. Swimming between the bar and the balcony: interns from Red Light and Paradigm, agents from William Morris, sipping whiskey sodas, their palms resting on the bar.

—His monitor wasn't in, Julien says. More a Simon issue than a band issue. And just because someone doesn't have perfect pitch doesn't mean they're tone-deaf.

—Well, maybe if we all grew up learning a *tonal* language instead of just English, we'd all have a better sense of pitch.

—Says the guy from Knoxville, I say. Don't you have exams or something?

Eddie shakes his head, blows smoke over his shoulder.

I pull out my phone and text Julien, even though he's standing right there: Do you want to push him or should I?

A muffled vibration and Julien tugs his phone out of his pocket, looks at the screen and then over at me, a small, focused smile.

Beyond us the city looks too small, the buildings squat against the obsidian sky. Part of me aches for something a bit more grand. Chicago or New York—a hulking skyline, glittery and boundless. I'm desperate for a drink, but—

I exhale smoke out into a snake of gray. The door into the main space swings open to a blast of Sleater-Kinneyesque howls from the stage, a song crescendoing up toward its tonic. Colt emerges, smirking as he meets my eyes. I look down and tense my stomach again, begging for cramps.

—Shut up, Eddie, he says, as though he's been listening to us the whole time.

For those three seconds, I love Colt.

—Has anyone heard any news on Justin Wilson? I ask.

—Who? Eddie asks.

—Probably OD'd, Colt says.

—We don't know that, I say.

He reaches out for a cigarette and I slide him my pack. His hand lingers for a moment. The breeze—sharp and then completely still. I pull my hand back. My phone buzzes: What if we push them both?

—Are you two fucking? Eddie says now, looking from me to Colt and then back at me.

—Jesus, I say.

—Fuck off, Eddie, Colt says.

Glancing down at my phone I catch Julien's ankle, twisting in a tight axle against the wood beams.

—His manager was at a show last week, but he didn't stay long, Julien says.

I try to catch his eye but he's looking out at the city, like he's trying to sketch the skyline in his mind.

—I feel like Esther's probably the only person who actually knows what's going on, and I think she's off the grid too. The rest of the band has been totally silent.

—Are they together? Julien asks.

—Justin and Esther? I say. I think so. Or they were. Or they weren't and now they are. Seems messy. I don't know, but I feel like she's sort of the woman behind the man. You know what I mean? Doesn't she do a lot of the writing?

Julien's the only person paying attention now, his eyes intently focused on me.

—I thought they wrote together, he says.

—Some songs, I say.

His eyes flick away from me, then quickly down to his hands. Another breeze, picking up a parking ticket in the lot below.

Andy pops his head through the door—a Wicked Weed Brewing T-shirt that looks like it's been washed a thousand times, a pair of jeans faded white around the knees. I don't know how old he actually is, but the reading glasses propped on his head make him look ten years older than that. I always assume everybody is my age—young—unless they look obviously the opposite. Or unless they tell me so.

—Can I steal you? Andy nods to Julien. Oh, and Hunter—don't forget your paycheck in the office. It's on my desk.

Julien stubs out his cigarette on the railing and flicks it into the parking lot. I imagine the cigarette as Eddie or Colt, their bodies tumbling to the asphalt, Julien and me laughing. The air is catching its first bit of fall, a heady relief from the never-ending stretch of steamy days, which had started to make me feel like I was sleepwalking. Julien slips back inside. A bit of quiet, then the sound of Kanye blasting from a car driving down Eighth, the repetitive echo of a nail gun from the construction in the Gulch. Andy hollers out to Colt something about the ice machine, and he goes inside. Eddie follows.

The beeping of a car in reverse down the alley. A helicopter slicing through the air, headed toward the Vanderbilt hospital. Tobacco ash—cheap vodka. A trio of girls, stumbling out from the show, staring at an image on a cell phone. Silky moonlight. Uncomfortable, truncated banter from the stage: a joke about Mondays. Lukewarm laughter.

—Got a light?

A tall wisp of a guy comes out on the balcony. Another break between bands, people swinging the door open, mouths wide with laughter and bullshit. Name-dropping, flirting. I recognize him immediately as the lead guitarist for a band around town, though I didn't think he was playing The Venue tonight. He has wild curly hair, Robert Plant's texture with Jimmy Page's color and Jack White's length. Flannel shirt over a Metallica T-shirt littered with holes. The fingernails on his right hand are long, delicate like a girl's. A guitarist's hands, like Nick's. Nails kept long for fingerpicking. It's hard not to immediately imagine them inside me.

—You're Dan Daniels, I say.

His head cocks left in curiosity. A cloud shifts in front of the moon. There are moments when I want to play it cool in this city—an actual celebrity, a musician I deeply admire—and there are moments when I can't be bothered to care, when being covert just isn't worth the bullshit.

—Have we met? he asks.

I pass him the pack of cigarettes and he plucks one out. His index fingernails are each painted a dismal shade of gray. My lighter flicks flicks flicks and he leans over to catch it.

—No, I just . . . I mean, I work here. You guys played back in February, right? The show with Steel City?

A guy in a camel suede jacket and a wide-brimmed hat swings open the door. He looks around, ducks back inside.

—Yeah, that was us.

Sloane had told me about Dan, an interview he'd done at Lightning earlier in the year. Something about a bizarre diet, marathon training, days in the studio fueled by only sparkling water and—

—Is it true you only eat sweet potatoes? I ask.

—You're sure we haven't met? he says, inhaling a long drag from his cigarette. He's leaned toward me.

From inside, a three-piece girl group is going on, their voices blending in a sultry harmony behind us. A line about crying in an airport bathroom, a twelve-string guitar ringing out.

—Well first of all, Dan says, that was a phase. I was *testing out* being a vegetarian. And turns out, I don't like most vegetables.

—Tough gig, I say.

—I was also testing out being single, though not necessarily by choice. Anyway. You are?

—Al.

—You can call me Al, he says. Where you from, Al?

—Michigan, mostly.

—Michigan seems like a dream to me now, he sings, in a voice that's higher than I'd anticipated, milky soft.

—It took me four days to hitchhike from Saginaw, I say.

I don't sing the lyric, even though it probably would have landed better in conversation with a melody. But Dan still laughs, his piqued interest as faint as perfume left on a pillow—slight but sexual, unignorable.

—Your shirt is the color of C sharp, he says.

I pull at his, a faint blue a shade lighter than my own. I am full of shit, but he smiles and watches my fingers pinch the fabric. I let the shirt fall back to his chest.

—So yours is what, B flat?

In the lot below us a girl howls in laughter, hanging on a guy in flannel and leather.

—What do you do when you're not here, Al? Dan says.

His eyes: intense and dark dark brown. He keeps them pinned to my face. I find myself shifting my glance from his face to his shoulders, then back up to his forehead, his eyelashes, his fingernails again.

—I write poetry, I say.

Not actually writing the poetry I tell people I'm writing. Not having perfect pitch. Not even being able to match pitch all the time. Not listening to enough Allison Krauss, Carole King, Dave Rawlings. Saying my favorite band is Mazzy Star when I've only listened to the album once, but I play Something Corporate on repeat. Not being able to keep rhythm without a metronome. Not being able to play when almost anyone else is listening. Not being able to get onstage, to even think about getting onstage. Caring so much about Nick's band that I stop writing my own melodies. Sleeping with the bartender knowing that you should never sleep with the bartender. Knowing the name of all the local lead singers instead of the founding members of Pink Floyd or the Who. Maybe someday I'll actually be one of them, but for now—

Down at the door, Julien gives me shit about Colt, about Dan, about some random guy who comes through and mercilessly hits on me.

—You're in love with everyone, he says.

A group of girls between us suddenly. Pulling wallets from Gucci purses, wiping the edges of their smeared lipstick.

—I'm not in love with you, I say.

The last album didn't really do it for me. Have they got Yuengling up there? Two months sober. Nobody hates that song. At Grimey's, Saturday. Is he actually missing? They're doing an after-party. Late night over off Charlotte. That guy is too tall to be standing in the front row like that. Why do people come to this shit if they're just going to talk the whole time? I need a new weed guy. You know if you haven't heard anything it's not good news. Yeah it's all free, whatever you want, baby.

A break: twenty minutes. I end up at the pharmacy closest to The Venue. It's late, quiet, traffic sparse after ten on a Monday. I take laps through the brightly lit store, weaving in and out of the aisles. Taking inventory, killing time. I've never actually bought a pregnancy test before. It seems like the kind of thing I should have asked Sloane to do with me. Or for me.

"Pour Some Sugar on Me" is playing—a song that should be illegal. The automatic doors at the entrance sound like they're on a loop: open, close, open, close, open, close. A surprising number of people shuffling in thirty minutes before close to buy half gallons of milk and toothpaste, pints of ice cream and room-temperature beer. The lights are too bright. I'm pretending I desperately need an ankle wrap as I glance at the tests; I didn't expect so many options. I need to be back at The Venue in ten minutes.

My phone buzzes with a text from Julien as I reach for the cheapest test.

Want to grab us a snack?

I start and stop typing several times, then finally respond:

Like what?

When I glance up from my phone, I look across the aisle and there, studying the tampons, is Jessika. It seems like a cruel joke.

—Oh hey, she says, not unkindly.

I don't know what to do with the box in my hand, which suddenly feels like a third limb. My whole body is hot, my temples pulsing. I should have driven to the East Side.

—How are you? she asks. Are you off tonight?

—I'm—yeah. Well, no. Break. I'm on a break.

—Who's playing? she asks.

She's wearing a light neon windbreaker, leggings. Her hair is pulled up in a messy bun. She's holding a giant sparkling water and contact solution. She's different, I notice, when she's alone. Not in front of Julien or one of her bands. Voice just a bit quieter, flirtatious energy reined in. Like she's offstage or something.

—Honestly, I can't even remember.

She laughs, that big honking laugh. There it is. The guy at the photo counter looks up, startled.

—You guys are there every night. I'm sure it's easy to lose track.

—I've been sent out for snacks, I say, and then immediately regret it, because now she's looked at my hands, which are of course not holding snacks. I might as well be handing her the box, asking her to carry it for me, to buy it for me, to pee on the stick for me.

Her eyebrows lift and then settle back down on her face.

—And obviously I've failed, I say. With the snacks.

She laughs again.

We both stand there for a moment. I tap the box casually against my hip. She takes her thumb and index finger then and runs them across her lips, zipping them closed. I shrug, let the unspoken weight hang there for a minute.

—How many days? she asks.

The doors at the front: open, close, open, close.

—Four, I say.

—Eek.

—And a half.

She nods, and I can't believe Def Leppard is still the soundtrack to this moment.

—You'll be fine, she says. I've taken probably a hundred of those in my life. Even if I'm, like, thirty seconds late.

I nod. Her response is so reassuring, like she actually knows what will happen. Like she has control over it.

—I gotta get back to The Venue, I say.

She pulls out her phone then and hands it to me.

—Put your number in, she says.

A couple walks by us and stops in front of the condoms, all of us quiet. I slide the test under my arm and punch my number into her phone and save my name.

—Cool Ranch Doritos, she says as we part ways.

—Hm?

—If Jules asked for a snack, she says.

A game Sloane and I like to play, or rather she likes to play: Pull up someone in your phone, she'll say, waiting patiently while I do. Then scroll back to the very first text exchange. What does it say?

Mine and Sloane's: The address of the house we now share together; then, before I could respond, another text: Thursday at The Basement—Free. I wrote back: Yes to all of the above.

Mine and Nick's: A text from me that said just Al Hunter, in case he couldn't remember my name.

Mine and Colt's: 7—my place?

Mine and Julien's: Evidence against us, if we ever murdered Eddie together; then a request for snacks.

Mine and Jessika's: You can text me if you ever need to buy one of those again.

2.

Some nights, when Julien cuts me from the door, I stay until well after close. Until the stage lights go up and the traffic lights down Eighth flash yellow. Because the interns are always there to close down Colt's bar. Shots of whatever is around—Four Roses or Jack. Jim Beam if they're unpaid. Eddie blends in with them, milking his free drinks and easy connections long after he's been cut. The actual talent agents are having kids now, passing off some of these late weekday shows to the new guys—Hot Topic teens turned new college grads, out here looking for a band that can make them feel as wild as the music they listened to when they were seventeen did.

Other nights, I immediately text Sloane. Tonight is Saturday, ten p.m.—a solo show for a folksy female songwriter and it's all too quiet, The Venue is too empty, not the way it should be on a show night. People are hanging in the back bar shooting pool. Eddie's trying to hit on a girl far out of his league on the balcony, talking so loud I can hear him describing his improvisation process from inside the office. Julien's still downstairs.

Up in the office, I grab my jacket and bag. There's a stack of vinyls on the coffee table, and I flip through them while I wait for Sloane. The last one stares mockingly back at me: an early pressing of Flirtation

Device's new album. *Cloud Cover.* My thumbs along the spine—it's gorgeous. It looks hand-drawn: waves of tangled, hay-colored hair, almost like a field of wheat. It's a drawing of his hair, I know immediately.

God—sometimes it feels like the night of the flood broke some levee between me and Nick and now he's fucking everywhere. I set the record down.

—You heading out? Julien asks from the doorway. He looks exhausted, a slight slump in his shoulders, a sheet of paper in his right hand, an amp cable wrapped around his upper arm.

—You cut me, I say.

—You don't have to defend yourself. I know. You're allowed to leave.

—Sloane and I are going to a house party. Well, dinner and then a house party.

—At Alex Molly's?

—You're going?

—Depends on what time everybody finishes loading out.

I nod. A song ends in the main space. Polite applause, a little mild cheering.

—So maybe I'll see you later, I say. Julien Black, out in the wild.

—You've seen me out in the wild, he says. You've been to my apartment.

—Once, I say, holding my index finger up. My phone rings: Sloane out in the parking lot.

—Oh, you can have that if you want, Julien says, nodding at Nick's record on the coffee table. It's just a promo from the label. I figured you might want it. Though I guess you can probably get an advance copy. Since you know them. Him, I mean.

I want to say no, to not reach for it, but I can't resist. I reach out to grab it—the cardboard square, the slick plastic—and try to slide it into my bag, but the corners stick out awkwardly, like an extra syllable that doesn't fit the rhythm of a song.

—You sure?

—Let me know how it is, Julien says.

To my knowledge, there is only one problem with music. Well, two, if you count the power of earworms, the fact that even bad songs can get stuck in your head. Okay then, three: the simple fact that once you've heard a song you love for the first time, you can never hear it for the very first time again. But the real problem—and this can fundamentally Fuck You, in my opinion—is the way a song or an album or a voice on the radio can fling you so authoritatively into the past. Songs are almost always slivers of souvenirs, recollections, and Nick's are no different. Maybe this is why his voice, to me, always sounds so much like a memory.

In the parking lot, Sloane dangles a cigarette out the window of her Wrangler. She's listening to an album from a new California band, Laurel Canyon harmonies slipping out into the night. Smoke out of her mouth like a frail ghost. She's wearing a plain black shirt and a short skirt, small gold hoops in her ears.

She's in one of those moods when she's being rich, which happens about once a month or so. Usually it appears in the form of designer jeans or some extravagant flea market purchase, but sometimes it's a meal we have no business eating. A night of eighteen-dollar gin and tonics and prime rib sliders at the Palm before a Ryman show, a bottle of champagne and filet mignon at the steakhouse that just opened on Demonbreun.

She passes me her phone—Mix #19—and says:

—Only additions for this one. No deleting. And no songs by people you've fucked.

For a moment, I think about telling her about the late period, the pregnancy test. But I can't, because it'll change the whole tenor of our evening. She'll probably make me take it right now, in the car, something crazy like that. Instead I scroll through her music, adding a pop-punk song I loved as a teenager, then slinking back into the seat. Sloane turns it up, sound pressing against the polypropylene, spilling into the night. Downtown skims by. Sloane's hand out the window, the energy of the night humming under my skin, like this is a warm-up for the rest of the evening, the rest of the week, the rest of the year. You know the feeling, like being on the precipice of something—the edge of a tall building but you know you can fly—where it seems like almost anything could happen, and we were still dumb and young enough to let it.

Sloane's parallel parking is divine. She finds a spot on Nineteenth, and when we empty out of the Jeep the breeze is mellow. An anemic leaf floats down facade of the condos on Division, the threat of a chill just palpable in the air as we walk into Giovanni's. Dark night into a darker entryway. Sloane hugs the hostess and I follow her to the bar. The bartender arrives, tall and freshly shaven, suspenders tight, his hands reaching across the bar quickly to Sloane's. Sloane says something I can't catch and then introduces me.

—Benny, this is my roommate, Al. She works at The Venue. Al, this is Benny. He works here.

Benny sticks out a large hand. I want to ask how they know each other. They look like old friends, their hands clasped, their frenzied side chatter. But this is just Sloane.

—Al also writes songs, Sloane says.

Benny gives me a smile, performative but vacant, but I can't return it. Sloane's never introduced me that way. *I've* certainly never introduced myself that way. But then, before I can say anything, she's leaning across the bar, showing Benny something on her phone. I get the sense that there are two Sloanes: the one I see, who lives in a normal house with cheap rent and a low-paying job, and the other, who splurges on three-hundred-dollar dinners and hangs backstage at Ryman shows and doesn't pay her own car lease. A Justin Wilson song comes on overhead. I briefly imagine him and Esther in a room together, a guitar in hand, parsing out the lyrics—

—No I don't, I say. I mean, I'm not, like, a *songwriter.* I've written songs. But I'm not—

Sloane doesn't even hear my response. Her hands are still clutched in Benny's, a platonic set of palms across the marble bar.

—What can I get y'all? he asks.

—Vodka martini. Dirty. Ketel One. Two olives.

—I didn't know you were such a regular here, I say to Sloane. Then, to the bartender: I'll do the same, but with gin I guess. You can make it with gin, right?

—You *should* make it with gin, Benny says, flicking his eyes dismissively at Sloane. Gin preference? he asks.

Nobody has ever asked me this question before. The gin I drank in college cost three dollars. I'm not sure I've ever ordered a martini proper before. Overhead, the song is still on, loud and haunting, an acoustic version of Wilson's album.

—Hendrick's, Sloane says for me. And you hate olives, right? At least on pizza? Don't get it dirty then. Dry. With a twist. Is this really your first martini? Trust me, she says.

The song ends, and before another one starts, quiet fills the bar in an awkwardly loud hush, like a server has dropped a stack of plates. A cocktail shaker rattling, a chair scraping against the floor. The phone rings at the hostess stand, but nobody picks it up. A credit card hits the bar.

—Why'd you tell him that? That I write songs? And how do you know everybody here?

—I told him you write songs because you *write songs*, Al!

—It's . . . misleading, I say.

—I know you don't want to play anything after the—ugh, the *Incident*—but it's been months now. Plus, I know you write. I know you've *been* writing, Sloane says.

—Privately, I say.

—Privacy is a privilege, she says.

—Oh my god. What does that even mean?

But Sloane was right: she did overhear me playing something I'd written, but it was something from college. And I didn't even realize she was home.

Our drinks arrive then, clear and crystalline on the marble bar. Sloane reaches for hers and holds it up delicately.

—I got a promotion, she says.

My hand is on the glass and I spill some of my drink, the liquor sloshing softly over the rim. Before we can cheers, Sloane has already taken a sip of her martini. I do the same. The gin is sharp and fragrant. My throat opens up and the evening becomes almost instantly a shade more pleasant.

—I didn't even know you were up for one. When did this happen?

I know I should be happy for her, but I liked the way our jobs felt similar—straightforward and easy, barely real. The bare minimum responsibility of The Venue is all I really want out of a job. I have no desire to climb any kind of career ladder; I didn't even know there were ladders I could climb. I thought Sloane was the same, that she didn't want to do something real either, but maybe I'm just being naive. Maybe eventually I'll be the only one left working at a place like The Venue.

—I wasn't really, she says. But Billy needed a new promotions director and I told him I was interested. We're starting to sponsor the free live shows downtown, and he needs somebody to take on that new work. So. You know. Blah blah blah. Boring work stuff, and voilà! I'm the new promotions director. Maybe now I can get us our own radio show, you know? Get some *women* behind the ones and twos.

—Well, shit. That's amazing. Is this why we're at such a nice restaurant?

—We're at such a nice restaurant because we're adults, Al, she said. And because it's a Saturday night and I just got paid and we deserve martinis and Benny promised to treat us well. Okay, she says, now what do we want?

She doesn't have any management. Do we want another round? It's the mixing and postproduction that's taking so long. Their drummer is a dick. I see him everywhere. He owns all the masters, everything. There's the weirdest party up on Love Circle. He said Caleb Followill was coming. He relapsed. I heard them on NPR. Wouldn't we know if he was dead? Nobody's cared about them for the last two albums. That voice will kill you. They're kind of a band's band. When is load-in? I think bus call is midnight.

We abandon Sloane's Jeep at the restaurant and she calls us a black town car.

We are daydream drunk and happy and warm. On the ride over we make grand plans for Sloane's promotion. She already had access, but now she'll have something better: *influence.* We talk about it like she's about to be running a record label or station of her own: the concerts where we'll be backstage, the musicians we'll meet, the radio show we'll eventually host together. It's all fantasy, all overblown, but fun all the same.

By the time we arrive at the dilapidated blue bungalow off Belmont, the party has spilled onto the lawn. A band has just finished playing a set in the living room, and guys in flannels and jeans are shutting the clasps on guitar and bass cases, stacking amps in the damp grass. Above: a bright moon, a nickel of light above the neighborhood. Cigarettes spotting the grass, the smell of weed drifting across the lawn.

—I have to pee, Sloane says, and takes off quickly through the crowd. Get me a beer?

The sound of drunken flirting, a distorted guitar from a window upstairs. I want a drink. That's the problem with martinis, I think, as if my first real martini half an hour ago has made me a connoisseur: they go down like water, and then all you want is more. I make my way inside.

The house is stuffy. Faces flushed, clusters of guys and girls huddled around holding Solo cups and cans of PBR and bottles of Yazoo. There's a nice, even ratio of men to women. Jessika is there, in the kitchen, surrounded by a group of guys. She stands tall and comfortable, singing along to a song carrying in from outside. They all look like they've known each other for ages. Probably all Belmont kids. She's braiding one guy's long, curly hair, a joint floating in and out of fingertips, its movement practically choreographed. When she laughs, it cracks through the room like thunder announcing a storm. She doesn't notice me.

In the kitchen, there's so much beer in the fridge it's comical. Like I'm doing these people a favor by taking some. When I take three, the refrigerator light splits into fluorescent white shards, the remaining stacked beers blocking the rest of the light. Behind me a shuffle of cards, the pop of a bottle top. I snake back through the party, passing Sloane on my way outside. I don't save her from the conversation she's already stuck in, though—it's too entertaining to watch her grin and bear it, talking to a guy with bright eyes who looks like he's holding a ferret. *Fuck you*, she mouths to me as I slip her a beer.

Outside I fall into conversation with a barefoot upright bass player named Tommy and an intern for Big Machine named Drew, a guy with gray eyes and a slight lisp. Tommy and Drew are debating the best Stones album. Tommy says it's *Some Girls*, everybody knows that, and Drew says it's *Exile on Main Street*, and I tell them it's *Sticky Fingers*, if only for the actual working zipper on the vinyl cover. I start rambling to them about an interview I read where Mick Jagger said it was called *Some Girls* because they "couldn't remember any of their fucking names." Beers are finished and crushed underfoot in the grass, only to be replaced by new ones handed off by acquaintances. The party is still pulsing, people arriving and leaving in minivan cabs, live music coming from the kitchen, a couple of guys messing around on guitar, bass. I think I see Julien across the lawn, but when I look again it's just shadows, a couple holding each other and swaying beneath an oak tree.

From across the lawn I see a girl with a gray streak in her hair leaving the house, walking toward a car parked up the street, staring at her phone as she walks. It looks like Esther Wainwright. I step away for a closer look, but she's already in the car.

Lukewarm beers, a dry joint passed, the twang of an acoustic guitar in drop D. Damp warmth between my legs—I think it's my period but it's not. Just sweat. A guy doing backflips in the grass, a playful shriek from the street. A firecracker pops on the sidewalk; a bottle crashes onto the concrete. Snippets of starlight, a neighbor threatening to call the police. A drummer, a guitarist, another drummer—

Sloane takes off right around the time my group disperses. She's going with her drummer, Jamie, to a late-night diner over on Eighth, like we didn't just drop $250 on dinner.

—I can send the car back for you, she says. Or Jamie can come back and get you? I mean, he'll have to drop me off first, because, you know, a motorcycle. But he can come back.

She's drunk but her words are sharp. She lights a cigarette, takes a drag, then passes it to me, tells me to keep it.

—I'm fine, I say. I'll get a ride.

—I can take her, says a voice behind us. It's Julien, appearing from a cluster of people as if we've summoned him. Seeing Julien outside The Venue—it's like seeing a teacher at the grocery store. Sloane pinches his cheeks like they're the oldest of friends, then traipses off and climbs on the back of Jamie's bike. I slide into Julien's front seat, wondering where his girlfriend is.

Songs meant for nighttime driving only:

"We Looked Like Giants" (Death Cab for Cutie)
"Just Like Honey" (the Jesus and Mary Chain)
"Runaway" (the National)
"Who Says" (John Mayer)
"I Will Be There When You Die" (My Morning Jacket)
"Everything in Its Right Place" (Radiohead)
"No One's Gonna Love You" (Band of Horses)
"Hammers and Strings" (Jack's Mannequin)

—I wish you could see the stars, I say, looking up at the sky as we roll up to a stop sign. Julien glances over at me, his eyes on me like a physical weight. Then back on the road.

He turns on the music, a burned CD he's slid into the console—an old pop-punk song I loved when I was seventeen, the kind of deep cut that makes me pause, look at him, ask:

—You know this song?

Memories of Michigan highways and cool, dry summers. A hand under a T-shirt, windows down, a fizzing somewhere in my chest.

—*You* know this song? Julien says.

—I haven't heard this in forever, I say. I didn't know anybody else still listened to these guys.

—I didn't know anybody else listened to them back then, either.

—We would have been friends in high school then, I say.

He takes us through the Gulch, though I don't know where we're going. Away from where we live, down toward the area where warehouses start to give way to new construction, sleek restaurants fading into empty parking lots, an Urban Outfitters sitting aglow across from the Station Inn. He flicks his blinker on; he's driving in circles just to let the song finish.

Waxing ivory moon—oily sky.

The volume is perfect. It's too tempting. Too much nostalgia—too much to drink—to not sing along. *Is that what you call a getaway?* I belt.

I'm louder than I need to be, the drinks drowning out my self-consciousness. Julien drums along on the steering wheel. He's usually a little stoic at shows, even for the bands he loves, but this—

I look out at the skyline: Technicolor lights in the distance down Broadway, all the honky-tonks bursting at the seams. Here on Division, though, we're the only car at the light, and Julien's full-on singing now. Outside, the shape of the city obscures the stars.

A low breeze out the window. The nylon of the seat belt pressing into my neck. Julien, looking over at me again, mouthing the words, fists still balled up on the steering wheel, right at ten and two.

And then the chorus breaks back through and he shrieks it, his voice carrying over the song, me right there with him screaming at the top of my lungs, the kind of volume where there isn't even pitch anymore, just noise and sound. Violent guitars and throaty howls, all our emotions emptied from our bodies.

When the chorus ends, Julien takes a breath. A bead of sweat appears on his temple.

—The light's green, I shout, and he turns left and swings onto Cannery, pulling into The Venue.

Car off, a hushed calm.

—Nightcap? Julien asks.

The parking lot has a lovely, ethereal glow, as if it's just rained, though it hasn't. The Gulch is deserted. It's after three. We walk up the back stairs to the balcony.

—Watch that step, he says, pointing out a spot where the wood is rotting.

I stand still, briefly grabbing onto the back of his shirt as he walks forward, like I'm following him through a forest. He unlocks the back door from a mess of keys clipped around his belt loop.

Pitch-black, eerie silence. *I will follow you into the dark.*

And even though he's warned me, even though I'm being careful—isn't that the true irony of all this, how reckless I am even when I think I'm being careful?—I trip. Knees onto warped wood, my purse poured out in front of me as Julien moves his hand along the wall, searching for a light switch that he can't quite find. And then light rushes over us, and he leans down quickly to grab my bag, the one I'd been carrying the other night, the one with—

—Are you okay? he asks, grabbing my wallet, keys, a couple of matchbooks.

I scramble for the cardboard box from the pharmacy. Why didn't I just take the test the night I bought it? I inhale sharply as Julien gets to it first, glancing down and then sliding it back into my bag like it's just a pack of gum. He passes me my purse and I stand up shakily. The quiet of The Venue is obnoxious, and I clear my throat to try to break through it.

—It's for Sloane, I say, ensuring the test is fully stuffed back into my purse.

He holds up both of his hands, as if to absolve himself of the conversation. Pale palms above his head, eyes wide and soft. I look at him for several excruciating moments, trying to read what he's thinking, but now his hands are down and his lips are closed and his face is back to its usual inscrutable.

—What happened to Jess tonight? I ask.

—Oh. Uh, she had to go home, he says. Early flight.

—Oh yeah?

—Don't act so excited.

—She's a lot, I say.

—Do you even know her? he asks, though it comes out as more of a curiosity than a reprimand.

—That laugh, I say.

—M-hm.

—Where's she going? I ask.

—Austin City Limits. Then on tour for a couple weeks.

—Denim? I ask.

—Yeah, or something, he says.

—You don't know? Isn't she your girlfriend?

—Do you want something? he asks. A drink? Or just water?

—You still have that secret stash of Yuengling? I ask.

In the office he grabs two beers from the mini fridge and hands one to me. It's too nice a night to sit inside, though, so we go back out on the balcony. We lean against the bricks; I prop my right heel up against the building.

—Have we ever used that second space upstairs at all? I ask. For photo shoots or, I don't know, anything, really? I know we rent the other space out for weddings sometimes.

—Not that I know of, he says. Though Colt just found out about it and now he wants to scope it out for a video.

—Of course he does.

The moon is high above the city. The air tastes like cold ash and yeast. A low chill, light shivers. Julien's shoulder next to mine, a few inches away, a low undercurrent of heat from his torso. There should be music playing but of course it's silent.

—What's up with, uh—What's up with you two, anyway? Julien asks. Is that—

My breastbone clenches.

—Nothing, I say. No. Why?

He takes a sip of beer and swallows quietly. The smell of brass and rotting wood, a scurry of an insect, a rodent, some other creature.

—Just wondering, he says.

—Nothing, I say again. Really.

—All right, he says.

—Nothing really. Not anymore.

It's obviously bullshit, like saying the test is Sloane's, but he nods, turning his ankle, digging the toe of his right foot into the warped wood of the balcony. My skin prickles at the base of my neck. I sing a line of what we were listening to in the car out loud without thinking. Molecules of air bouncing off bricks—sound.

I look over at Julien. He's looking at me and—

Eyes brackish like floodwater, almost wet. He takes another sip of his beer, glass against teeth, our mouths full of bones.

—You told me a couple months ago that you had someone like . . . I trail off, not wanting to say Nick's name. From before you met Jess? You know, like, a person, an ex, a *someone*, who . . .

He blinks, his eyes closed for a moment. He glances away and clears his throat.

—Someone from back home, he says.

I nod, trying to ignore the sourness that's settled across my chest.

—Do you still talk? I ask.

—Here and there.

He looks away then, and I can't tell if the acerbic taste in my throat is from all the beers or the conversation, the thought of some girl Julien has in the back of his mind, like he doesn't also already have a girlfriend, like—

I exhale, then hum another line from the song we were listening to in the car to break the silence.

—I can't get that song out of my head now, I say.

He opens his eyes and looks at me again:

—When do I get to hear one of *your* songs?

3.

~~*I don't like her gold hoops*~~
~~*her red lips, her attitude, I don't like the way she's looking*~~
~~*at you*~~

On the floor of my bathroom—the acoustics round and silky—the tile is cool against my thighs. Seven days late. I toss the notebook aside. I've lost my melody again, like I'm trying to draw a shape without lines. Lou Reed pokes his head through the doorframe, looking hungry. My phone buzzes and I swipe out of the Voice Memos app.

Nick.

Can I send you a song?

The timing is laughable, as if he knew even from afar that I was in the middle of trying (and failing) to write one of my own. I want to throw my phone across the bathroom. I want to scream. I want to say *fuck you*, crawl back into bed, tell him *no.*

Of mine, he says.

I toss back the dregs of my gin and tonic and turn up Steel Train and type back:

Maybe.

At my feet, Lou Reed has made himself a nest on the bath mat, nudging it with his nose and pawing at it repeatedly before collapsing into a perfect spiral. Is there a way to say no to Nick? Perhaps there is, but I don't know it yet. A low-grade mania coursing through me—pricks of energy heating up the tops of my ears, my jaw, spreading down across my chest. The idea of getting unreleased Flirtation Device singles is still too exciting, too tempting—all that intimacy and access. Or maybe Nick is just drunk.

It's rough, the next text says. Truly just a demo.

Send it, I reply, walking to the kitchen, filling a glass halfway with gin, topping it off with tonic like a fizzy afterthought. Sloane's still at work. The house is too quiet, but she's texting me updates from an interview she's doing at the station.

My phone buzzing again. Nick: I wanted you to hear it first.

Thoughts I have but don't send: *Am I the only person you're sending it to? Does Allison have it too? Has anyone else in the band heard it—or is it just for me?*

Fifteen minutes pass and my email sits silent, like The Venue after hours. Under my skin, a louder hum of misplaced energy, like I've missed a step walking up the back stairs to The Venue, or swerved into the wrong lane driving. My body bristles again, this time my palms and fingertips, little desperate pads of anticipation. Colt's given me a toothpick box full of benzos and other goodies, and I chew up a child's dose of Xanax and let the bitterness coat my tongue before downing the next gin and tonic.

I scroll through social media, waiting on Nick's email. Jessika has added me as a friend, and my curiosity is insatiable. I click on her profile—a photo of her standing in the alley outside the Ryman, a pass hanging from her neck—and flick through her photos while I get ready for the party. She is stupid fucking pretty, which of course I already knew but which now settles over me with a fresh clarity as I click through picture after picture after picture. The kind of pretty that requires no makeup, that looks good in dresses, in skirts, in men's oversize shirts, in sweatpants, in baggy jeans and ponchos and ill-fitting swimsuits. Fake leather and family photos.

She has all her work experience and internships listed, and it seems impossible for someone who's only twenty-five to have already done so much. Sony and CAA and Red Light, a couple of others I haven't heard of. There's a picture of her on a panel at last year's Tin Pan South Songwriters Festival, and apparently she even sat on the board of some young music professional organization.

There are only a few pictures of her and Julien. Casual. In the cutest one, he's standing behind her, his elbow hooked sweetly over her shoulder and around her neck, his fingers wrapped around the lip of a Yuengling, a PBR tall boy in her hand. Her mouth is open in a wide toothy smile, his lips closed but warm. It's from months ago and there haven't been any posted since. I'm trying to figure out where it was taken—one of their houses? At a bar? A friend's house? Julien's living room. After sex, maybe. I look at the picture for a very long time, finish my drink, then head off for his party.

When I get to Julien's, the night is nice, still a little warm, the trees starting to flicker *fall.* The maple on the corner of Lawrence is so red it matches the rust on the chain-link fence. It's quiet for Halloween, just a few cabs and a band rehearsing on the corner of Twelfth and Edgehill, either covering Bon Iver or thinking they are. I walk even though nobody else does, putting in my headphones and flicking on a mix of Taylor Swift songs that Sloane made for me. She keeps insisting Taylor's one of our generation's greatest songwriters, but I'm still on the fence.

By the time I get to the party, though, I've listened to one of her six-minute tracks five times. As usual, Sloane's probably right.

At Julien's, the party is not a party. At least not in any way that's visible or audible from the porch, where the giant rocking chair sits empty. The lights are off in the upstairs window, so I let myself in a side door—which puts me directly into Julien's room. Piles of beige boy clothes and Springsteen records and show paraphernalia. Springsteen seems a little vanilla for Julien—but then I'm still listening to Taylor Swift, so maybe I should shut the fuck up? The room is small and dark and the emptiness of it is a little sad. I wonder how long he's lived here, if the decor is a product of not being settled or if this is just how he likes to live. There's a certain coldness to the space, like a doctor's waiting room, but with Springsteen posters. My throat is tight. I need a drink.

From upstairs, finally, evidence of a small party—low electric guitars, a few rumbles from boys' voices.

—People know you can just drink? I say out loud to no one, arriving at the top of the stairs. You don't even have to have a game.

—Ladies and gentlemen, Al Hunter! The Spirit of Halloween.

Julien's cheeks are pink. He's wearing a black suit, black-rimmed glasses.

—What are you supposed to be?

—Guess, he says.

—You look like a used-car salesman.

The table bursts into laughter. The music in the background is unrecognizable. Probably one of those bands everyone pretends to like but no one really does. Cool to like, boring to love. Arcade Fire, maybe.

—Elvis Costello, he says. Drink?

—Please.

He gets up from the table and passes me a Sierra Nevada from the fridge. The boys continue the next round of whatever game they're playing, and silence slips around me and Julien for a second like a hand. This loopy, buzzed version of Julien is new to me—no books or trumpet or ratty messenger bag in sight. It's like he's unfolding.

—What are *you*? he asks.

—Like, what's my sign?

—No, weirdo, your costume.

—Oh, I'm a musician.

He laughs quietly—kindly—and takes a sip of beer, wiping the back of his mouth with his hand. My face warms as I drink my beer half down. The vibration of my phone in my pocket is impossible to ignore: Nick. The song. I'm woozy, like I've been picked up and set back down into the conversation. Sometimes in moments like this, it's like I'm plucking feelings for Nick off my skin like dog hairs off an old coat. Weeks, months, years after you thought you'd gotten them all, that the fabric was clean—

Julien has said something but I've missed it.

—What? I ask, putting my phone back.

—Nothing, he says. Take your call.

—I don't have a call. I'm here.

—It's not a costume.

—You know I hate Halloween.

—That's not what I mean.

My phone is a hot coal in my hand.

—I'm here, I say, planting my feet. Julien takes another drink and then so do I.

—It's not a costume if you're dressed up as something you already are.

The heat from the phone spreads to my palms, then up my arms into my chest and down through my core. I tense my calves to keep from shivering.

—Stop fucking with me, I say, and Julien just smiles, lets his eyes get all squinty.

—Did you meet everyone? he asks, pointing over my shoulder to the table.

Elvis Costello. Buddy Guy. Springsteen. David Bowie. Prince. Sting. Stevie Wonder. Stevie Ray Vaughan. Paul Westerberg. Kris Kristofferson. Lucinda Williams. Loretta Lynn. Patti Smith. Morrissey. So many songwriters I don't know shit about, so many legends I wouldn't recognize if they walked into this party and sat down to play me a song.

Jess is still on tour, so it's mostly a bunch of Julien's friends from college. They're a real mixed bag, and he's the best-looking of them; the rest of them are fine, forgettable. Two of them are wearing fleece; they immediately become one in my mind. The third, dressed up as Yoshi, has a warm smile, and the childish costume makes me like him easily.

—Wanna play? he asks, holding up a deck of cards.

—I want to drink, I say.

Another friend arrives, though, and to my relief the game collapses before it begins.

—You don't like Halloween *or* drinking games? Julien asks.

—I don't need a game to help me finish my beer, I say. And then: Sorry.

—Feisty tonight, he says, but he's smiling.

A half dozen people pour in from a side door, in varying degrees of costume.

—Do you know everyone here? I ask. A thought crosses my mind: if

I had a party, the only person I'd know to invite, besides the guys at The Venue, would be Sloane.

Julien shrugs.

—Small town.

Shrieking from the back balcony. The sound of the fridge: open, shut, open, shut. A pint glass shatters in the sink, water rushing over the glass. Snare drum, a bass lick that's familiar but unplaceable. A text from Sloane: she's going to the East Side for a bar crawl, I should call her if Jujubean's party is lame. A girl yodeling. A guy forgetting someone's name and trying to cover it up.

After an hour, the party finally settles into a rhythm of its own. The music is all backbeat and radio rock now, the kind everybody knows, the kind that starts to feel like it's bad for you the more you listen to it, like grocery store candy against your teeth. The ratio of guys to girls is in my favor, though no one in particular has caught my attention. I know literally no one here except for Julien, which doesn't bother me as much as it should. For much of the evening, I slip in and out of conversations like a ghost.

Yoshi is telling stories about Julien, half-baked ones he looks guilty revealing, like how Julien was the lead singer of a hard-core band in high school that he still played with occasionally in college, or the fact that he lost his virginity listening to the Postal Service. Or maybe he just wanted to. Yoshi seems surprised that I don't know these things already—haven't I spent most of my evenings working side by side with Julien for the past nine months? He's right—I'm surprised too. That pinch of envy again around my ribs.

I get up from the conversation—in theory to pee, but in reality to find another drink and in truth to find Julien, who's in the kitchen talking to a girl dressed—how did I miss this?—in a cheap-looking Snow White costume.

It's nearly eleven. Another text from Nick.

Let me know when you listen.

The refrigerator light is dim, blocked by a tray of Jell-O shots.

—Are these up for grabs? I ask, pulling the tray from the fridge and poking my finger into the neon jiggle, testing for doneness like it's a birthday cake. I'm well past the point of needing another drink, but for one blissful moment I'm able to convince myself that a Jell-O shot is not a drink at all. I grab several, loosening one and letting the shot slide down my throat.

In the bathroom, the text from Nick is still hanging there, and now there's another. I slurp down a second shot.

Why don't we live in the same city?

I want to say, *You're never even there.* I want to say, *We could have.* I want to say, *We still could.*

Instead I type back: I hate the winters there.

Still, the back of my neck shivers. Arousal at the hypothetical. The clarity and calm of a solid buzz slipping around me like a shield. I'm irritated but turned on, and there in front of the mirror I take off my clothes slowly, purposefully, like I'm being watched. My underwear is still spotless as it drops to the ground. I let out a protracted exhale. In the background, someone has put on bad country music.

My hip bones are visible in a way they haven't been since high school, my hair is long and thick and can nearly cover my chest, my tan from the summer is still a faint glow on my skin. I don't know what to do with my face, so I let the flash obscure it. Julien's voice is audible over the din, somewhere nearby, though I can't hear the girl. I don't over-think it.

Will listen when I get home. For now . . .

In the picture I send to Nick, my nipples are hard, but my face is just a shadow. I delete the others and put my clothes back on. Opening my Notes app, I type in a few lines about the party, annoyed to hear them rhyme but unable to stop it: *Snow white at your shoulder / felt the night growing colder / send nudes in the bathroom / swear this isn't about you.*

I'm either a genius or a total amateur. Back inside the party, the noise washes over me. Shouting about a show that just ended at the Basement, a drunk girl on a phone call, voices debating whether to go to the dive bar down the street. People have splintered off to corners of the kitchen, the living room, the back porch. I flick my phone off and scan the party for Julien.

The people in this town swirl together. Most nights, the sheer amount of creative energy—all in one place—is a deluge. The guy in the corner who plays in a folk band is maybe the same guy from the house party who also plays in a jazz trio, a pop band, a metal band, an alt-country band. A guy dressed as Townes Van Zandt is a friend of a friend of a friend of Sloane's; he lives in an efficiency apartment on Belmont and writes horribly beautiful sad songs. A girl who chain-smokes on Monday nights at The Venue is in the corner, dressed up as Marie Antoinette or maybe Edith Wharton or maybe just an old lady; she sings backup and lead, but I can't remember the name of her band. A guy who looks like Ezra Koenig, and who once told me he writes songs about the new American South, is now here at Julien's, across the room, dressed like Moby. Everybody does something, nobody has a salary. Everybody writes songs, but only some of them are songwriters.

Julien is in a mood.

For much of the rest of the night, I am sure he's flirting with me—real, bona fide flirting, like he doesn't have a girlfriend, like I'm a stranger he's just met or we're actually exes. Intimacy like this comes only at the extremes on the spectrum, and I'm not sure which one I'm closest to. It's hard not to slurp down drinks, but they just keep coming and the Snow White girl is gone and a guy dressed as Jim from *The Office* confesses to having built an ice luge out back and then another guy dressed as Don Draper passes around an enormous joint and then someone puts on Amy Winehouse and Julien is singing at me in the living room where a Christmas tree is already—still?—up and the air is stuffy but the ceilings are high and we are singing to only ourselves.

The song changes and my voice cracks at the high notes, aching over the volume of the music, but I don't even care, I just sing. Julien is singing too. His voice is pretty in an unpracticed, maybe-he-doesn't-even-realize-it kind of way. I didn't totally register it in the car after the house party, when he was shrieking, but now his voice is bright and confident, his cheeks stop-sign red, his face buoyant and dotted with sweat. Woozy, breathless, the song carrying us along on the current of the melody. Sharp aftertaste of vodka. Julien's throat open, teeth coffee-stained and crooked, the glint of a retainer beneath his tongue. My lungs trying to keep up with the music, with the water, until finally Brandon Flowers's voice fades out and a song I hate comes on, and I ask Julien if he needs some air, and even though he looks disappointed and I can tell he wishes we were still singing along to the song together, he says: Sure.

On the porch you can hear the low murmur of the night. We sit in the giant rocking chair, and I cross my legs like a child and he does the same. It's almost conspiratorial out here like this, all his friends inside debating different Bowie albums and reminiscing about drunken nights from undergrad. He offers me a cigarette, even though he rarely smokes, and I say no and then yes and then no again and then shrug and take one.

—Was that your friend from the door? The guitarist? He nods at my phone. Earlier.

—Oh, it was—no.

The lie slips out so easily, and I don't have the heart to follow it up with a correction, that Nick is a lead singer.

The air is cool. My cigarette has gone out and I lean over to Julien with it between my lips, expecting him to light it with the neon green lighter he's flicking around in his hand, but he leans forward instead, the ember on the end of his cigarette a hazy orange, and touches it to mine for several beats until mine lights in a slow glow. A shiver runs from my shoulder blades down my arms as he blinks his long eyelashes, fingertips close to mine. And then he pulls away and I realize I haven't been breathing. A siren howls over by Horton Avenue and then the night is quiet again. I lean back.

—I heard you used to be in a hard-core band.

—Oh god, he says. Were you talking to Matt?

I laugh, nod. I crack my knuckles, run a hand through my hair. My phone is dead in my pocket.

—How'd you get from there to the trumpet?

—I contain fucking multitudes, he says.

My laugh is loud and sharp.

—Are you gonna stay here? I ask.

—Like, in the house?

—No, like, *here* here.

—In Nashville?

I nod, inhale.

—For now, he says.

—What does that mean?

—I don't know. This year, anyway.

—There's only two months left in the year, I say.

—You know what I mean. Probably for the foreseeable future.

—How long do you consider foreseeable? I ask.

—I don't know, Al.

—I'm just curious.

—Why, are you planning to leave? Are you quitting? Don't tell me you're quitting, he says.

—I'm not qualified to do almost anything else, I say. Of course I'm not quitting. I love it there.

—Good.

—And it's barely a job.

—I'm not moving, Julien says. Not anytime soon.

—That's cool.

—Is it?

He puts his cigarette out.

—This is fun, I say.

—Good party, he says, and I just look up into the fractured light of the porch and say, That's not what I meant.

4.

The next morning, my period finally comes. Heavy and forceful, my stomach aching all morning. I relish it, lying in bed with the heating pad until midafternoon. I throw out the pregnancy test, take the trash out before Sloane gets home. I don't want her to freak out, don't want her to wonder why I didn't tell her earlier. She'd scoff at Colt, I know, but then again: Who wouldn't? When I go to change my tampon, I consider saving it. Framing it. Handing it over to Colt as he stands there clueless. Instead I text Jessika and say: safe.

Back at The Venue, up in the second space, a few days later. Bare feet on paper napkins, I slide across the wooden floor, dancing to an old Death Cab song in my head. Downtown glimmers through the window. Wet cardboard, old beer. I take a hit from the tail end of one of the joints from Andy's drawer and sit in the windowsill with his guitar.

> ~~*don't waste your time on me*~~
> ~~*you know I'm only looking for novelty*~~

The melody is too loose, though; I'm not even sure what key I'm in. I keep getting stuck in the spaces between notes—the melody meandering until it's nothing at all. When I open my eyes, Julien's across the room, a blank look on his face. Black jeans and a navy blue Modest Mouse shirt, the two shades clashing slightly in the sunlight. Emo front-man cute, I think.

—What the hell? How long have you been standing there? I ask.

His face is hard to read from across the room, the sun slanting in from the window behind me and briefly turning him into a silhouette. I set the guitar down and stand up, but in my haste the instrument slips and hits the hardwood with a horrible smack.

—Me what the hell? *You* what the hell? What are you doing up here? Aren't you off today?

—Aren't *you* off today?

—Just bringing back some chairs I snagged for the party, he says. What song was that?

—Nothing, I say.

Julien and me on his porch—a warmth in the tops of my cheeks—and then he asks:

—Did you smoke up here?

He starts stacking chairs, the clink of metal on metal filling the space.

—Probably Eddie, I say.

He knows I'm lying, though, and we laugh. I slide Andy's guitar back into its soft case.

—He keeps trying to show me his tight five on his phone, I say. It's him rehearsing the bits in front of a mirror.

—Tight five?

—Yeah. He's working on a stand-up routine. He hasn't tried to make you watch it?

—Oh god, Julien says, laughing. No.

—Lucky, I say.

—Probably because he doesn't have a crush on me.

—Gross. He's barely legal, I say. Plus, he knows you're taken.

Julien smiles and runs a hand through his hair, though the strands fall back across his eyes immediately. He *does* look like he's getting ready to go sell merch at Warped Tour—swooping hair and dark jeans and all. *Oh I would kill for the Atlantic / but I am paid to make girls panic while I sing.* Something in my chest tightens, and he bends down to adjust the tongue of his sneakers.

The zipper on the guitar case is stuck, but I sling the guitar over my shoulder anyway, half open. Julien clears his throat and it echoes throughout the space. We collect a dozen or so chairs, stacking them the way we used to after church when I was a kid.

—You found it there at the end, Julien says.

—What?

—The melody. That last bit.

My face is hot, and I have to look away for a moment. The sun is starting to dip slightly off to the west, a firestorm orange beyond the skyline.

—I don't think so, I say.

He shrugs.

—I'm just saying. It sounded like the start of a song to me.

Waking up and feeling like I'm underwater. Preferring drinking over eating. Relishing the dark headlines, wishing for rain, for the sun to go down. Not getting out of bed until noon. I've been here before—stuck in the kind of looping sadness that blurs the days with a milky film of ennui—but I'm still not sure what to do except listen to sad music and crawl back into bed. I can turn it on at parties, when I'm drinking, when the alcohol mutes the melancholy a bit. But at home I sink into the sadness, let it course through my body like blood.

At home, I get a text from Julien that says: For someone so private about her songs, you sure play out a lot.

An abandoned storage space is hardly playing out, I respond.

We haven't even texted enough for our texts to be scrollable yet: just this exchange and our back-and-forth about the snacks and pushing Eddie over the balcony. He sends back a dumb, old-school emoticon smiley face. My phone buzzes again, but this time it's a notification from a Google Alert I set up. *Esther Wainwright Asks for Privacy During this Difficult Time.* There haven't been many updates lately about Justin—maybe his inner circle is small enough that whatever is happening can be truly kept under wraps. Or maybe he just wasn't well known enough for people to care in a public forum. Maybe I'm one of the only people who are this invested.

There's a chance Colt's right. Wilson may just have overdosed. He could be sitting in some hospital, strung out in a hazy in-between of life and death. The family has all but said something of the sort; it's been months now. Wilson and Wainwright had apparently just started recording something new too, and the thought of the unfinished songs sends a pang up through my shins, my pelvis, settling into a hollow corner of my stomach. If I died today, I wouldn't leave even a single finished song worth hearing. My old notebooks, pages I used to fill with pedestrian poems and half-scribbled verses of songs I never finished in college—all of them just bulky place mats to catch crumbs from break-and-bake cookies.

I pull up Wilson's appearance at the Americana Awards from a year and a half ago. It's a shaky video that I haven't watched in a while. A full band performance, but it might as well be solo—the spotlight's on him alone. He's a little staggery, clearly intoxicated, and when you get a glimpse of the band, their faces are clouded in concern. You can tell people are wondering if he should be up there at all. He looks possessed—though that's probably the drugs—like he could fall over any moment, but it would all be worth it, just to get these last breaths of song out into the air. It's mostly a cappella; his fingers are too clumsy with the guitar. When Esther's voice comes in—her high harmony just barely hovering in the background—it's otherworldly. You'd think they were singing to save their lives. When I look up the songwriting credit for the song, "Off the Ground," I see it's Esther's. She wrote it alone and Justin recorded it for his debut.

I replay the video a few times, letting the song wash over me. I scribble down the lines I love as I listen—sparse lines about the heavy weight of depression, but Justin and Esther have somehow made the pain poetic. The performance itself is a little hard to watch, not just because Wilson is so fucked up but also because he's still so *good* despite being so fucked up. His hypnotic stage presence, that bellowing baritone voice on the cusp of cracking or crying or both, the hand Esther places on his shoulder when he seems to stumble backward, his neck craned and eyes closed, sweat beading on his temples as he sings the last words of the bridge and Esther's harmony swirls in, their voices together subtle and soft, like cream into coffee. I pause the video and take a deep breath, still wondering where he is right now. If he's okay, if he's alive, if—

For weeks I've slept poorly. Late nights after shows, drinks well after nobody needed another drink, coming home just before dawn—the sun slinking menacingly over the horizon. On the nights when I'm not out, I wake up in the middle of the night, unable to get back to sleep for hours. In the mirror, my eyes are somehow gaunt and puffy at the same time, something I didn't even know was possible. Online I look for a fix. Google *sad eyes*, delete it, google *tired eyes*, *bags eyes*, fall down a rabbit hole of dumb shit I could do, though nothing that will actually help except sleep and becoming seventeen again.

Just as I'm about to click on that link about Wilson, a text from Nick:

> Well, what do u think?

I toss my phone onto the bath mat.

The songs I listen to when nothing else will do, when no one is around or everyone is around and nobody cares, in no particular order:

> "Callback" (Flirtation Device)
> "Bruised" (Jack's Mannequin)
> "The Best Deceptions" (Dashboard Confessional)
> "Love Story" (Taylor Swift)
> "Konstantine" (Something Corporate)
> "I Thought She Knew" (NSYNC)
> "Hey There Delilah" (Plain White T's—let's keep this to ourselves)
> "Swing, Swing" (the All-American Rejects)

Later that week, I crack open a Yuengling and sit on the edge of Sloane's sink while she's getting ready for a date with the drummer. Her laptop on my knee, I'm flicking through a playlist.

—How was Jujubean's party the other night? she asks.

—It was fine, I say. Though I did think I was pregnant the whole time.

—At the party? What the fuck, Al?

—For the last three weeks, I say.

—Jesus. Why didn't you tell me?

I take several large gulps of beer.

—Nick? she asks.

—I wish, I say.

—I know you do, Sloane says.

—Colt.

—Yikes.

—See, that's why I didn't tell you.

This is why it was easier to tell Jessika—she didn't know me well enough to comment, to judge. She was a blank slate.

—I'm kidding! Sloane says. Wait, is that a thing? Is Colt, like, an ongoing thing?

—No. Not really. Not anymore, I say.

—I don't believe you, she says.

—Jujubean found the test, I say.

—Wait, not, like, the one with piss on it?

—God, no. The box. I never even took it.

—Oh my god we are going to the pharmacy right—

—Don't worry. My period finally came. Earlier this week.

She lets out a lengthy exhale and starts to unscrew her mascara.

—Thank god, she says. We cannot be raising that drug-dealing barback's baby.

—He's not a barback. And I'd hardly call him a drug *dealer.*

—He's a music video extra, Sloane says. And that's just because he doesn't make you pay for the drugs.

I laugh and roll my eyes, glancing back at the playlist.

—Avett Brothers or no?

—Don't change the subject. Did you make out with anyone at the party to celebrate your empty womb? Sloane asks.

—No chance. I'm celibate now, I say.

—Oh I'm sure, she says, laughing.

Lou Reed is looking up at us, hungry as always.

—Did you feed him? I ask.

—Don't let him fool you, she says.

Lately she's been cooking him ground turkey in the morning and sprinkling it with Maldon salt because—as she says—*dogs need salt too.* But he looks starving, eyes wide and desperate. Unclear how my beer disappeared so quickly; Sloane hasn't touched hers. I change the song on my phone.

—Who is this? Sloane asks, looking at me in the mirror.

—It's appropriate to the fall theme, I say.

Nick's voice—peaking into its upper register, cresting over a note in the bridge, a line about morning frost and something lost.

Sloane parts her lips in the mirror; suddenly she looks both five years younger and older at the same time.

—Goddammit, Al. We're not giving your ex any more airtime, she says. And I told you. No more adding guys you've slept with. What, did Colt slip you a demo too?

She sighs. Lou Reed shakes himself off, then comes in and curls up at Sloane's feet. I lean my head on her shoulder for a moment while the song plays out. Her phone buzzes on the counter but she doesn't reach for it.

—Ugh. Fuck. It's good, she says.

We let the song play for another thirty seconds. Sloane swipes on a little bit more lipstick and then presses her lips onto a piece of toilet paper. Blood red on the tissue—the color I'd been waiting on for weeks.

—So, what did Juju say when he saw the test? she asks.

—I told him it was yours, I say. Sloane cackles, and I add Nick's song—the one he texted me—to the playlist.

Never knowing—really knowing—how to change my own strings. Never having sat in the balcony at the Ryman. Accidentally buying the obstructed view tickets at the Ryman. Not spending enough time on the East Side, at the 5 Spot, the French Quarter Cafe. Not being able to harmonize on the fly. Not being able to harmonize even after someone feeds me the notes, even after practicing, even when I'm alone. Confusing a blues scale with a standard minor scale. Forgetting what makes a pentatonic scale pentatonic. Having no real vocal range. Breathing from the chest, not the diaphragm. Not really doing coke. Not liking tequila enough. Forgetting the words to "On the Road Again." Not thinking Tom Petty is a god. Not recognizing a Tom Petty song when it comes on the radio. I don't know what makes someone legitimate enough to live here, to call themselves a musician or a songwriter or a writer at all, but I don't think I've crossed the threshold. I'm not sure I even know where the threshold is.

It's close to midnight and Sloane and I are leaving the twenty-four-hour spot off Elliston. I pass her a bite of a weed brownie from Aunt Izzy. *Start with half,* she whispered as she handed them over.

We slide into Sloane's Jeep, freezing. Her Rhode Island bones are built for a different kind of cold, a resilience to temperature that I never picked up in Michigan. She lights a cigarette while I shiver and blast the heat.

—Did I tell you I saw little Jujubean at the William Morris thing the other night? Sloane asks, turning onto Twenty-First. He's everywhere. I should have told him that was absolutely *not* my pregnancy test.

—I'm pretty sure he knew I was full of shit anyway. What was he doing there?

—I don't know, I didn't really talk to him. It was a networking thing. Jess was there too, but not really with him, I don't think. Are they still together?

—As far as I know.

—She's cool, Sloane says. I'd never talked to her before, but I ended up in a corner with her for half the night, ducking all the douchebags. She may have been flirting with me? Anyway. You didn't tell me she worked at Red Light. She's very legit. I thought she was just, like, a hot girl who was Denim's friend-ager.

—I don't really tell anyone anything about her.

—And yet you can tell me the exact coordinates of Nick's location at any time, Sloane says.

—Anyone else there that we know? I say, ignoring her.

—Not really. I spent the rest of the night telling Billy he should give me my own radio show. He made it sound like someone would have to die before he did.

—Is this the National? I ask, pointing at the dash.

—Seriously? This guy has the most recognizable voice in the world.

—He was *screaming.*

—Shit, aren't you from the Midwest? They're, like, the coolest thing to come out of Ohio, maybe ever?

—Michigan and Ohio are not the same place, I say. Who do we have to kill to get a show on Lightning?

—Oh, you're cohosting now?

—Yeah, I say. I'll explain to the listeners who the National is.

Sloane laughs—accidentally snorting, her whole body leaning forward as she pulls up to the light. Matt Berninger's baritone bleeds into the night. Frost on taillights, a few rogue guys in Carhartt jackets smoking cigarettes outside the brewery, shoulders ducked into the cold. The song fades out and Sloane throws the car into park.

Midtown, well after last call. Curing my hangover with pineapple vodka, then some kind of alcoholic milkshake. Colt's at the bar looking dangerously good, but wearing a hat that makes him look bald. I consider telling him about my period, about the test—why was I the only one who had to think about it, to worry about it?—and then a stranger tugs at my elbow and . . . *I'mworkingonmyfaultsandcrackstheskybluesky.* Julien's still at work—I doubt he'd ever come here anyway. Someone famous—snakeskin loafers, an eleven-thousand-dollar watch—is playing tabletop shuffleboard in the back. Low amber light, everything a bit fuzzy. Sloane is talking to a woman in the corner; she looks familiar, but the shapes of their faces are a blur. Spinning. A CD skipping ad nauseam. Sleater-Kinney comes on, and I wander out to the front deck—a rush of crisp, black fall air. Practically a rebirth after all the cigarette smoke.

I text Julien, but when I look down at my phone, the letters are gibberish.

Eddie's in the corner of the deck, laughing like a lunatic, but when I look again, it's not him.

Sorry, Izzy, we did not start with half.

5.

A warehouse somewhere in Germantown—you have to climb a ladder to get in. On the fire escape down at the record store, in the back parking lot, the crowd staring up, up, up. Inside the shop, the line out the front stretching all the way down Eighth. After-hours—two a.m.—Station Inn, Sloane and I there early, standing on the toilets in the curtained bathroom stalls while they try to clear everyone out from the midnight show. Rock Block: cigarette smoke pouring out of the Gold Rush. Springwater: so drunk we almost broke into the barbecue place next to Centennial Park. Downtown on the green in front of the courthouse. At a warehouse off Charlotte, a warehouse off Fourth, a warehouse off Chestnut. In the backyard at the Groove, somebody's living room tucked back behind Eighth. At a house party down on Granny White, on Wedgewood, on Woodland, on Holly, on Elmwood. We try to go to all the local shows, but there are only so many hours in the day, so many nights we have free from The Venue.

In early November, Flirtation Device add a few new dates to their tour: the Theatre of Living Arts in Philly, the Knitting Factory in Boise, the Orange Peel in Asheville—and The Venue. Of course. It's December, and the schedule doesn't leave any wiggle room: they're in Atlanta at Eddie's Attic the night before, the Southgate House in Cincinnati the night after. Last week, when I turned on *Grey's Anatomy*, I heard one of their songs. I wondered how much the placement paid, but not as much as I wanted to know if the song was about me. Remembering Nick was like accidentally biting the inside of your lip: at first it hurts, and then in the following days the spot becomes sore and swollen, making it impossible to avoid biting it again and again and again and again.

Because, the thing is, the song on the radio *and* that demo Nick sent—they were both about me. Definitely. I listened to the demo that night, on the walk home after Julien's Halloween party. That night, I still had my doubts—maybe I was just buzzed, a little turned on, coasting on some inflated sense of self after flirting with Julien. But now I listen again and there's no mistaking it.

It's barely seven a.m. when I wake up. My sternum is tight, like someone has pressed their palms against my chest. I blame my late night last night. Or daylight saving time and the shorter and shorter days. Or serotonin. A dream I woke up from—gasping for air, body drenched in sweat. My underwear, T-shirt, sheets damp. I pop one of Colt's Xanax and slip back under.

By ten, when I wake back up, the day has taken on a new, vaguely more welcoming shape. I peel myself out of bed. Concrete sky out my window. Temperatures have dropped to just above freezing for the first time in months; daylight hours are suddenly a priceless commodity. The Venue is closed tonight for a private event. A text comes through from a phone number I don't have saved, asking if I'm coming to the photo shoot tomorrow. Can I bring The Venue stamp? They want every detail authentic. Or, more likely: they also need extras in the background of the video.

Jake, John. No. Jay? Jaylen. Jay. That's it, Jay, a guitarist I met at a show last week. He asked for my number, then texted me repeatedly to follow up. A photo shoot over in Wedgewood-Houston.

Please come with me, I text Sloane. I don't want to go alone to this. I add a link.

She doesn't respond, but she'll be there.

Later that day, heat cranked too high in the car, my palms burn against the steering wheel. Two new Justin Wilson songs have appeared online. The chords are elegiac, the fingerpicking is broken, sporadic—the way someone might play if they were learning a song for the first time. A true rough demo. Outside the clouds are slipping all the way down into the sidewalk, until sky and ground are one vast, disorienting canvas of gray.

Prescient, if a song itself can be prescient: the pre-chorus is the line he posted months ago: *going away away away, always better this way.* I can hear Esther's voice braided into his, hollow and sad, but still beautiful. The first of the songs is short, the recording full of static, like a vinyl record playing through a fire. The second—unfinished, cut short, a build to a chorus whose crescendo never comes.

Without meaning to, I linger at the stoplight on the corner of South Street and Eighth, and I cry.

Some people don't pay attention to lyrics. They're all about melody, rhythm, timbre—their heads melting at the sound of a riff or the pulse of reverberation, the vibrations of a note throughout space. Not me. I am always lost in the words, transfixed by what they're saying. And now it's my obsession with words that has fucking fucked me. I'm so consumed with the poetry and the slant rhymes and assonance and the tender bits of alliteration that I forget about what it means to make a melody work, how to stay within the confines of a key. And yet—

My eyes are blurry, but I manage to pull into a spot in the parking lot of The Venue. The Justin Wilson songs have ended. Silence—and suddenly a different melody comes to me out of nowhere. First it seems to be somewhere in the back of my head, like I'm remembering it, a kind of melodic déjà vu. And then just in front of me, like a mirage on the horizon, a shimmery something I'm trying to reach out and touch—

Lines of my own:

> ~~*This ain't a holiday, It's a fucking cliché*~~
> ~~*Dressed up like somebody you already are anyway*~~

Voice Memos on, and I hum it into the black void of my phone. It's not the same, but for a second it sounds like the song I was stumbling through up in the second space. A new iteration of it, maybe? I press STOP.

Songs so aching you can only listen to them once a year:

> "Both Sides Now" (Joni Mitchell)
> (All of them) (Elliott Smith)
> "Everybody Hurts" (R.E.M.)
> "Hallelujah" (the Jeff Buckley version)
> "Halah" (Mazzy Star)
> "The Blower's Daughter" (Damien Rice)

"Limousine" (Brand New)
"The Work" (Frightened Rabbit feat. Archie Fisher)
"Casimir Pulaski Day" (Sufjan Stevens)

After Andy hired me, it took a full month for me to slip away from the door to catch a bit of a set. It was Dan Daniels's band; I'd never seen them before. On a night when you were working the door, you could usually catch little moments of a performance—during a break, on your way to the bathroom, going to grab something from the office. By ten that night, the door was dead. Colt's barback had already gone home, and I'd probably get cut soon. Danny was training Simon, who was bug-eyed stage-side. Eddie hadn't started yet. The crowd was young, expectant—entry-level Sony guys and Belmont band-aid types. The collective musicianship in the room was absurd. So much talent in one space it was practically simmering. It was the tail end of winter, when you know there's relief around the corner. Everyone's holding out just a few more days—weeks at most—for spring to come. The days will get longer. The nights will get warmer.

I stood in the shadow of the stairwell. After a while the band left the stage, and it was just Dan up there, a little Taylor acoustic in hand, almost as small as Andy's. I hadn't been expecting—I certainly hadn't been *meaning*—to cry. In hindsight, I blame the night, the weather, the whole goddamn winter, to be honest, but what Dan sang sent me into some kind of emotional trance. All of us, really. The kind where the crowd is so quiet you can hear a stranger clear her throat across the room, where even the sound of the bathroom door swinging open or ice rattling in a plastic cup is an interruption.

When I came to—the only phrase I have for returning from wherever the song had sent me—Andy was at my side. I panicked, apologized, remembering our interview: *You are at the door, not in the audience.* But he just looked at me and nodded, his eyes onyx and misty, a faint dreamy smile on his face. I walked back down the stairs.

Now he's on the couch in the office, a mug of coffee steaming into a wisp of silver in the air. Dark jeans and a Rush hoodie, a binder and some papers in front of him, a few records stacked up next to an open laptop. One of Eddie's button-downs—this one forest green—is draped over the arm of the couch. Andy stands up and opens his arms, offering a hug. I'm still coming out of a bit of a *moment* with the Justin Wilson demos, and he can tell I'm not myself.

He pulls me into a quick side hug.

—Aren't you off tonight? You doing all right?

I stand up straighter.

—All good, I say. Sorry to interrupt.

—You're fine, what's up?

—Do you mind if I borrow the stamp today? These guys want to use it for a photo shoot.

—What guys? Eddie asks, spilling through the door. You got some guys?

—Go away, I say. He flicks me off, but to his credit he grabs his button-down and walks out.

—Are these the ones who emailed? Andy asks.

—Probably? By the way, it's really beautiful up there in that storage space. Do you know the capacity?

His eyebrows lift just slightly.

—Around fifteen hundred square feet. Hold a hundred and fifty standing, maybe? Seventy-five or a hundred banquet? Not that we're trying to have a banquet up there. It's still not up to code, not for anything real. Why do you ask?

I shrug.

—Just seems like a waste.

Everybody here is always working on something. There's the guy who lives over on Nineteenth, putting together a magazine, looking for writers, photographers, designers. The blues band, getting ready for a European tour, working on their GoFundMe. The photographer, the one you see at every show, shooting stuff for the *Scene* and *American Songwriter*, even *Rolling Stone*. Another local magazine, this one looking for editors, advertisers, countless pitches. A food festival, supposedly sponsored by a Very Big Band. A songwriting space, cheaper than anywhere on Music Row. A streaming platform that isn't Spotify. A mini festival—Road to Bonnaroo, 8 off 8th, Next Big Nashville, AmericanaFest, Record Store Day. Everybody is always planning something else, something bigger, something they need everyone's help to get off the ground. Musicians, sure, of course, but also sound techs and security, copywriters and essayists for their zines, lighting directors and door guys, promoters and photographers, club owners and city councilmen. Some days it really does feel like It's All Happening.

—What the actual fuck are we doing here? Sloane asks.

She's holding a brown paper bag of something, but pointing her keys at me. Like if I don't back away she'll plunge them right between my eyes.

—I just saw someone pissing on the roof of a booted car over there, and the train around the corner has been stopped for at least thirty minutes. I'm leaving before the sun sets, she says.

—What's in the bag?

—Oh, I stopped at this bakery pop-up around the corner, she says, pulling out a couple of chocolate chip cookies. Want one?

—I'm good, I say, turning down the cookie.

I haven't been hungry in days. Lately the only thing I've been wanting to eat is blue-box mac and cheese in the middle of the night.

—I got a galette too, Sloane says, chomping.

—Let's just go get a drink, I'll drop off the stamp and—

—And then we will get the hell out of here. I gotta go to a thing at the Five Spot in, like, an hour. Billy's gonna be there. I'm giving him one of our mixes.

—You burned him a CD?

—Flash drive, baby, she says, waving a tiny thumb drive at me from her key chain.

I expect her to invite me but she doesn't.

—I promise, I say. Just one drink, I'll deliver the stamp, then we'll go.

—God, this place looks sketchy as hell. Why is there a bathtub in the parking lot? Is that supposed to be art? That's not art. Do any of the streetlights even work in this neighborhood? Or did the city just give up over here? *Hello?* she says, shouting up at the flickering streetlamp overhead. *Hello!* It's fucking *dusk*!

Inside the warehouse, the Whiskey Riders—about as stupid a band name as I've heard, and there's competition—are having a photo shoot. They needed a few extras, which seems like the type of thing Colt should be doing, but he left on tour with some friends of his last week, doing god knows what. Plus, I assume they wanted women. Bodies in the background in exchange for beer.

The place is freezing inside, and decorated bizarrely: Technicolor mushrooms made of papier-mâché, against a green-screen background. The band is already there, dressed, improbably, as Oompa Loompas.

Jessika's there too, her camera slung over her shoulder, laughing loudly with the lead singer and the bass player in the corner as they huddle around a laptop, pointing and talking about something we can't quite hear. She's wearing a chunky sweater that hangs loosely over her frame, her curls pressed beneath a black beanie.

Another of Colt's pills in my pocket, and I pour four fingers of whiskey into a red Solo cup and down it.

—I can never predict what you're going to drink, Sloane says.

—What do you mean?

—You don't have a standard order, she says. Shit, you don't even have a standard liquor.

—So?

—Is there anything you don't drink?

The hot, comforting sharpness of the liquor hits my throat. Molasses and smoke. I'm glaring at Sloane. She opens a beer with a clumsy bottle opener.

—Milk, I say.

Her laugh is sharp and throaty. Jess and the bass player finally see us and come over to say hi. The bass player kisses me on both cheeks like he's a French movie star.

—Good to see you, I say, and I introduce him to Sloane. He shakes her hand, then points us to more alcohol and a small spread of questionable-looking drugs.

—You guys know Jess? he asks. Actually, I don't know why I asked. Of course you do. Everyone knows Jess.

Jess reaches out to hug me. How are you feeling? she says quietly.

That shift in her voice—she's stepped offstage again.

—Barren, I say, and she laughs like herself.

—Thank god for that, she says.

Sloane misses the exchange between me and Jess; the bass player has pulled her into another conversation, I can hear him explaining the concept of the video to her.

—How was ACL? I ask Jess.

She looks at me skeptically for a second and then responds:

—I mean, not bad if you like festivals. You should go sometime. Better than Bonnaroo. I don't know why anyone would ever have a festival in Tennessee in the middle of the summer, but whatever. The guys were great though. How'd you know I was there? Oh sure. Jules.

—Julien, I say.

She narrows her eyes just slightly.

—I gotta go take a few test shots before we lose light, she says. We're all going to get beers later, by the way, if you want to come. I can text you.

—Okay, yeah—

—Don't lie, she says.

My chest tightens and I reach for a strand of hair at the base of my neck.

—I'm not lying, I—

—If you're not going to come, it's not a big deal, she says. Just don't say you are if you already know you won't. No pressure either way.

Her tone is friendly, but her directness still throws me. I get the sense that Jessika has almost never held back any of her thoughts, that whatever she is thinking at any given moment, she says. And she usually gets away with it, because she is beautiful and competent, and people want to trust her, want to tell her things—want to have sex with her. Even when she's a little bit mean, a little bit forward. Then people just want to have sex with her more.

Sloane tugs at my arm.

—Al likes to keep her options open, she says.

Jessika runs a hand through her curls, then gives me a look I can't read. She shrugs and says: Oh believe me, I get it.

6.

Freezer aisle at the grocery store: me looking for a pizza, Julien suddenly in front of me in a black hoodie, holding a half-full basket, tugging earbuds out of his ears. I've just left the weird photo shoot, still toying with the idea of taking Jessika up on her invitation.

—Hey you, I say. What are you listening to?

Overhead, a mid-aughts soft-rock band has come on—the kind of song that's so ingrained in your memory, where you know all the words but for the life of you can't remember the name of the song or even the artist, just a flash of memory from an earlier life. A boy's passenger seat, a window down on a Michigan highway, a fingertip pressing into a hip bone, a day on the beach when you were sixteen—

—Postal Service, Julien says.

—Cute, I say, and resist the urge to make the obvious joke about what Yoshi told me at the Halloween party.

He laughs, barely.

—What are you doing tonight? I ask.

He shrugs and shifts the basket in his arm, tamping down a box of fancy spaghetti that's threatening to fall out.

—I was going to make dinner, he says.

—For yourself?

—Yup.

—Sounds a little lonely, I say, shrugging at him.

—You think doing anything alone is lonely.

—Isn't it?

—Some people like being alone, he says, and then takes an unexpected step toward me to let a large—large—man pass behind him. The man lingers there awkwardly, looking for something behind us, leaving the two of us standing quiet and close, our bodies only seven or eight inches apart. My face, chest, the back of my neck warm, and I suddenly want to press my fingertip to his collarbone, his cheek, the jut of his hip bone. But my palms are too sweaty, and I am overwhelmed by the desire to be somewhere less public, somewhere I could stand even closer—

For the first time, I notice large scars on Julien's earlobe. A piercing that had closed up? Healed skin that will never be smooth again. This close, his face delicate and pale—you almost want to pull him out into the sunlight. Fluorescent lights flashing, a piney whiff of cologne. When the man behind us finally sighs and settles on a lasagna, Julien relaxes a bit, but he doesn't step away from me.

—Want to hang out? I ask.

I have the odd urge to stand on only one foot, like some strange grocery store flamingo. Instead I bounce up and down on my toes, let the blood travel up through the arches of my feet, my calves.

—Do we need wine? I ask, before he's answered.

Things I missed: A pewter ring he wore on the middle finger of his right hand. His block-caps handwriting, the words covering every centimeter of the mix CDs he still played in his car. The absence of an aux cord in his car. The way all his CDs skipped. The choppy, jarring sound of being pulled in and out, in and out, in and out of a melody. Cheeks that flushed peach when he got too warm, most nights at The Venue. His short, filed fingernails. Green eyes, sometimes, and then other times definitively hazel. The way he was always listening, waiting, showing a patience for others that I could only aspire to. He had a way of walking through the world like a dancer, elegant and intentional and poised, but then he would stop somewhere—in a parking lot, working the door at The Venue—to pull out his phone or pick up a dirty napkin, and his shoulders would slump and break the spell. The way he always wanted whatever would make things easier for someone else. And here I am, not even knowing what I want.

On the way from Kroger to Julien's house, I flip through the CDs in his car. Most everyone else has switched over by now—to aux cords and Bluetooth, anything but CDs. But Julien and I seem stuck in 2005, both our cars full of burned CDs, scratched and ruined, like we've run them all across concrete. In the front of his collection is a silver CD, a burned one, with *JwK #11* written in black sharpie across the front. I put it in and Julien glances over at me at a stop sign. A last streak of sunlight pierces through the window in a line of golden glitter. Belle and Sebastian comes over the speakers, and I can't read the expression on Julien's face.

Julien carries in all the groceries even though I offer, even though it's way too much for one person, even though the bags are too tight around his wrists, his forearms, his biceps as he makes his way from the car. On his porch, a can of San Marzano tomatoes rolls out, a clang of metal on wood as it rolls down the front steps. I haven't been to his place since the Halloween party, and the trees in his yard have turned into vibrant, wild creatures in the past two weeks. The maple looks like it's been set aflame. A bubblegum pink sunset starts to fade into indigo—evening.

—Sorry, it's a little messy, he says, opening the front door.

It's not, though. Not at all. His trumpet is out, leaning against the lip of the couch, a worn-in chambray color I didn't notice at the party. Records are stacked on the coffee table, atop the small TV. There are books and graphic novels spread out on the couch, as if he were reading them all at once. And yet they appear almost thoughtfully arranged, as if they were styled by some designer for a picture.

—It's not, I say. You've obviously never seen my room.

—I haven't, he says, and I wonder if I hear a hint of a suggestion.

Plastic bags onto a small kitchen table. A *New Yorker*, several bills, a copy of the *Nashville Scene*, a coffee mug from the place on Twenty-First, day-old tea at the bottom. A set of guitar strings, the high E missing. I pick it up and twirl the pack in my fingers.

—I always break the high E, I say. And then I'm screwed because I'm terrible at changing my own strings. So I'll just play without it for weeks.

Julien is still unpacking all his very adult groceries. Pork chops, loose greens, lemons, shallots.

—I can do it, he says, not turning around, the refrigerator light casting a weak halo around him. If you ever need a hand, he says.

—I forgot. Your hard-core band. Of course you can change a string on the fly. What was their name again?

Now he turns around, stares at me.

—So Much Man, he says. And then: Shut up. Shut up.

I laugh.

—Wow. So Much Man. Okay. That's not what I was expecting. How old were you? I mean, it's not much worse than Flirtation Device.

My throat constricts—I immediately regret shoving Nick, however loosely, into the conversation. Julien's face is straight.

—That's true, he says, pointing the corner of a box of granola at me, a faint smile registering as he turns back to the cabinets.

—Want to put something on? he asks.

Out of his jeans he pulls an iPod, unplugging the tangled headphone cord. When he passes it to me, the smudges from his fingers cover the surface of the screen. The pressure to choose music for us rises up between my lungs. I turn on a song about a one-night stand, and then, for some reason, I ask:

—Do you know how to have casual sex?

Julien chokes out a startled laugh. His cheeks flush light pink as he glances over his shoulder at me.

—Excuse me? Do I know *how*?

He's holding a can of tomatoes in his palm, the label facing upward, like he's about to do a bicep curl. He waits.

—Yeah, I say. I just . . . I've tried. I don't think I'm very good at it. I don't mean, like, logistically or physically. Well, I don't know. I mean emotionally.

—I'm not, Julien says. Good at it.

—Casual sex, or sex in general? I ask.

He laughs.

—Do you want me to cook you dinner or not? he says, turning back to his cabinets.

—What about with Jess? I ask.

Julien opens and shuts a cabinet, then glances over his shoulder again at me. I wonder if we'd be having this conversation if his back weren't to me.

—What about her? he asks.

—Would you call that casual?

—I wouldn't have called it serious, he says.

—Wouldn't *have*? I ask. Past tense?

The kitchen is quiet; the refrigerator emits its soft hiss.

—What about Colt? Julien asks.

—I don't want to talk about it.

—You brought it up.

—Did you and Jess break up? I ask.

—Put something else on, he says. And then: Will you eat salad?

—Sure. Yeah, okay. In the mood for anything?

—Dave Matthews Band.

Now it's my turn to give him a dead-eyed stare.

—I'm kidding, he says. Though there was definitely a point in my life where I probably wouldn't have been. Do you want a drink?

He pauses, and then:

—I know that's probably a silly question.

The comment is subtly loaded. I let it pass and say:

—Yeah, in a minute. Which is maybe the closest I'll ever get to turning down a drink. Postponing it, perhaps. My tongue still tastes like syrup, an aftertaste of the warm whiskey at the photo shoot. I check my phone and there's a text from Jess: Headed to Melrose now. See you there? Or not:)

—And yeah, we broke up, he says. Right before Halloween.

Halloween. The night Julien was loopy and drunk, when we sat on his porch and smoked together. I slide my phone back into my pocket.

—I'm sorry, I say.

—Oh, it's really okay. Turns out she mostly likes women. I think I was more of an experiment.

—Really?

—I mean, kind of.

I nod. And flip through more music on his iPod, desperate to ask more questions. Instead, I say:

—That was weeks ago. You didn't tell me.

—I'm telling you now, he says.

—Okay, but—

—From what I've gathered there's plenty of things you don't tell me.

Our eyes meet and then I break the eye contact and look down at my hands—it's too much. He turns back around and opens and shuts more cabinets, pulling out pans and spices. I clear my throat and ask:

—Have you heard the new Justin Wilson demos?

—I don't think so.

—There's two songs up on Bandcamp. Hang on, let me find them. I downloaded them today and, well, let's just say: I was not emotionally prepared. I don't know how he—how they—do it. Seems like so much pain wrapped up in two and a half minutes.

Julien nods.

—Do you think he's dead? Like, these are just old demos someone's digging up and releasing now? And soon . . .

I stop and look to him, as if he might know how to finish the sentence.

—I don't know, he says. I feel there would have been an announcement or something, right? Maybe he just wanted to go off the grid.

—I know, but there's been nothing. Like, *nothing*. And he was kind of fucked up anyway, you know. I hate saying this, but it wouldn't be surprising. If something happened. I mean, did you see him at last year's Americana Awards?

Julien shakes his head.

—It's kind of a mess, but even so.

—That voice, he says.

—Yeah. But she wrote the song. Esther did.

—That's right, Julien says.

—And honestly, when she sings with him—

He nods, like he wants to say something else but doesn't. My chest clenches as he turns back around, the stove flicking on. Hot oil and the searing sound of a melancholic melody pouring out of my phone. A motion sensor light glows caramel in the back alley through the window, then: pitch dark, the window a midnight sea.

Julien turns back around and sets an onion on the table in front of me. He looks directly into my eyes, very seriously, as though he's about to—

—Can you slice this? he asks.

The air gathered in my chest collapses.

He hands me a pair of swimming goggles.

—If you need them, he says. I usually do.

Panic, for me, always comes in wild, messy tears. Not a heart attack but an absolute meltdown. That hollow fist in the back of my stomach, the certainty that everything, everyone, everywhere is fucked. Late at night at The Venue, cleaning the toilets, wondering why I got a college degree just to clean up somebody else's vomit. In my closet. On the floor. In my car, bed, bathroom. In the alley behind The Venue. At Robert's. At the Ryman, the Exit/In, the End, the 5 Spot. At 3rd and Lindsley, the bus stop bench on Woodland on the Fourth of July. In the bathroom at The Venue, after Nick showed up but before we left together. Now, in Julien's kitchen, head bent over a pungent white onion, as the demos fade out. The only sound the hiss of meat against cast iron, the click of the knife against wood. I should be able to predict it by now.

The moment Julien uncorks a bottle of wine, dribbling it lightly into glasses, I have to excuse myself. I duck out onto the front porch. The sun has set and the studios of Music Row are sleepy, tucked beneath the leaves drifting down with every bit of breeze. Because I have to, because I have no choice in situations like this, because my body and my brain do whatever they want whenever they want to, I let the panic rush over me, let the tears run down my face. A fist to my mouth to quiet myself.

It's six in the morning over in Korea, but I dial my parents' number anyway. It's a matter of pure, primal instinct. The phone rings and rings; nobody answers. I start to dial Izzy, but then stop. Inside, a pan crashes into another, water running in the sink. Thirty more seconds: finish crying, take a deep breath. I dig back in my pocket, find another Xanax. It dissolves under my tongue in seconds. Maybe it's just that simple to feel better. Maybe it actually is that easy.

—Everything okay? Julien asks when I walk back inside. He's at the stove, still cooking the pork chops.

—Too many onions, I say.

His eyes narrow and I run the back of my hand across my own. Damp.

—You sure?

—I had to call my parents.

He nods, but he's not convinced.

—Are they in Michigan? he asks, looking over his shoulder at me, ignoring the meat sizzling on the stove. I look down at his Chucks—god, doesn't he have any other shoes?

—Korea, I say, and he finally breaks eye contact.

—Really? What are they doing there?

—Foreign service, I say. And then: Actually, they're missionaries. Foreign service just sounds . . . I don't know. Yeah. No. They're missionaries.

He's sliding the pork chops onto a plate, the juices pooling against the china.

—They've been there for—two years now? They moved when I was in college.

I don't say the rest: the loneliness, the distance.

—My dad was a pastor, Julien says.

—No shit, I say. Is he still? In Minnesota?

—He—uh, he actually passed away.

I start to reach out to him and pull my arm back into my own space. He looks at where my hand was and then back at me. His eyes are the color of fresh, fertile dirt.

—I'm so sorry, I say.

Here I am crying in Julien's kitchen, on his front porch, about absolutely nothing, when his own father is actually dead.

—It's okay, he says. I mean, it's not, but I'm okay. I mean, you don't have to apologize.

—When was this? I ask.

—In high school, he says.

High school seems like both yesterday and a million years ago.

—I'm sorry, I say again.

He turns his back to me again as he reaches for the wine. My face is very warm. The crickets on the porch are so loud it sounds like they're inside.

—Do you want to play some music after we eat? he asks.

He opens the fridge, the dull light briefly bathing the room in a shallow fluorescent glow.

Julien hands me a ceramic plate and we go out to eat on the porch with the plates in our laps, our feet over the steps. It's still a little cold, and the sun is long gone. Suddenly I remember that he mentioned stopping by a show later tonight. Doesn't he have plans after this, I ask, and he just says:

—I'll be fine.

The meal is surprisingly good; I didn't know I liked pork chops or salad, or maybe I'm just buzzed enough to eat anything. But the pork chops are tender inside despite the crisp edges, and the salad is bright and balanced, and I find myself practically slurping off the dregs of the dressing. When we finish, Julien slips inside and comes back with a bar of dark chocolate—the fancy, six-dollar kind—and we pass it back and forth, breaking off pieces of it and wiping our cold fingers on our jeans. We share a joint, and the tops of my ears are cold, and I hope he isn't really going to the show. It occurs to me how little time he and I spend completely alone like this, outside work, wrapped up in the silence of Music Row at night.

—Would you ever want to have a spot of your own? I ask, moving to the rocking chair.

—Like, a house?

—No—

But the misfire has thrown me off. Julien is unwrapping the chocolate bar to break off another piece.

—No, like, a venue.

He looks up.

—Somewhere smaller, he says. Maybe.

—Yeah. I like the—I don't know. I don't like big shows. Even the Ryman is pushing it.

—Yeah, I like the intimacy, he says.

I nod, my fingers pressing into the weathered wood of the rocking chair, sliding back and forth as if I'm trying for a splinter.

—Would you? he asks.

—Me? No way. I don't ever want to be in charge. I don't want to be responsible for—I don't know, fixing the air-conditioning or something. I don't want to have to pick up my phone when shit goes wrong.

—You need a phone guy, he says, eyes on me, a sleepy half smile.

—Exactly, I say. But it could be fun to help with somewhere a little smaller. More acoustic shows, songwriting rounds, more women. I don't know. Third and Lindsley does that live broadcast once a week. Something like that could be cool.

He smiles. The joint has kicked in and the night has lovely aqueous, fuzzy edges.

—You like the boys, he says. The boys in the bands.

It's innocent enough. Coming from Eddie or Colt, the comment might have sharper corners, but Julien . . .

—I like the music and the people. I like—well, yeah. I guess I like the bands. Which are mostly boys.

—It's not a bad thing. Maybe if you were better at casual sex—

—Fuck you, I say.

—Your words, he says, laughing lightly. He leans a shoulder softly into mine.

Warm wine, cool night. Hot acid down my throat as the wine dries out my mouth, my tongue briefly a slab covered with sandpaper, asking me to take another sip. A jet rushes overhead, then the neighborhood is just us again. We climb out of the giant rocking chair to sit on the steps.

Julien brings me an acoustic guitar and a flimsy electric one for himself and starts to play a few licks without saying anything, so I follow, trying to figure out how my fingers fit against the wood, trying to find the key he's in. The action is low and the strings are light and now Julien is letting me lead, and before I realize it I'm playing without thinking, without worrying about who's listening or whether the melody is working or the chords are right. His notes are twangy and distant while a few cars pass by, and I wait for the silence of the street again, closing my eyes and letting the tension in my knuckles loosen, the muscles moving without effort, our playing the only sound on the street. When I open my eyes again Julien is lying down with his back on the porch, his eyes closed, his eyelashes black and delicate like maybe he's wearing mascara, grease from our meal still caught on his top lip, reflecting in the porch light as I hum, quietly, so far under my breath that even I can barely hear it, and he says softly then: *Keep going.* Our legs are touching and he is lying back and my fingers are cramped and cold but I keep singing, slow and self-consciously at first, the sound emerging from a distant corner of my lungs and then swelling up in me a bit, angry and restless and frighteningly sad, and I know I'm not hitting notes and I've messed up the chorus but Julien is still playing and the cars on Seventeenth are hardly there and I stretch the song—my song—as long as it can go, and when it's over I'm exhausted, like after a long hike or an endless run, and we sit in the silence, the outsides of our thighs still barely touching.

He sits up—I can hear him shifting—and my eyes are still closed but his shoulder leans into mine again and I turn to him and kiss him first. He meets it, a little too soft for my liking, like maybe if the kiss is good enough I can convince him to return it. His mouth is salty and soft and a little oaky and I like it more than I expect to, and then my mind goes a bit blank, like waking up in a dead dark room only to find that it doesn't matter if your eyes are open or closed, you can't really see anything anyway.

Side Three

1.

Justin Wilson is alive. My phone pings with the news, in a text from Julien, who has sent a link from the *Nashville Scene.* A crashing headache—like someone playing Metallica full blast, forever and always—threatens to crack through the front of my skull. I read the news in bed.

He was hospitalized, and it's unclear from the article whether what happened was intentional or accidental, but yes, substances were involved. There was a lengthy, private stay in a facility in East Tennessee. Off the grid, of course. And now an outpatient rehab facility in California.

The article is only a paragraph or two, and I scroll back through the sparse updates from the past several months. I wonder now if there was so little information simply because people didn't know—whether he was going to live or die, whether it was purposeful or accidental. Maybe people really can keep a secret when something is serious enough. Regardless, he's alive. Whether he wants to be or not.

Right after my open mic—the Incident—I kept saying to Sloane: *Kill me.*

She laughed and rolled her eyes, saying it really wasn't that big a deal.

It wasn't as bad as I thought. But the night had been so humiliating that all I could think about were ways to scrape the memory from my consciousness, or scrape my consciousness altogether.

She'd convinced me to play at a little spot that served two-for-one drinks on Thursdays, right down the street from our house. Divey, but actually new, just across from the old Belcourt Theatre. A storm had been rolling in, over-puffed cumulus clouds crowding the dusk sky. Distant lightning flashing as we walked.

The bar was emptier than I'd expected, and only one other person had shown up to play the open mic. A high schooler, I thought: hunched shoulders and greasy skin, a nicer guitar than I had. When the bar manager announced the songwriting *evening* (generous word), I heard an audible groan from a group of Vanderbilt kids who'd ducked in to avoid the storm.

I felt ill, anxiety seeping out of every pore as I settled into the chair on a covered pallet in the corner. This, apparently, was the stage. I wore jean shorts and a flannel, and already I could tell I'd made a mistake—the shorts tight, my legs sticking to the leather of the chair, my Taylor acoustic pressing uncomfortably against my thigh. I looked to Sloane and took a large sip of beer, then another and another. I knew my fear was an overreaction; this wasn't the fucking Grammys. But this was worse, right? Playing for people who absolutely did not want to hear you play? The bar manager eyed me again. I looked for Sloane but she'd disappeared. More students poured in, shouting cheap beer orders to a suddenly weeded bartender. The bar was neither full nor empty now.

When I spoke into the mic, my voice was shaking but booming. Far too loud over the quiet bar. I felt like I was interrupting every conversation. A cluster of girls glanced at me, sighed, then pulled their stools into a far corner. Where the fuck was Sloane? Feedback over the mic, a few people placing their hands over their ears. Everyone in the bar had crowded to the back; they were already drunk, and I was not drunk enough. I heard someone say *Let's gooooo*, and the manager looked at me like: *Well?*

Now my headache is still pulsing. Load-in is in forty-five minutes.

Nick is in Nashville.

I need to pull my life together. At least right now.

The city is a muted slab behind me as I drive to The Venue, the sun a low sliver of citrus in the sky. Sloane and I have just gotten back from Thanksgiving with her family in Rhode Island, and when we landed it was officially fucking cold. The winter days here, I'm learning, are desperately short. The sun sets even earlier than it did in Michigan. Sometimes, by the time I wake up and shake loose my hangover, walk Lou Reed, and start to feel like an actual person, there are just a few hours of sunlight left.

It's frigid when I step outside the car, my leather jacket useless. We're supposed to get snow tonight and it's all anyone can talk about. Grocery store clerks, baristas, the mailman. Suddenly everyone's an armchair meteorologist, preaching about dew points and barometer measurements and the meager amount of road salt the city has on hand. Andy and Julien have been at The Venue all day, talking to artists, vendors, distributors, promoters. Trying to plan for shows that are happening later this weekend. People are canceling flights, moving dates, preparing for some kind of apocalypse. Sloane's even purchased a dog parka and little snow booties for Lou Reed and filled our fridge with Yuenglings and frozen pizzas. Inside, The Venue is barely warmer than the parking lot.

The caustic cold reminds me of Michigan, of the winters on campus when cheap beers would freeze on back porches, and your breath would fog the path before you on your way to classes that were never canceled, however brutal the cold. I'd met Nick on a night like that. Here, though, the cold was a personal affront. A bitchy, anemic insult after weeks and weeks of "winter" that barely dropped into the low forties. The mild temperatures we get in December are supposed to be our gift for the cruel summers.

Upstairs in the office: Andy, pale in the weak winter light, wearing a flannel over a T-shirt. Julien still in a flimsy coat, practically a windbreaker. Eddie, thankfully not on the schedule tonight. The rest of us are wildly underdressed for the weather. We don't know how to brace for it, where to buy sweaters that actually shield us from the elements, coats that can actually cover our bodies.

—Hunter, there you are. Can you grab a few space heaters out of storage? HVAC guy is on his way. This should tide us over till doors at least.

—Sure, I say. How many do you want?

I look to Julien but he's barely looked up from his computer since I walked in.

—Two or three is fine, Andy says. I think there's four up there. Load-in is in twenty. Headliner's running a little behind. These are friends of yours, right?

—Yeah, the headliners. Sort of. Hi, I say to Julien.

I haven't seen him since we kissed. His fingers stop typing, and he glances up. Finally.

—Hey, he says. Welcome back. How was Rhode Island?

—It was good, yeah, Sloane's family is wild. I'll tell you more later, I say.

Andy pulls a key off a set of masters—they must have started locking the second space—and hands it to me.

—Storage space, he says. I think you know how to get up there, yeah?

Ice cold, my fingers numb, my steps quick, hoping my body can collect some heat if I walk fast enough. This time, the lights work up here when I flick them on. The cold presses against me, a freezing hand to the face. Two space heaters—hulking, ancient—sit behind a ten-foot bar with a peeling linoleum countertop. A cockroach scurries into the darkness across the bar. Outside, feathery bits of snow are starting to fall. I palm a bit of condensation off the window; Nick's van isn't here yet. For a moment, my whole body is so cold I wonder if I'll ever be warm again.

At my staff check-in with Andy, he asked me how I was feeling. I wanted to say: I've cried on the porch at Julien's, the floor of my closet, my car; my ex-boyfriend's music is following me everywhere; I haven't talked to my family in months. I almost had your bartender's baby. Sometimes I wake up certain that I'm underwater. I can't breathe. Sometimes I'm sure that I'm dying.

Instead I told him I couldn't stay away.

—From? he asked.

—From all of it, I said. The artists. The songwriting. The bands. The Venue, I guess.

He laughed, a crease in his forehead like a slice of shadow. For a moment I wondered how old he was, if I would ever be that old.

Then I said something I didn't even see coming, surprised to hear myself ask:

—You know that second space we have? Upstairs?

—What, that storage room?

—Yeah, I said. I think we could do something more with it.

—Like what? he asked.

In the office, the afternoon is fading quickly. Dim violet light shifts through the fogged-up windows. Colt is back behind the bar, but he doesn't see me. Back from tour, I guess, and barely even a hello. Julien is still on his laptop. Dark green corduroys and a black Bowie T-shirt, his flimsy jacket now on the lip of the couch. His lips are too pale, the color of an overused pencil eraser.

—Hi again, he says. Sorry. Today's a mess.

—Sorry. Is there anything I can do to help? Besides, I guess, just my actual job.

He smiles, the room warms. His porch—hot wine, cool night. Did I want to kiss him again? The sound of a van door closing in the parking lot. My body pulls toward the window, but I stay still.

—How was your—did you go to Minnesota? I ask.

—I didn't, he says.

—Oh.

—Had to work.

We were only closed for Thanksgiving proper, and I thought Julien had headed home, to Minnesota, unfathomably far away. He looks tired now, faint circles of indigo beneath his eyes, his lips irritated from the cold.

—I can't believe Justin Wilson's alive, I said.

—I know.

—You got a case! I say now, spotting a horn-shaped plastic thing in his bag.

—I did, he says.

Colt pops his head in.

—Anybody got a lighter? he asks. And then: Oh, hey you. When did you get here?

—A few minutes ago, I say. How was tour?

Andy tosses him a lighter; Colt's eyes are lit up. Too shimmery—high—for the moment. *Later*, he mouths at me.

—All right, we got two of three pulling up for load-in. Let's get these guys situated and then everybody can take a break before doors open.

No sign of Nick on my phone, just a text from last week that he'd see me today, would I be working? Downstairs he's still not here. The openers are Goodnight, Goodnight and the Last Relay, both bands unloading their gear as the snow falls steadily in the waning afternoon light. The doors to the two vans are thrown open, their black instrument cases looking like little dominoes beneath the dusting of snow in the lot. A bouquet of cigarettes, weed, and fried food pours out of the vans. Guitar straps and plastic grocery bags and a roll of paper towels. Danny helps them carry most of their own shit up the back stairs and I slam the doors to the vans behind them, taking in the Mexican blankets and dream catchers, the loose joints and water bottles and sour straws and gas station coffee cups.

Nick and me in the tour van, the parking lot of the Blind Pig, dysfunctional parking lights flickering on and off and on and off overhead. A shitty hotel—Best Western? Doubletree?—outside Detroit. In the shower, up against the off-white tile, coming so hard my atoms felt rearranged. Cleveland, in an alley behind the House of Blues. Chicago, backstage—the Vic, probably—on my knees. Drunk. Reckless.

Nick, in my city; Julien over my shoulder.

—I need you to talk to the bands, Julien says. The guest list is too long.

—Okay, which one?

He seems—

—Headliner, he says. Your, uh, your friend.

Angry. He seems angry, his words clipped like he's trying to preserve syllables. Stressed.

—How many people do they have? I ask.

—Too many, he says. One person per band member, not five.

—So *now* we're getting tight on the lists?

He looks at me like I'm Eddie and I stare back, hot.

I want to argue, but I know I won't win. Julien usually handles the guest lists, deals with the issues. And then I think: Who else in Nashville is Flirtation Device putting on this fucking list?

—Fine, I say, holding my hand out.

When he passes me the sheet, it catches in the web of skin between my thumb and index finger, quick and ruthless, leaving a slice the color of the inside of a grapefruit.

Campbell Brannen. Ellen Carpenter. Alyce Hampton. Garret Effler. Ellen Porter. Chelsea Majoy. Allison Harris. Allison Hunter. Jenni Zenaro. Ted Forrey. Bo Stubner. Jessika P. Julien's not wrong. The list is too long. Obviously I don't need to be on it, but if you're gonna put me on it, at least spell my name right. I scratch out the extra *l*, then scratch out my name altogether, like I don't even exist. It's three thirty—still no Nick. Andy tells me to take a break, come back around sound check at five, after the heat's fixed. Colt tries to get me to have a drink with him at the bar.

What I say: No, I need to get out of here.

What I mean: If I stay, I'll spend the whole afternoon looking out the window for Nick.

—If the list is too long, why don't you take Jessika off? I ask Julien.

He glances down at his phone, then back up at me.

—I'm just saying, I assume she's your guest, not the band's. You know the band's people take priority.

—She works with the opener, Julien says. She's not my guest.

—Without her, it's eleven.

—What's your deal with her? he asks. I thought you two were—

—What's yours? I ask.

—We need to get it down to eight, Al.

—Ten is fine. I obviously don't need to be on it.

I cross Jess's name off the list. Above us: the sound of microphones being tested, amps buzzing with feedback. I pass the sheet back to Julien and he shakes his head, our hands lingering for a moment on opposite corners of the paper. He'll let her in either way, I know. Jess is one of those people—like Sloane—where it doesn't really matter if she's on the list or not. She'll get in.

Have I thought of Julien in the two weeks since we kissed? Of course. For the first half of the holiday break, it was all I thought about. The intensity of the kiss itself, the slow, sober determination of it. The fear wrapped around all the feelings expanding in my chest as his tongue pressed softly against mine, thinking that I hadn't even been sure he liked me all that much until that exact moment.

We texted over the break—more than our usual short exchanges, starting with him sending a simple: dinner was fun the other night, to which I responded: it was. And when Sloane's mom overserved me one night, I even wrote out how I was actually feeling to him: I kinda wish I was at the venue with u right now. But before I could send it, I stumbled on a photo he'd recently been tagged in online. Julien's eyes a little bloodshot, a wide-eyed blonde next to him in one of those casual but intimate poses: her head on his shoulder in the booth of a cozy-looking bar. It didn't take long to work out that this was an old friend—an old flame?—someone he'd gone to high school with, maybe. I thought of our conversation months before, when he'd mentioned someone from back home, someone he talked to *here and there*. If he wasn't in Minnesota, had she been in Nashville while Sloane's mom was pouring me another negroni in Rhode Island? Had she been there just to see Julien? My chest collapsed in a kind of confused, ethereal sadness. So yes, of course, I have thought of Julien—the kiss, the dinner, the playing, the kiss, the kiss again. But then I think of the picture, or of Jessika, or a song of Nick's comes on, or a friend brings up the show or I get a text from Colt, and then I am—where was I?

I head off to the coziest place I know: a brewery taproom tucked in the same factory building as Sloane's office, behind the railroad tracks in a dilapidated offshoot of downtown, all warehouses and gravel lots and empty commercial real estate. It won't be this way for long. The city is morphing before our eyes, little bits of land snatched up, filling up with steakhouses and condos and juice bars and condos and taquerias and condos and yoga studios and condos, and then more condos, a few more condos. But right now the taproom is still here, and all I want is to be somewhere warm. The bar is so tiny that even when the line for a drink is only four or five deep, people start spilling into the echoey brick hallway. A space this small and crowded can't be anything but warm.

When I sit down, the bartender slides me a pale ale before I even order. He's an older guy with long, dark hair in a ponytail. He grins and I want to marry him. Sloane arrives moments later, quicker than I expected.

—I thought you were working tonight, she says. I thought tonight was the big night or whatever. Your BIB is in town.

—My BIB?

I take a sip of my beer. Almost instantly the pain in my forehead starts to fizzle and fade.

—Your boy in a band, Sloane says, motioning at the bartender, mouthing her order. Nick seems worthy of an acronym—even though we're actively trying to forget him. Right? We're still trying to forget him?

—He's not *mine*, I say. And no. Not tonight. Lost cause. We'll be trying tomorrow.

Sloane nods. Another coppery, frothy beer appears in front of us and she slides a debit card across the concrete bar.

—Sure, Sloane says. Fuck tonight. And you have to keep a deep bench. Remember? A good orbit. Minus Colt. Colt's off the bench. I can only stay for ten minutes, by the way. We're prepping for an interview tomorrow and I'm not really off yet. Oh, did I tell you?

—Tell me what?

—I'm doing it. I mean, *we're* doing it. I'm working on Billy to give us a slot for a show. Seriously, Al. I'm writing a *proposal.*

—As in an actual radio show?

—No, a *Broadway* show. She rolls her eyes and takes a slug of beer.

—I didn't know you were actually serious about it, I say.

—Where have you been? And yes, an actual radio show. I do work at an actual fucking radio station, right? Just imagine: we can play whatever we want. And it's not like you have to get onstage to do it. No one will know who we are.

—But don't you need to be, like, an actual DJ to host a show?

—Please, Sloane says. Like hosting a radio show is a real job. Speaking of—shouldn't you be at The Venue? What time are doors tonight?

—It's fine. Andy told me to take a break. I needed to get out of there anyway. It was freezing. I was just waiting around. And Julien's being weird.

—Waiting around? You *work* there, Sloane says. And yeah, I'm sure Jujubean is being weird. Considering you almost had a barback's baby, smooched Julien, then disappeared with me for the holidays.

—Well when you say it like that, I say.

Sloane nods, takes a slug of her beer.

And now your famous ex is playing a show where he's working.

—Nick isn't famous, I say, pulling the words through my teeth with effort. And by the way, how's Jamie?

Sloane rolls her eyes.

—Don't project! Or redirect or circumvent or whatever. No no no. Tonight is not about me. And Jamie is *fine*. I'm on the list for tonight, right? I'm supposed to go to a showcase at the Basement, so it doesn't really matter, but if it's as horrible as I'm expecting it to be, I'll text you. Okay, you can finish that, she says, sliding her beer my way. I gotta run.

—Seriously? Already? You just sat down.

—I told you I couldn't stay. Give Nick my love. I'm sure you will.

—Fuck off.

—Love you.

And she's gone, and I'm drinking alone. But is it alone, with all these people around, all these warm bodies so close to one another? Sweat pricks at my temples, a pint glass shatters somewhere behind the bar. The windows are fogged over, so I can't really tell if it's still snowing. I finish my beer, I order another round, I never want to leave.

And then:

Wilco comes on. Two A-listers walk in and everybody in the small bar pretends not to notice. And then, Nick texts me: where are we getting a drink before soundcheck?

I'm drinking the same beer I was that night, at the open mic, at the little bar down the street from our house, indifferent students milling around as I sat there with my guitar in my hand, thunder in the distance. I couldn't find Sloane's face anywhere, I couldn't find my capo, but I started to play anyway, because it was better than sitting there silently, surrounded by irritated staring faces. My voice started to crack into the mic:

—Hey, uh, I'm Al, and I guess I'm gonna play some songs tonight. Well, not just me, a few of us are—

Someone shouted a drink order at the bar and I stopped talking, distracted. I cleared my throat and it sounded like a hacking cough when it came through the mic.

—But, like, not too many songs, so, you know, but this one is, uh, I'll just start I guess.

I looked around wondering, again, where Sloane was.

The manager nodded at me, eyes saying *go on*, and I strummed, already hearing a slightly out-of-tune note in a chord as I sang, *Watch the traffic lights swaying down on Eighth—*

But I wasn't hitting any of the notes I'd written. The melody felt so loose, so distant, I could barely follow it. Panic pressed up on me. *Where the hell is Sloane?* I thought again; I think that maybe I could do this if I could see her, but then I hear a guy laughing, a guy from a band I recognize, a keyboardist, and he's looking right at me—right at me—and that's when it starts to click, that I'm in the wrong key, I can't hit these notes without the capo, without shifting the melody up or down, no, and the crowd isn't even a crowd, they aren't even listening, so it doesn't even matter. I just do it, without even realizing, I'm launching into lyrics I remember but not ones I wrote, with a melody that isn't mine, no, not at all, and I don't know how it happens, like my brain is glitching and I'm mashing something up—*I'm watching the clock in a haze . . . it's been stuck at three for days and days*—and I hear someone say, loudly, *Jesus, she can't even sing*, and it sounds like they're shouting but it's probably just talking, somebody else saying *nobody wants to hear Rob Fucking Thomas* and that's when I realize, I'm playing "3AM"—the chorus and the bridge over and over, like I'm frozen in some awful early-aughts musical loop, a pedal effect I didn't mean to put on, and I see the keyboardist from the band standing under a soft light, laughing again, looking right at me, not even trying to hide it, and five or six kids walk out, thunder rolling as the door opens and then closes, and then Sloane is in front of me nodding, no, shaking her head, a little grimace on her face, a drink in her hand, and something lodges in my throat, like a bit of dust has gone down the wrong pipe, and I cough into the mic, a slow-motion cacophony of sickness, grasping for water.

Then, for a moment, a horrible quiet. A low laugh from the corner, someone talking into a cell phone at the door, the next songwriter quieting the high E string he's accidentally plucked. My hand is still trembling, and I've lost Sloane again, she's gone, she's left, no wait she's here, but where where where, there are too many fucking faces in this fucking bar.

And then, I lean forward to look for her face again and the neck of my guitar knocks the mic stand over—a scream of feedback, a clatter so loud and gruesome and mortifying I can't even see straight—and everything goes black black black.

2.

Oh, I used to play in a little jazz trio around town. That's none of anybody's business. I hear they're closing it down. You can't start a fucking band in your thirties! Do you have a guy? I might have a guy. I don't know if there's any good sushi in this town. I heard Miranda throws the best Christmas parties. They're doing the show in their basement. Double bass, I think. Nobody listens to Can except that guy. All they gave us were these meat wipes and now I'm fucking starving. You know who I'm talking about. Tour bus broke down, right on I-24, out by Whites Creek. The Delta Saints, next week! People are going to be skating down Broadway. Supposed to get more snow than we've had in a decade. She needed an extra uke for the picking party. He can put you on the list.

Nick arrives at the bar wearing a peacoat and a beanie, his cheeks ruddy and damp, looking like the warmest person in the room. Gloves without fingertips—who needs them? His grin from across the small room is a sliver of white gold, honey. When I stand up to hug him, my legs are loose and wobbly, like I've been sitting for weeks. The beer rushes from my head down to my arms, to the tips of my fingers. I steady myself with a damp palm on the bar, then reach back to finish the beer Sloane left me.

—Look at you, so warm, I say, as Nick folds me into a hug. He smells unfamiliar.

He pinches at my leather jacket. My shoulder blades, the back of my neck, shiver. He brings his hands to my cheeks—his fingertips freezing along my jawline. Like an animal, my clit pulses. Smoke on his breath, beneath artificial spearmint.

—Look at you, so cool. Hi, he says again.

For a moment I'm sure we're going to kiss. My lips part unintentionally. I'm wet, just like that. The scraping of a barstool against concrete, the belly laughter of strangers. Nick pulls his hands away. The heat in my chest dissipates, trying to find a place to rearrange, like a blocked electric current searching for a new source.

—How is it out there? I ask.

—Everybody's freaking out. They've obviously never experienced a Chicago winter. What are we drinking? he asks.

He sits close to me and I point out the beer menu. He takes off his coat, revealing a chunky sweater. I want to wrap myself in it. The music overhead is a touch too quiet, and I'm trying to follow it—the opening chords of—

—What time do you need to be back? I ask.

—An hour, he says.

Our windows of time are always so paltry. How could anyone possibly sustain something like this? With so little oxygen, so little time?

—Sixty entire minutes, all to myself, I say, dragging my bitterness through a half smile.

Nick looks around. He doesn't register the irritation in my voice. He runs a hand through his long hair, on the cusp of scraggly. He's been on the road too long. I tell him about the A-listers in the corner, behind him.

—Who? he asks.

—Never mind. You need a haircut, I say, taking the ends of his hair between my fingers.

—Do I? he asks, leaning in toward me slightly. People like it right now, I think.

What I want to say: *What people? Who? Am I going to get you to myself tonight? Do you still live with the girl who has my name? Are we going to—*

—Oh hey, he says. I think we're going to record that demo I sent you.

—Really? Will you do it here in Nashville?

—Oh, I don't know, he says. Hadn't really gotten that far.

I wait for him to say more but he doesn't. A beer and a half is enough, my chest lighter, my hesitation dissipating like clouds scattering.

—Guess what, I say.

—What? He smiles back, light, amused.

—I finally wrote something. Or, well. The start of something. We'll see. But it had been a minute.

—Yeah? he says, looking right at me, eyes glinty and sharp.

The look has me ready to surrender, to tell him about the song, every nascent, sloppy bit of it. He squeezes my leg and every inch of me warms.

—It's barely—

—You want another round? he asks. Before I head back?

His beer is somehow already three-quarters gone, and he glances at his phone. The light in the taproom dims slightly. An old Big Star song comes on.

—Looks like they're bumping sound check up fifteen. Oh hey, I put you on the list, right?

The snow muffles the city.

People stay home, traffic piles up on Charlotte, Twenty-First, Eighth.

The heat kicks back on at The Venue, but it won't be warm enough until the space is full. I want whiskey and blankets, soup and endless beer. Cotton beanies, heated front seats in expensive cars, tissues by the bedside, grilled cheese that stretches neon orange when you pull it apart. Hot coffee, hot tea, hot toddies, hot baths. New gloves, a new coat, a new car, a new—

—Did you fix the list? Julien asks.

—I'm going to go talk to the band about it, I say.

—Doors are in less than fifteen, he says.

And even though I know he's just doing his job, trying to make sure someone is *actually* in charge, that someone is *actually* working—

—I know, I say.

—Fifteen, he says.

—Heard you the first time, I say.

He's looking down at his phone as I head upstairs. The Venue is still quiet now, but energy is starting to collect, little pockets of warm air gathering throughout the space. The bartenders lining up, Colt haranguing everyone about properly closing out their tabs at the end of the night, merch guys straightening screen prints on the tables in the back, holding beers and unlit cigarettes.

I knock on the greenroom door, like a fan. Timmy answers and looks at me for a moment like he doesn't recognize me, then gives me a lackluster hug and says *Good to see you again*. Nick is sitting on the couch with his feet up. Open Rolling Rocks dotting the coffee table, Styrofoam cups of cold coffee, an open bag of tortilla chips.

—Come hang, he says. He pats the space next to him on the couch.

I sigh, looking at his hand against the worn-in tweed. Doors are in nine minutes. It seems like just long enough to—

—One drink, he says. Like we didn't just have several.

—You know I'm working.

—So am I, he says.

That easy fucking grin. You want to grab it, try to hold it in your hands.

—Right, I say.

But I do it. I go and sit next to him, and when he leans to open a beer for me, I lean back, letting my hip bone press into his.

—Tough gig, he says.

—Oh please, I say.

We take a sip and I wait for him to actually say something, to contribute to the conversation, to actually advance the plot. When he doesn't, I say:

—Doors are in five; I really can't stay long. I should go back downstairs.

He turns to me then.

—Did I tell you about Coachella?

Four minutes. I take several large gulps of beer to swallow down my . . . surprise? Envy? Irritation? Nick's looking at me eagerly now, his eyebrows high, his face bright bright bright.

—No. For . . . wait. Are you fucking with me?

He takes a long pull from his beer. Doors are in three—or probably in two, or probably in one, or already happening, who knows, because I always lose track of time when Nick's face is in front of me. He reaches across us and starts to adjust my necklace then. My chest warms quickly, prickling, like placid water about to boil.

—It's not a huge slot or anything, he says. Saturday, though. Not the smallest stage, obviously not the biggest. Right before Mumford.

—Seriously?

He's twisting at my necklace now, his fingertips callous against my collarbone.

—It's tangled, he says.

—That's amazing. I mean—

He looks at me closely, his fingers unclipping the necklace.

—We're not supposed to tell people yet, but—

—I'm not people, I say.

He laughs quietly. He rehooks the necklace around my neck.

—You're—

—Doors, Julien says, appearing in the doorway. Irritated. My body flashes hot. I turn around quickly, catching Nick's thumb on the necklace he was just fixing. The cheap, fake metal tugs and then gives, snapping quietly.

—Fuck, he says.

The necklace slips off my neck.

—Sorry, I say, though I don't know who it's meant for. I'm coming, I say to Julien.

I look down at my beer, then at Nick, then at Julien. Nick's holding my necklace in his palm, passing it to me like it's a broken guitar string. Something you've used and worn out—something to toss.

—We're late, says Julien.

I look over at Nick and say:

—Congrats.

Downstairs, Julien asks:

—Did you fix the list?

—Fixed it, I say, which of course is a lie.

The show is sold out, so the door is a nightmare. The entryway to The Venue is horribly icy, people coming through with slush sloughing off their cowboy boots, their Vans, their cheap Target shoes. Lips are cracked and cheeks are flushed. Everybody everywhere is fucking freezing, but I'm edgy with Nick in town, and I can't stop bitching. I swear I'm the coldest. I swear I'm the victim. I swear I'm the only one. Here I am working the door—Nick's a floor above me, and I'm stuck hoarding in strangers.

I've stamped barely a dozen hands when a girl in a skirt and a jean jacket slips outside on the sidewalk. She's on the ground, wailing. It's unclear if it's her arm or her elbow or her wrist or her shoulder, but something is *broken*, she shouts. People slip past as she screams; Julien is on the phone talking to the paramedics; the first band is going on. I've lost track of Nick—he's upstairs drinking backstage, surely. Four people come in with three tickets, begging us to let their friend in anyway. Two people who aren't on the list swear they are. They weren't even on the first draft, the one where my own name was spelled wrong. Jess never comes, but one of the guys from Denim does, using her name to get in. When I tell him he's not on the list, he just keeps spelling her name for me, saying *k* like it's a secret password.

And then he looks at me and says, Hey, did you do an open mic a few months back? Over in Midtown? Aren't you the girl who—

—Go ahead, I tell him, rushing him through. It's fine, you're in. His laughter—is it echoing up from the stairs or from last year?

Andy comes down thirty seconds later with some underage kid I let in, and I get a short lecture about ID'ing properly, about the exorbitant fine we can be charged for something like that. Do I have ten K? he asks. No, I don't fucking have ten K. I haven't seen him this irritated since Eddie started, his temples pulsing in the shadowy light, his cell phone in his hand like it's connected to his palm.

Our sound guy, Danny, wouldn't come out in the snow, and the bands are pissed at having to do everything themselves. Simon's here to run monitors but he's drowning. Flirtation Device tours with their own guy who offers to help the openers, but he's drunk and edgy and precariously too close to fucked-up to be manning the boards alone. I can tell all the way from the door that something's off with the sound. The heat is back on, but everyone is bitching about how cold it is, even with all these people, even with the heat cranked up.

I barely see Julien all night. When I finally catch his eye, at ten fifteen, a few minutes before Nick's set, he looks exhausted, frustrated, his face drooping, his ankle twisting in a constant circle, the toe of his Converse squeaking into the slick, slushy linoleum.

—How'd you meet him? Colt asks at the bar.

Nick's onstage now. I'm still on the clock but getting a drink, waiting for Julien to cut me. The band is starting into a new song, and now I'm trying not to look in the direction of the stage. Colt's face is dotted with sweat, his cheeks bright.

—Michigan.

—I said how, not where, he says. Look at you, all shy. Are we going out after? Snowmaggedon, baby.

—I don't know. Can I just get a Four Roses and a High Life?

The song is picking up energy, all thrumming bass and exquisite harmony. I want to ignore it but I can't.

—You have any Xanax? I ask Colt as he slides the drinks to me. A bit of whiskey splashes out, and he wipes it down with a white bar rag. The song is trailing off, and Nick is bullshitting with the crowd while his lead guitarist quickly works to fix a broken string.

—All out, Colt says, his voice carrying across the bar.

—Come on.

His eyebrows lift and he shrugs. A small girl with a pixie cut elbows her way to the bar on my right.

—I have some other shit I can give you, though. It's close enough. Come by, he says.

The next song starts, one from the first album that I love. The beat is urgent, the kind of pulsing that begs you to participate, to clap, jump, shake your head. The crowd quickly starts stomping along, singing loudly—so many eyes fixed on Nick. We're all overcompensating for the cold, dancing and shouting, manic bright sunshine energy on a snowy night. Nick walks into the crowd, not once but twice, and our lights guy isn't prepared to follow him. The spotlight searches and falls short as Nick jumps around, singing in the dark, the crowd's collective voices drowning him out, his long hair framing his face and his throat pulsing in the light of the shadows, all that strained effort of singing without a microphone. I hate how much I love him right then, somewhere in the hazy in-between—friend, lover, ex, fan—as I watch him sing his songs, everybody else screaming along, his words on our mouths.

I go out for a cigarette as the crowd starts to dwindle after the show. Lights are up, spirits are too. Maybe it's just me—I've always been prone to exaggeration when it comes to Nick—but it's been a buzzy show. High energy and low inhibitions, everyone trying to stay warm beneath the lights as the city gets colder.

Julien's in the parking lot below, hunched over and talking through the front window of a car. He's not wearing a coat; he must be freezing. I don't recognize the car, though I do recognize the wild laughter that pours out of it. The loud cascade of joy you can hear from all the way up here: staccato sixteenth notes.

My cigarette won't catch with the wind this strong. I stand out there anyway, though, the cigarette cold in my lips. Down below, Julien leans into the car; then the door on the balcony swings open behind me and Timmy walks out.

—Great set, I mumble.

—Hey, thanks, he says.

He flicks on his lighter and the balcony is silent for a moment. Without Nick physically present, Timmy and I have never had much of anything to say to each other. Down below, the sound of tires on concrete, a red Jetta flicking its blinker on—Jess driving away, Yeah Yeah Yeahs pouring out of her window.

—I should probably get back to work, I say to Timmy.

Do we matter? Shooting the shit with the band or out there in the crowd, our faces blurry, pixelated. Sometimes enthralled, enchanted, luminous. Other times apathetic or distracted, staring at our feet or our phones, maybe even actively uninterested, maybe laughing. In the blissful moments, it could be transcendent there in the audience: drunk, howling, finally putting words, notes—music—to a feeling. But the band matters more than we do, right? Inherently, they do. We pay money to see *them*, to hear *them*. And yet they can't exist without us. There's no show without an audience. There's no them without us.

Inside, the night cleaning crew is bagging trash and sweeping up neon wristbands and damp napkins, plastic straws and paper tickets. Colt and his crew are running receipts in the back, looking ragged: T-shirts pitted out, sweat glowing on their foreheads beneath the bar lights. I go to the office to get my things, wondering if Julien is ever going to actually cut me, wondering if he was leaning into Jessika's car to kiss her, if maybe they're the kind of people who keep kissing even after they've broken up, if maybe they both miss each other, still want each other, still think about each other. Even if she does prefer women. Even though he just kissed me.

Someone knocks on the office door, and before I can say anything Nick is there, electric, the adrenaline of the night still shimmering off of him.

—Holy shit that was fun, he says.

He's glistening.

—It was great, I say. Lights couldn't keep up with you.

He walks across the room quickly now and takes my right elbow into his palm so that I am standing in front of him, our bodies close.

—I'm glad you were here, he says.

—I mean, I live here. I work here.

He laughs and shakes his head.

—Shut up. I know. But it just made it, I don't know. All the better. Knowing you were out in the audience.

He hooks a single finger into the collar of my shirt then, tugging me toward him. Like I'm on a leash, like I'm his.

—Hi, I say.

—Hey.

He presses into me then, mouth hot with whiskey. He tastes like the past. I run a hand up his neck, into the long mess of his hair, like I can pull us into the present. He's already hard—too easy—and I wonder if it really even matters that it's me he's kissing, if he's thought about this moment as much as I have, if I really could just be anyone right now. Any stupid girl in any stupid town who loved his stupid band.

He slides a hand under my shirt, his hand slick with sweat, my bra slipping up easily. His fingers on my nipples, then up to my neck, then back on my chest. But I am still in the office, I am still at work, I am still—

—Let's go, I say. Somewhere else, okay?

I pull back from him and his frustration comes off him like heat. He kisses me again.

—Where are we going?

—Come on, I say, pulling away from him. I gotta clock out. I'll meet you downstairs, okay?

At the door, I'm waiting on Nick, who's run into fans by the merch table—the kind who linger. Julien is running a mop across the floor, trying to remove some of the clinging, desperate slush.

—How was it? he asks. I didn't get to see much.

—It was good. It was fine. Is that girl okay?

Julien shrugs.

—She'll be fine. What a mess.

—Seriously. Thanks for dealing with the ambulance. I can't believe we've never had to call one before.

—*You've* never had to call one before.

—Like I said, I don't want to be in charge.

Julien nods.

—Did Jessika end up coming through after all? I ask.

—You're cut, by the way. I can get the rest of this.

He motions to the mop, the stubborn slush on the floor.

—You sure? I can—

Nick: on the stairs, a Rolling Rock in his hand.

He is still bright, his body looking elastic, free. Julien's shoulders are stiff. The mop sits propped up under his elbow.

—Do any of y'all need a ride? Andy asks from the top of the stairs. Things are getting messy out there.

—Do we? Nick asks.

—Julien, Nick, Nick, Julien.

—I think we'll be fine, I say to Andy, not knowing how we'll get wherever it is that we're going.

He nods and disappears into the stairwell. Julien puts his hand in the air, an animatronic flick of the wrist. Nick says:

—Hey, man.

—Julien works here, I say. With me. You met, or, well, you saw him earlier.

—Yeah, I thought so. Thanks for everything. Great spot. Good crowd tonight.

—Glad to hear it.

—Sorry I made your partner in crime late for doors, Nick says. Wanna get out of here then? He looks at me.

—All right, I'm gonna make sure everything's closed out upstairs, Julien says, and starts up toward the main space, meeting my gaze for just a moment. We share a quick, uncertain look—eyes that I can't read, lips that are holding something back—before I follow Nick out into the freezing night.

I stretch my legs out and make sure our knees touch. The van is supposed to leave at midnight, but it's never going to happen. The roads are a disaster; the rest of the band is downtown; Nick doesn't even want to drive to his hotel. The streetlights glow softly through the windshield as we pass a joint back and forth. I'm already higher than I want to be—every noise, even muffled beneath the snow, surprises me. The van is cool and smells like sweat, stale bread, fatigue.

Nick presses his knee into mine and exchanges the joint for a small bottle of cheap whiskey. It's been a long time since we've fooled around—ever since he started seeing the other girl with my name, I've been good. Even in May, I was good. It helped, of course, that we didn't have enough time. We never have enough time.

But now he reaches for my leg, lets his fingertips graze my knee and then drop, drumming his fingers along the floor, like his touch could have been an accident. A car engine starts somewhere in the parking lot and I tense up, my legs pulled into my chest and then extended again. This time, I'm more obvious about touching him. I press my hand to his ankle, run it up the inside of his leg and then back down. He glances up and we look at each other quietly for a moment, his hair in his eyes. He presses a hand more intentionally to my shin, my calf, the back of my leg. He grabs, runs his hand beneath my jeans. I inch toward him so that his hand can reach my thigh.

I reach between his legs, watching as he grows hard against his tight jeans. I run my fingers across the denim. He leans forward; someone calls out a name in the parking lot, the light rushing amber and golden through the windshield. I sit up and then so does Nick, and we pause there for a moment, our faces very close, our breath choppy, as if we're trying to see how close our lips can get without actually touching, and then his lips are on my neck, running hot across my skin, my jawline, my ear, but not my lips. I go to meet his mouth with mine and he finds my chest. I reach for his belt buckle; he leans into it and kisses me everywhere but my mouth. I want to scream. I find his lips and he pulls away, some coy bullshit that should make me hesitate, make me stop, make me want more than this but I will take any of this: I have him, we are here. I press my lips to his chin and neck and chest and nipples, the convex curve of his ribs, his waist, then tugging down his briefs, I put him in my mouth. The snow falls silently.

His dick is very big, slightly curved, it is hard to take him all the way into my throat but I do it, whiskey and sweat and strain. He presses his palms lightly against my head, pushing me down just barely as I bob—first hungrily, then with a gritty determination, then eventually with irritation, anger, frustration, and then, finally, my jaw sore and my eyes watering, he comes into my mouth, with so little warning that I gag as he hits the back of my throat.

I swallow. There's nowhere to spit anyway.

3.

Songs that should be listened to only in the winter:

"River" (Joni Mitchell—perhaps obvious, but deserves mention)
"Snow Day" (Matt Pond PA)
"The Latter Days" (Frontier Ruckus)
"We Looked like Giants" (Death Cab for Cutie—yes, again. Ideally should be listened to at night *during* the winter.)
"Woods" (Bon Iver)
"If It's the Beaches" (the Avett Brothers—counterintuitive, I understand)
"Cold Cold Ground" (Tom Waits)
"I Want to See the Bright Lights Tonight" (Richard and Linda Thompson)

Drizzly blue daylight, my chest pounding in the cold of the second space. A memory of Nick, now several weeks old, hazy. Regret. New Year's Day, and everybody's somewhere doing nothing. A memory of Julien then, soft lips on mine, my palm pressing into porch as he kissed me. The show tonight is a local thing, three up-and-comers I haven't heard of, but it should be pretty quiet. Andy says he doesn't really need me at the door. We aren't expecting much of a crowd.

The whiskey from last night—and the gin and the beer and the cigarettes—gnaw at the back of my throat like a rancid echo. I'm all out of Colt's benzos. Andy's guitar is cold to the touch, slightly out of tune. The song in my head is finally my own, but it hasn't convinced me, not yet. The hook settled in quickly, clear and confident—cocky, even, about as egotistical as a melody could be. But I'm still mapping my way through the verses. Every time I think I've got something, it disappears.

Told me that I'd fallen in love with everybody who came through
I pretended it was nothing, said at least I didn't fall in love with you

The space heater kicks off and the A minor of the last lick lingers, quiet reverb off the empty walls. Two partial songs now, with weeks of no full ones. Last night, at home after a party Sloane had snuck us into, I sat in the living room trying to smash the songs together, forcing the fragmented melodies into a drunken mess. It was sonic carnage.

Colt's horizontal in the office when I get downstairs, a cowboy hat over his face. The room reeks of potent weed, and he doesn't see me slide Andy's guitar back under the coffee table, a swish of nylon against the hardwood.

—What'd you do last night? I ask.

—Drugs, he says.

Without even removing his hat, he points with a sad finger toward Andy's desk. The remaining half of an expertly rolled joint is perched on a copy of *Anna Karenina*.

—Is Julien here?

Now Colt looks up.

—The two of you are always asking where the other one is, he says.

—No we're not.

—No, he's not here, sorry babe. It's just me. Don't kill the messenger. Just smoke that, and then I'm getting us a beer. It's the only way through to the other side. What do you like? Rolling Rock, right?

—Yuengling, I say.

—You guys know Tolstoy hated music? Eddie says, appearing in the doorway.

—Jesus, Colt says. When did you get here?

Eddie's hair is shorter, but his facial hair has taken over the bottom half of his face; he's shaved it into a Fu Manchu and somehow it's grown in even redder than before.

—I've been here. Upstairs.

—Where upstairs? I ask.

Picturing Eddie in the second space is like finding out he's had sex in my bed. Colt dips out to the bar for our beers.

—Getting a space heater from the closet, Eddie says dumbly, running a hand over his mustache and grinning. Why? What's up there?

—Nothing, I say.

—What the fuck did you do to your face? Colt asks as he reappears in the doorway.

It's hard to tell what triggers the rush of relief in my chest—Colt appearing with my beer and mocking Eddie, or Eddie not knowing about the other space yet. A text from Sloane pops up on my phone: talking to Billy (officially officially) about our future slot tonight. Get ready DJ queen. I roll my eyes and slide the phone back into my pocket.

—You good to be solo tonight? Andy asks me from the doorway. Surprised to see all of you here.

He's got a generic-looking to-go coffee in his hand and his fleece hangs loosely on his frame. He looks cold; for that matter, we all do. All winter, everyone in their thrift-store T-shirts, threadbare beanies, flannels, thin jackets. Wondering why we're always so cold when we do nothing at all to keep ourselves warm.

—Yeah, sure. Julien's not coming?

—She's obsessed, Colt says.

—Jealous, Eddie says, and Colt lifts a middle finger toward him.

I knew it would be a slow night, but for some reason I still expected him. He went to Minnesota over the holidays and I haven't seen him in almost two weeks. Just two shifts together since Nick's show. Twice, over the holidays at Izzy's, I *almost* got drunk enough to call him, to text him that I was thinking of him, but then I woke up with all the lights on in Izzy's guest room, my phone dead in my hand, Julien's number pulled up but not called.

—No guest list tonight, he says. I'd be surprised if we do more than sixty or seventy. Eddie, you know you're not getting paid to be here tonight, right?

—Capitalism, man, Eddie says.

Andy looks at him with a mix of confusion, irritation—regret.

Behind the bar, Colt leans over, shaking ice loose from the machine, stacking cups, restocking bottles. As I'm heading over to the greenroom, Andy calls me back to the office. The last band is finishing up a sleepy sound check and looped guitar slips into the room. Danny is half-dead in the sound booth. Our whole team looks functionally ill today.

—You can borrow it, you know, Andy says.

—Shit. I'm sorry, I say, turning to him. I mean. I have my own at home. It's just—yours is nice.

—I thought you didn't play, he says.

—I have an old Gibson that was my aunt's. But it's too big for me.

The action's too high. I don't know. I can't write much on it. Though that's probably not the guitar's fault.

—What are you writing?

—Nothing finished, I say.

—Take it home sometime, he says. If you want. Or you can just keep playing it upstairs. Not a problem. Just give me credit, he says. You know, if you write a number one single on it.

I roll my eyes. Through the doorway, Colt's waving a beer at me over Andy's head.

—I'm gonna go restock the greenroom, I say.

The night is slow, listless. I should have stayed home, but Sloane is at Jamie's and I would have hated the silence seeping through the floorboards, into the walls. Eddie's sitting at the bar drinking a Mich Ultra with Colt, talking animatedly with his hands while Colt stares numbly into space. Without Julien here, I pass the time just staring at my phone, flipping through a copy of the *Scene*. There's a review of the Flirtation Device show, with a byline I don't recognize. I start to text Nick a picture of it but then stop. He's back to his life that doesn't involve me. Our nights are just miniature detours from his actual tours. Instead—

I text Julien: What are you doing? Doors are dead.

He doesn't respond.

I text Sloane back about the radio show: only if we get a prime-time slot.

She responds immediately: well obviously.

Colt comes down and asks me for a light. I pass mine to him and he takes the lighter but doesn't step outside.

—You know you're free to do whatever you want, he says, the cigarette loose between his lips like he's posing for a photo.

—I do know that, I say, turning the page of the alt weekly, not looking up.

—Don't get me wrong, I like our . . . our evenings together. But if you're—

I glance up. He looks like he's cut his hair even shorter in recent weeks, which barely seems possible.

—I got it, I say.

He pauses and then looks at me closely, taking the cigarette out of his mouth. He says: I like that you don't even know you're hot.

—Excuse me?

—Or maybe you actually do, and that's the whole ruse. It's sexy, though. Even if the humble thing is bullshit.

—Someone here has to be humble, I say, and Colt laughs.

I glance at his feet—a lazy pair of New Balance sneakers—planted firmly into the floor.

—Go text your emo prince, he says.

I roll my eyes.

—Go smoke your cigarette, asshole.

Upstairs, the first band has gone on, and quiet fuzzy guitars echo down the stairs. There's a piece in the weekly on a local school board member, a bit about some flood recovery that's still in progress. On my phone, Julien still hasn't responded. Nick's just played a show in Philly. Sloane's back home; she texts to ask if she should save me some pizza. I pull up the photo I saw of Julien from over Thanksgiving with the blond girl. I zoom in on his face, then slide my phone back in my pocket as someone shoves an ID in my face.

A couple of people come through the door over the next half hour, a parade of cold January frowns. A girl I recognize from the Belcourt comes through, but she doesn't seem to know me. Two guys then, eyes bloodshot. Danny's girlfriend, natural deodorant and dreadlocks. A redhead who does lights for the National, off tour for the winter. A middle-aged man who used to be in a "famous" Christian band—I recognize his name when he flashes his ID. And then, oddly—Esther Wainwright.

At first I'm not sure it's her. Dark hair with a prominent gray streak. But her name is fresh on my mind, the recent news about Justin Wilson. It's so perfectly Nashville, to be suddenly face-to-face with someone you were just thinking about. For the first time all night, I'm fully aware of my body, the cold, the physicality of being a person walking through the world. A person sitting on a stool, wearing a fake leather jacket.

—Esther, right? I say, remembering Andy's distant advice—*never guess*—and as usual ignoring it.

—Hi, yeah, that's me. Do we . . . know each other?

—No, no. I'm Al, though. I've been following along with the—keeping up.

Should I apologize? The way I did to Julien, after my comments about his dad? Suddenly I wish he were here. Somehow I'm sure he'd help me through this conversation.

—I'm glad he's okay, I say, then start to doubt myself. Or well, I mean, I don't know. I'm glad—

—Thank you, Esther says. Me too.

She reaches across the ticket stand to me, her hand impossibly soft.

—Esther, she says. Which you already know.

—Sorry. I feel like a stalker.

—No. I didn't mean it like that. You sure we haven't met? she asks now.

She adjusts a simple gold necklace around her neck, pale skin dotted with rosacea, silver chipped nails pressed against her chest.

—Maybe? I say. I'm around a lot.

—Were you at the house show over on Horton? Back in—maybe just before Halloween? I recognize this jacket, she says, pinching at the shoulder of my neon windbreaker.

—I was.

—Maybe that was it. I had a writing gig over near there, she says. And then she sighs and says: Nashville.

—Nashville, I agree.

Shots of Four Roses, a Miller High Life and then another. Esther floating in the back, like a ghost. Another shot, the room warm, the music on a reverb-saturated loop. A girl onstage, sing-screaming about getting sober while I drift blissfully away from any such condition. Danny suddenly in charge of load-out, of closing, of everything. Andy off to the emergency room, his daughter's wrist broken in a basketball game. Colt: red cheeks, puffy eyes, buzzed head, too many rings on his hands. Why would one man need so many rings? Eyeing myself in the bathroom, looking for whoever it is that Colt has seen. Maybe he is right—something about the way the sheen of sadness radiates through the alcohol, a milky lightness left in its wake. The humility, though, he was wrong about that—or maybe I'm just drunk. No dinner. The night taking on the shape of a walking dream, *January blues, I wish I had a river snow day snow day I could skate away skate away skate away from you—*

Two a.m. A pizza place off Music Row that's been closed for hours, but we're still here: Colt, the local bands from tonight, a street artist who's working on a mural downtown somewhere, Sloane, two other girls from the radio station. Sloane's head is thrown back, her teeth white, her neck long. Always making friends with the women at tables, pulling them in as I push them away. Bottles of thick, hot wine. Broccoli rabe and sausage, cheese that stretches into the night. The room spinny. Colt has solved the hangover problem because now I'm fucking wasted. His hand on my leg, tracing the thick denim at the crotch of my jeans. I want to run my fingers along the outline of his dick. Wet heat—it could be this easy.

No way they'll sell that place out. I swear to god, it was him, I saw him. He was wearing suspenders! We have a hockey team? He has almost no rhythm. Did it come out on vinyl? Apartment three eleven, come on over. Close me out while you're up there. You know that song is about John Mayer, right? Michigan, I think. Yeah, they're getting some buzz. Flotation something. Can someone pass the water down here? Well, fuck him then. Flotation Divorce? No that's not it.

Julien, walking around the corner off Edgehill—I can see him coming from the patio of the restaurant. No, wait, can't be. Julien's at home, asleep. Peaceful under his posters of the Boss. The lights are low and my inhibitions are lower, the whole scene is taking place underwater, sound warping in quiet echoes, people becoming fuzzy, slippery versions of themselves. Press my palms into the stiff wooden bench, shift my leg from under Colt's hand. The room still tilts. Is it too warm in here? A hand on my shoulder.

—Hi.

—Hey. Hi.

I have to pull the words out of my mouth like candy stuck to my teeth.

Julien.

—Where have you been? I ask. You didn't text me back.

—Home, he says.

—Do you want some wine? I need some water.

—Ah, the Emo Prince, Colt says. She was asking about you all night.

—Ignore him, I say. He's drunk.

—He is?

Sarcastic. I try to sit up straighter.

—What are you doing here? I ask.

—Mallory needed a ride, he says, nodding to a girl down the table that I don't recognize.

—Mallory, I repeat, like I'm chewing the word.

The patience in his face flickers on and then off and then disappears completely.

—My friend Mallory, he says. Don't do that.

He shakes his head, looks around the restaurant and then down at his hands.

—What? Don't do what?

—Don't, he says. You know.

—I'm sorry, I say. Are you sober?

—I am.

—Incredible, I say. Valiant. Majestic.

My mouth is full of marbles and bullshit.

—Hunter, Colt says, I'm gonna close us out. You good? Want a shot of Fernet for the road?

He puts a hand at the base of my neck, somehow hot and cold at the same time.

—Of what? No, it doesn't matter. I'm good. I'm good.

Colt turns away; Julien looks around the space, briefly lost.

—We're not together, I say stupidly, and he looks back at me, his eyes watery, tired.

—Neither are we, he says.

4.

We drink until we don't anymore.

We don't cross the river. Not tonight, not most nights. It will be years until we discover the other half of the city. But we are young and naive and we ignore whatever streets we aren't walking, ignore the restaurants we aren't at, ignore the places outside our six square blocks, our two square miles of city, ignore the people with normal jobs, the bands we've never heard of and the bands everybody's heard of. We ignore the warnings and reminders and the alarms, beyond this week, this day, this show, this night, this hour, this drink this face—

A dive bar in Hillsboro Village and I've lost all sense of time. Minutes have slipped away, and so has my group. The bar lights are up. Colt is wasted, insisting he can drive. Sloane's off with her drummer, and Jess—Jessika—is sitting next to me, telling me she can drop me off, that she hasn't been drinking tonight. Julien was there but I can't find him now. It seems late, but when I check my phone it's not even ten. Colt and I day-drank, and now we're both a bit underwater. *I should never have told you how hot you were, now you're getting cocky*, he says. I ignore him and drink more.

—I can take you, Jess is saying, but I'm looking past her. I'm looking for Julien. When did he slip out? He was with us earlier; it was our day off.

—Where'd Julien go?

—Julien left, she says.

—Julien, I say again, like I want to say more about him but either I can't or I won't.

—All right, babe.

She's smiling at me, but it's cracked. Judgment? Or maybe—concern.

—I'm fine, I say. I'll walk.

—Where do you live?

I wave uselessly in the direction of my house.

—Okay, no, Jess says. I can take you. It's on the way.

—You don't know where I live.

—It's Nashville, she says. Everything's on the way.

We walk around the quiet block; winter is a cocoon across the city. It's a Monday, and we're the only people partying this hard. A streetlight flickers and the breeze rushes through, lifting a napkin, a plastic bag off the ground. Briefly, the two items are suspended in the air before rustling back to the ground. Inanimate, silent. The cold is sobering—I open my eyes wider, as if I can let the wet night in under my skin.

—Sorry, she says as we step into the car. There's shit everywhere.

It's a relief that her car is messy, that it looks almost like the inside of my own. A water bottle and a receipt in the console, a roll of film and a few CDs—CDs!—in the passenger seat. A plastic Jesus wearing a rainbow robe hangs from the rearview.

—It's fine, I say. This isn't even dirty. What were you doing tonight?

—I have been hungover all day, she says. So I've been doing exactly nothing tonight. Hence the not drinking.

—What are you doing here then? I ask.

—Denim had a thing over there.

She nods at the bar next door, the same one where I did my open mic. This was the last place I'd wanted to be tonight, but two-for-one beers all day Mondays and Thursdays is a powerful argument. I was overruled.

—I usually just drink through it, I say. A hangover, I mean.

—Not this one, she says, shaking her head.

She turns on the car and a familiar song fills the space. She adjusts the volume.

—Okay, so where am I going? she asks.

I point her toward my house, glancing down at the two CDs I picked up off the passenger seat. There's writing on them, but I can't make out what they say.

—I think Julien's mad at me, I say.

Jess glances over at me and then back at the road and says:

—Grumpy little Jules.

She takes a sip from the bottle in the center console—Sprite—and in the glow of a stoplight I can see how pale she looks for the first time. It all somehow softens me toward her.

—He is, isn't he? I say.

—It's not you, she says.

—How so?

—He was probably annoyed that I was there.

—Is there anything still going on there? I ask. I mean, I know you broke up. But is it one of those breakups that isn't really a breakup at all? Like, do you still—

—Oh, no. Not—no. I don't think so. He just asked for some space afterward, so—

—He asked for space? *After* you ended things?

—Kind of an impossible request in a town this small. Like, what the fuck, there are only two places to get an actual decent drink here. Of course I'm going to run into him. We're in the same industry.

So am I, I almost say, but instead I ask:

—How old are you?

—Twenty-six, why?

—Is that why you already have such a legit job?

She laughs and shrugs.

—I'd hardly call it *legit*, she says. It's really not as sexy as it sounds. Sometimes it's basically babysitting. The free shows are nice, though.

I nod.

—What are we listening to?

—Good, right? Esther Wainwright. God, she's one of my favorites.

—Really? Her solo stuff? I ask.

—You don't listen to her?

—What about him? I ask. Justin—

—What about him? she says.

I shrug and let the comment hang there. Outside the moon is bright and heavy.

—Turn right on the next street, I say, and Jess flicks her blinker on.

—Are you still into him? I ask, as she pulls onto my street.

Julien's already answered this for me, but I want to hear it from her. The house is dark and gloomy. I wish Sloane or I had thought to leave a light on. I wave vaguely toward my house and Jess pulls over.

—Jules is only pissy with people he feels comfortable with, she says. People he likes. He gets like that sometimes.

She hasn't even remotely answered my question.

—Don't lie, I say.

She laughs.

—I'm not, she says.

The soft acoustic song intro fills the car as Jess shifts into park. The stillness is briefly disorienting.

—This was cool of you, I say. Thank you for the hangover ride. I owe you.

It takes effort not to slur the words together. She laughs and I almost startle—the volume of it is always a surprise, a jolt of loud energy into the night air.

—I can't promise next time I'll be sober, she says, and I swing the door open, tucking the CDs from her passenger seat into the pocket of my coat.

A JwK playlist, stolen:

"On Ice" (Chris Thile)
"Snails" (the Format)
"I Can't Tonight" (Esther Wainwright)
"Flowerparts" (Bob Schneider)
"Jolene" (Dolly Parton)
"Talking Shit About a Pretty Sunset" (Modest Mouse)
"Samson" (Regina Spektor)
"Hangman" (Cadillac Sky)
"The Book of Love" (the Magnetic Fields)
"Good Deeds" (Owen)
"Maps—Four Track Demo" (Yeah Yeah Yeahs)
"Tim McGraw" (Taylor Swift)
"You Can Call Me Al" (Paul Simon)
"Buttons" (The Weeks)

It probably goes without saying, but I have a somewhat slutty winter. Colt, a softball, a hookup of convenience. A boomerang of sorts. Dan Daniels, sweet potato king of the Southeast. A keyboardist from a California band, an inch shorter than me but desperately beautiful—just a kiss. A singer from Denver who wears exclusively deep V-neck shirts but gets away with it because his face and his voice are so perfect. A barista—a new one—at the place on Twenty-First. The door guy at the Basement, the bartender at the burger place, the bartender at the pizza place. Leather jackets and tight jeans, phone numbers left on bar tabs and forgotten in the morning. I am making a mess but I swear I'll clean it up next week, next month, next—

Wednesday, three days into the New Year. An alt-country guy with a solid local following is on tonight. Andy's gone.

—How's Jake Barnes? I ask Julien.

I can't believe he's actually reading Hemingway in the ten minutes before doors open. The cover is the color of fire, the same edition I had in college. But—finally—it's one I've read. Even rarer, I remember the names of the main characters.

—Bathrooms done? he asks.

—Bathrooms are done.

—Mirrors?

—Yes, Julien. The mirrors too.

Outside, car doors click shut. Downtown flickers neon in the winter night. Julien keeps reading, running his thumb along the top of the pages, down the side, like a kind of ritual. I stare at my phone.

—Do you want a drink? I ask.

He looks up.

—I'm not drinking.

—Ever?

—This month, Julien says.

It's the third of January, which means he is not drinking for twenty-eight more days.

—That's long, I say, and then: I hate this idea.

—Of course you do.

—What's that supposed to mean? I ask.

—Nothing, Julien says. He reaches behind him to get a leather jacket—not warm enough for the night.

—Are you smoking? What are the parameters of this little sobriety sabbatical?

—It's a drinking sabbatical. A sobriety sabbatical would be, I don't know—a bender?

—Boring.

He shakes his head.

—Are you mad at me? I ask.

What I don't say: You could be. Maybe you should be.

—Am I mad at you? No, he says, though the tone is unconvincing.

I take a breath.

—Are we going to talk, ever, about the fact that we kissed?

—It sounds like we already are, he says.

—You disappeared, I say.

Like it's all on him, like I didn't go somewhere for the holidays too.

—I went to see my family. And anyway. You had—

—I had what?

He sighs.

—Never mind, he says. Doors are in two.

—Did you see any old friends? I ask.

He looks up at me, eyes narrowed.

—Who?

—I don't know, blond friends. Friends who put their heads on your shoulder at a bar.

I'm shameless, but I can't help it—the words are just coming out. He nods, just barely.

—I know who you're talking about. And no. She doesn't live in Minnesota anymore, he says.

—I thought she was someone from home? When I asked if you—

—She's just a—she's a friend. Our moms are friends.

—She's very pretty.

He smiles then, skin around his eyes scrunched and crinkled; I want to press my fingertips to it. He cocks his head slightly and asks:

—Were you stalking me?

I roll my eyes.

—The photo was tagged. So, what, did you kiss her on New Year's? I ask, practically slipping into the grave I'm digging myself.

—Stop it, he says, but he's smiling still.

—Here, I say, reaching for his hand.

I flip his palm and push the long-sleeved waffle tee up his forearm. There are faint scars along the insides of his wrists, his veins running violet underneath his skin. Upstairs, the house music is too loud.

—What are you doing? he asks, but he doesn't move his arm, his palm resting in mine lightly. My hand is sweating and I press the ink of the stamp into his inner wrist. It seeps into the skin. His pinkie moves, ever so slightly, as if to wrap around mine. I start to do the same—

A horn screeches out front, and I pull back.

—Good, I say. Stamp still works.

Latkes and Irish coffees and sour cream. Shepherd's pies on the East Side while we try to avoid Eddie, who's on a date at the other end of the bar. Someone trying to get us to go see the Opry Christmas lights while they're still up. Avoiding the coffee shop down the street and the V-necked lead singer everywhere we go. A DVD that plays the sounds of a crackling fire on our living room TV, even though we have a fireplace. Whiskey instead of tequila, Sloane giving me shit for being from Michigan and not owning a pair of real snow boots. Julien and I working, at some odd impasse. Like we never kissed. Like neither of us is even thinking about it. An invitation to go skiing with a friend of a friend at Big Bear—Sloane takes it and I stay behind, sink into the silence of the house. Lou Reed relishing his frigid walks, like he's some kind of Siberian husky. New Year's resolutions—I don't even pretend to make them; January is not a time for reinvention.

—Please tell me you're not taking me back to some Oompa Loompa photo shoot, Sloane says as we drive down Eighth. I just can't with these acid heads. I'm not in my psychedelic phase yet.

—Shut up, I say. No Oompa Loompas. I left my phone at work last night.

—Oh, Billy told me he wants to see a sample playlist for our show.

—We don't *have* a show, I say.

—Sure, yeah, whatever. It's not like there's even an open slot, technically. But if and when one opens up, he says we should be ready. Plus we have a million playlists, so this isn't going to take, like, *effort*.

Sloane flicks on a Strokes song and starts humming under her breath. Outside, the day is mild. The branches in the neighborhood look like broken arms, everything covered in a layer of moisture. It's unseasonably warm today. Sloane ties her windbreaker around her waist as we step out into The Venue parking lot, the doors latching shut with a muffled *mmph*. It's lunchtime, and nobody else is here yet.

Inside, a chill. And then: mildew, stale cigs, cheap liquor. I lead Sloane to the back hallway, feeling around for a light switch.

—Should I have shared my location with a friend? she asks warily.

—Who would you share it with besides me?

—Billy, she says. My dad. I don't know, Lou Reed. Jamie. Jessika.

—Jessika? Wait, are you guys friends now or something?

—Kind of, Sloane says.

I turn to try to read her face, but it's obscured in the dark hallway. She's quiet as we wind back through the hallways and up the stairs to the storage area. When I open the door, daylight swims through the west windows, the sun breaking through the clouds outside in a crack of golden light.

—What is this? Sloane asks.

—Nothing. I say. Storage, supposedly.

I spot my phone over on the windowsill where I was playing yesterday. It's dead, with a half-finished song buried somewhere in the Notes app.

Sloane steps away from me, looking around, her shadow stretching long behind her. She looks tiny, all that emptiness swathing her. She hums a melody I don't recognize under her breath.

—What are you singing?

She shushes me, continues to hum. The melody carries quietly in the space, and I imagine it as water, flooding into the shape of the room.

—I'm not singing, she says. I'm listening.

Not calling Izzy enough. Not going to any appointments that she helped schedule for me. Not remembering where my parents' health insurance card is, not responding to their emails, to Izzy's texts, to the voicemails my dad's left on my phone. Not being able to say no to Colt when he offers me a free drink, like anything is ever free. Not being able to finish a song, not being able to remember the chords to my own song, not being able to follow the low or the high or the *whatever* harmony of anybody else's songs.

—Play me what you wrote, Sloane says later, at home. It's sunny outside, hazy golden light drifting through the windows. Julien is out there somewhere, eleven days sober; we're drinking Two Buck Chuck. My guitar is on the end of my bed, Lou Reed at my feet.

—The Incident was forever ago. It's behind us now. It's just me, she says.

—Nothing's finished, I say.

—So? Is anything ever finished?

—How existential.

—You need a writing partner. A collaborator. You think Taylor Swift wrote her debut all by herself?

—I have no idea, did she?

—Her *third* album, sure. But maybe you just need someone to bounce ideas off of. Someone to help you tweak things. Edit. Harmonize. Oh my god—you need a Liz Rose. Do you know how many people in this town have publishing deals and we don't even know their names? And they're making idle fucking income, all from a bunch of songs they wrote sitting stoned in their living room. We need to get you one of those.

—Wait—she wrote *Speak Now* all by herself? I asked. Every single song?

—Okay, I'm hungry, Sloane says. Can we go get food? That space you showed me the other day is dope, by the way. I like it better than the actual fucking Venue. We should put on the show up there.

I give her a look.

—Jesus relax, *you* don't have to play it. You ready to go?

I keep watching the Wilson performance on my phone, over and over and over again. Studying the way he staggers to the mic, then stands very still, and then—eventually—starts swaying. At one point Esther reaches toward him, like she wants to steady him, but then she just raises her hand into the air, like a trilling pop star, catching the high harmony. Wilson's eyes are glassy, but his voice—god. Their voices, together. If I'm ever on a stage again, I know I don't want to look like that. And I know I'll never sound like that. But maybe—maybe—

Tonight at The Venue, it's a tenth-anniversary tour stop for a punk band that flew under my teenage radar. Eddie says he's never heard of them. Julien says he listened to them a bit. It's sold out, though. Up in the office, we've got twenty minutes to kill before doors.

—What's a band you would never recognize without their lead singer? Andy asks.

—Maroon 5, I say.

—Coldplay, Julien says.

—Oh, good one.

—U2, Eddie says, running his thumb and index finger over his Fu Manchu.

—Seriously? You wouldn't recognize the Edge? Julien asks.

—Who's the Edge?

—Bull fucking shit, I say.

—No way. I do not believe you, Julien says. Andy shakes his head.

—The Killers, somebody says.

Jessika is at the coffee shop on Twenty-First—the one that's also a smoke shop, convenience store, liquor store. The clientele's a mix of Vandy freshmen and Bible studies, teachers from the private school down the street, chugging stale drip coffee to stay awake as they grade papers. I hear the barista call out her name before I see her, and then she's next to me, sliding a beige sleeve onto her cup, saying:

—I'm so glad I ran into you again.

I'm always surprised by how she talks to me, like we've been friends for years. She reaches to give me a hug, and I return it warily, my hand limp along the small of her back.

—I think you left a glove in my car? Bright orange? she asks.

—Oh, yeah, that's probably mine.

—Are you staying? I can go grab it. I just gotta run to a meeting in a minute.

—I'm heading out, I can come with you.

We walk out into the day. Blistering cold—cracked lips, skin peeling and turning red, the sky blindingly bright but doing nothing for the temperature. Jess unlocks her Jetta and roots around in the front seat; my ears are so cold that they feel feverish.

—Et voilà, she says, handing me the sad-looking glove, a hole in the pinkie finger. I stuff it into my pocket.

—Thank you. For this—and again for the ride the other night.

—Anytime, she says. Well, anytime I'm sober.

I laugh, glance over my shoulder. A siren has started up in the background, church bells ring somewhere to the west.

—Hey, can I ask you something? she says.

My chest tightens and I nod.

—You don't have to answer if you don't want to—

—So I can lie?

She laughs loudly but quickly, her face changing back to serious so fast it's like she didn't even smile at all. She adjusts her scarf and I catch a glimpse of a tattoo, the head of an animal, on her collarbone.

—I've just been wondering. With the pregnancy test.

I glance around, like the cars buzzing down Twenty-First are listening in. The church bells continue on, making me think of my parents. I wait. Jess pulls her beanie down over her hair, her curls tightening beneath the cotton.

—I just . . . It wasn't Julien, was it?

I start to speak and then stop, the cold catching my breath. And just as I'm about to tell her the truth, her phone rings in her hand and she looks at it, rolls her eyes and says: Shit, sorry—I gotta take this.

5.

Are we going to see the sun this month? He fell off the stage. Literally, just fell right off. Oh, yes, he's definitely an alcoholic. Would we call that famous? You should really keep that in a case, you know. With a humidifier. The wood's gonna get all fucked. I think you'd like Escaped Cookie Mountain. The PD they gave us was pitiful. What does a person have to do to get a goddamn cab around here? Those guys were the good precursor to a bunch of worse bands. They're opening a new spot on Twelfth. Have you been yet? She has solo stuff too, like, three albums. Sold out doesn't mean shit. If anything, he should be paying me. Do not shit on the bus. I think it was on purpose. Is the Opry open yet? I want a martini.

Songs from Sloane pile up in my inbox. She sends them at all hours of the day and night, along with name ideas for the show. I think I'm the one with insomnia, but she must be up too—scouring sites like Hype Machine and *Brooklyn Vegan*, clicking away all night on her laptop in her room down the hall. It's one of the more comforting parts of living with someone else: the simple knowledge that you're not the only one there.

—I got you a present, she says one afternoon.

Another shadowy day, the sun already low behind the tree line west of the house. Losing light and it's not even happy hour.

—Just because? I ask.

—Valentine's, Sloane says.

She's making tea for us, grabbing two mugs out of a cabinet, tearing open the teabags on the counter. Sober on a Thursday—I feel like a nun. She flicks on the stove, then ducks into her room. From the doorway, she tosses a vinyl at me like it's a frisbee, shrink-wrap still slick and tight. The National's *High Violet.*

—Aw. You didn't, I say.

—*Boxer* is better, or honestly even *Alligator.* But they weren't in stock.

—I didn't get you anything, I say. Am I a bad girlfriend?

—You still have two weeks, she says.

The kettle starts its shrill, shrieking soprano. I claw into the plastic and put the record on immediately. I don't even remember to thank her.

I don't set out to get a drink with Jessika the following week, it just sort of happens. Sloane's on a date with Jamie for Valentine's Day, which isn't technically until Wednesday, but tonight is Saturday, and everybody who's got somebody is going out.

At the beer bar down the street on Twelfth, I sit in a corner bar seat and pretend to write, even though I'm actually just sitting there with my notebook open, watching reality TV. The taproom is mostly empty—despite a scattering of fake plastic roses, this is not a romantic place. While my eyes are glued to the stilted advances of several single men and one eligible bachelorette, Jessika slides in next to me. As if we planned it.

—Well well well, she says. She stands back up to give me a hug, and I return it uncertainly, still surprised to think we're even at the hugging stage. She smells like Sloane.

—Are you stalking me? I ask.

—Absolutely, she says. Am I taking someone's chair? Are you with someone?

—I'm really not, I say.

She laughs too loudly—always—which makes me laugh too, somehow. She looks pretty, of course—very little makeup, her hair back in a loose bun. A mauve lipstick that's faded so much I wonder if it's just the natural color of her lips.

—Are you meeting someone? I ask.

—No no no. One and done. I have a showcase down at Twelfth and Porter in, like, an hour. Jules give you the night off?

A beer arrives that I forgot I'd ordered.

—I swapped a shift with Eddie, I say.

—Oh, Jesus. That fucking guy.

Now I laugh loudly.

—Jules hates him too, she says.

—Yeah, I know.

She nods and lifts her eyebrows, shifting away from me to study the menu scrawled on the chalkboard behind the bar. I can tell my tone was too harsh. She asks the bartender for a couple of samples, then turns back to me.

—How'd you like the mixes? she asks.

The bartender is faster with her, slinging her tasters of various beers, which she sips thoughtfully while I try to find my footing.

—I . . .

—Johnny, this is—no. Absolutely not. This tastes like pennies. You're serving this to people? And this one has too much strawberry or something. I don't want a milkshake. I want a lager.

She pushes two of the samples away and takes a sip of the third.

—I don't care, she says to me then. I'll make you one if you want. A mix.

I want to ask if they're duplicates, if I'd just end up getting the same one she made for Julien, with the Belle and Sebastian song on it.

—Isn't that just a you-and-Julien thing? I ask as she sips at one of the samples. Sorry—Jules, I add.

She narrows her eyes almost imperceptibly, but seems otherwise undaunted.

—Doesn't have to be, she says.

The light catches on her face, her eyelashes briefly sparkling, like she's coated them in glitter.

—I'm good, I say. I can grab them out of my car. I was just, I don't know. Drunk. Curious.

—Oh, I don't care, she says.

Of course she doesn't. It's a kind of prerequisite of cool—this absolute nonchalance I'll never have. I pick up a guitar pick someone left on the bar, spin it between my fingertips. She finally orders a pint after trying two more samples, her nose pinched up and judgmental until the last one.

—Picky, I say.

—Not worth drinking something you don't like, she says.

I nod, taking a sip of my beer, realizing that's almost exactly what I'm doing.

—Do you play? she asks, nodding at the pick.

—Doesn't everyone here? I ask.

—I don't, she says. God, I could never.

The softening in my chest—relief?

—Yeah, but no, I say.

She laughs loudly again; Johnny rolls his eyes at her from down the bar.

—Which means? she asks.

—I do, but not like that. Not out. Not in public. Not really.

—Not really? Ever?

And maybe it's the single beer on an empty stomach, or maybe it's the impossible warmth of her flawless fucking smile, or maybe it's just that I want to talk about it out loud, to tell somebody who isn't Sloane, because then I say:

—I played out once. In town. It was kind of a mess. I fucked it up pretty royally. So, yeah, not sure I'll be doing *that* again.

—Oh yeah? Where at? she asks, completely unfazed.

I tell her the name of the spot.

—I accidentally ended up playing, like, a Matchbox Twenty song.

This makes her laugh suddenly after taking a sip, and she covers her mouth with her hand, little dribbles of beer bursting between her fingers.

—Nothing wrong with that, she says, laughing still, wiping her mouth.

—One of the Denim guys was there, I say. The keyboardist? God, he was laughing. Which, like, maybe he should have been, but fuck.

—Who, Bo? Bo is *always* laughing. Because Bo is always *stoned*. I'm sure he wasn't laughing at you.

—I don't know about that, I say.

Jess is shaking her head.

—They told me not to come back until I had my own songs to play.

—Those guys are idiots. You should try again somewhere else. It's basically a rite of passage here to fuck up an open mic. It's your *Behind the Music* or whatever. It would be weirder if it went perfectly.

—I don't think so, I say.

She shrugs.

—Jules told me you write, she says.

—Everybody in this city writes.

—Not really a reason not to do something, she says.

—It wasn't, I say.

—Hm?

—Julien.

She nods.

A couple sits down at the far corner of the bar, coats swishing onto the backs of chairs, the cold rushing in and then just like that: gone.

I make so many mistakes. There are the big ones, the obvious ones, like Colt, Colt, Colt again. Nick. Nick again. Forgetting to renew my license, to fill up my gas, to get Sloane a Christmas present, to order new checks so I can pay my rent on time. And then there are the small things: the glove in Jessika's car, forgetting to take my guitar in for a setup or to change my address so that I'm a legal resident of Tennessee. It's exhausting, exhilarating, endless. Am I learning everything, I wonder, as I finish my beer and pay my tab—the unreadable look on Jessika's face still on my mind—or am I learning nothing at all?

Julien's sober month ends on a Thursday. He did at least a full week extra. Instead of getting a drink, he wants to go to the Frist, to see a Warhol exhibit that's closing soon. I know nothing about visual art, but Sloane tells me I better fucking go, it's Warhol.

He picks me up—late, which I'm fine with, because it limits the amount of time we'll have to spend Experiencing the Art. The weather is mild, but I dress the same way I have all winter: fake leather jacket, beanie, a swipe of drugstore mascara.

—Dad was a big Warhol guy, Julien says, as we flash our college IDs for free access to the exhibit. I look over, trying to read his face, searching it for cracks of sadness, grief, but he's looking the other way, trying to figure out which gallery to enter first.

—A pop art pastor, I say, and then wish I had a string to pull the words back into my mouth. I slide a Xanax under my tongue, let it dissolve into a film of bitterness.

—My parents weren't into art, I say. Or even music, really.

My voice carries. The museum is quiet, all heels and hushed whispers. Should I be bringing up my living parents when he's just mentioned his dead dad?

—So how did you end up getting so into music? he asks.

I shrug, and he points us into the exhibit.

—A friend in high school, I say. She introduced me to a lot of bands I probably should have known already, being an emo teen and all. You?

—I was more like the friend in that scenario, Julien says. Though I was also the emo teen.

I laugh and look over at him, but he's already off checking out the first stretch of paintings. As always, with visual art, I feel like I'm not looking at it hard enough, like I don't know *how* to look at it.

—I was a mess in high school, I say.

He nods.

—Yeah, same.

We see some art, see some more art. I try to seem thoughtful and moved, but my mind drifts easily in the quiet, and soon I'm thinking about Julien as a teenager. In the large white hall I can hear the breathing of strangers, their quiet footsteps, the sound of someone whispering to someone else, the click of an iPhone keyboard. An older man clears his throat. A brochure is dropped on the hardwood, then scooped up. We walk in countless circles. For several minutes Julien says nothing at all; I try to mimic his silence, the sincerity with which he takes in the art, but the whole time I want to scream—to fill the void with some kind of sound.

The last room, though, is full of Warhol's music collaborations, and suddenly I find myself interested. Julien starts talking about the Velvet Underground—another band I think people pretend to like more than they actually do, but Julien really does love them. He starts telling me about something called the Exploding Plastic Inevitable, and I nod and smile.

At 8:42, I remind him that the museum is closing soon. He wants to circle back through one more room, a durational film of the Empire State Building at dusk. The room is empty, dark, and we stand a few feet apart and stare. I shift my weight back and forth on my feet, pressing the dead nerves of my toe against the sole of my shoe. When I look at Julien, he is lost, his face given over to ethereal focus. The reflection of the video catches against his face, and his eyes look like pools of water.

In the car on Broadway, traffic lights swing in the breeze. Julien puts the windows down, turns up the Velvet's *White Light/White Heat*.

The city passes by us out the window. The bad bars in Midtown, the college kids in coats too warm for the weather, the hipsters spilling out of songwriting rounds and open mics and taco spots and frozen yogurt shops. We pass a club whose marquee reads *We love you, Justin Wilson*, and behind us the city flickers under a constant sway of cranes.

—I think about it a lot, I say.

—What?

—Justin Wilson. The whole thing. I don't know. It's just—it's so morbid. It's just—I know we don't know if it was on purpose or not. But still. I just can't imagine getting to that point. Even though I'm always, like, thirty percent depressed.

Julien nods, changes lanes.

—Always? he asks.

—I mean, I'm depressed and nothing bad has ever even happened to me.

The next song starts and Nico's voice fills the car.

—Bad things happen all the time, Julien says.

The distorted guitar fades to a light fizzle over the speakers.

—Just hard for me to picture getting to that point. I probably wouldn't do anything besides drink more beer and turn up a Wilco record.

Julien laughs quietly. The light changes, and he shifts into second, third gear.

—That's good, he says. You're—that's good.

He nods, he's not finished.

—Have—

I start to speak and then stop. A car cuts him off near Nineteenth and he comes to a sudden stop at the intersection.

—Sorry, I say. That's—never mind. I shouldn't just go around asking people casually about the range of their, I don't know, their suicidal ideation.

He laughs again. The breeze rushes in through the windows.

—It's fine, he says. It's been a long time. But I've been there, I guess you could say.

Pricks of rain start to dot his windshield and he flicks on his wipers. It's not enough rain though, and the rubber screeches against the glass. Julien shifts in his seat, clears his throat.

—I'm glad you—

—Yeah yeah yeah, he says, waving a hand in the air as his blinker disengages.

Other things I miss, dots I didn't connect at first: The scars on Julien's arms. The look in his eye while we sit at the stoplight on Broadway. Like he knew he could tell me this, like he'd been waiting to. An air freshener hanging from the rearview mirror, the same color as his eyes. A cut on his index finger as he drums on the steering wheel. I want to pull it to my mouth, put my lips to it, feel the cool of his fingertip against my tongue. Instead I move my hand to the center console, my pinkie trying to reach for him. He glances over at me, then at my hand. His hands stay on the wheel.

When he pulls up to my place, I invite him up. He hesitates, eyes fixed on the stillness of the speedometer. It's only nine; what does he really have to do? He puts the car in park, sighs a little, then opens the door without saying anything.

Sloane has left a pot of rice remnants soaking in the sink and a freshly packed bowl on the counter, with a note reading *smoke me*. The heat is on high, too hot for the night. I offer Julien a beer, but he says no, and the noise of popping the cap off my own seems awkwardly loud. We stand in the kitchen and suddenly I don't know what to do with him.

—Do you want to go sit on the roof? I ask.

—What's on the roof?

The truth is, nothing, but you can sometimes watch the neighbors across the street who are always shouting at each other, the sweet old couple who drink wine together on the porch on warm nights, the cars that run the stop sign over on Tenth. He sets his keys on the kitchen island and the evening shifts. We go upstairs and climb out, the night wrapping around us like a blanket. We sit close, our knees touching. The moon glows blood orange above us.

—You know, I wrote something new, I say. It's not finished, but I'm stuck.

—You gonna let me hear it? he asks.

The distant hum of a band rehearsing down the street floats up. Julien's breath, steady and quiet. The night has finally dipped back into winter, the breeze a little crisp for roof sitting. I crawl back inside and drag out my guitar and my notebook and my beer, which I drink half down. The song is still ragged, unfinished, but he doesn't say anything as I move through the chords, my voice cracking as he's sitting too close, my pinkie throbbing, red, not callused enough as I get lost in the playing, closing my eyes, improvising a few couplets, fumbling toward an ending I haven't really written, the last cadence of chords making it sound like a CD that skips, clunky and pedestrian. But when I finish: a small pinch of relief, like someone has let the air out between my ribs.

—I haven't figured out that second verse, I say.

—What if . . .

He holds out his hands for the guitar and I pass it to him. He plays my chords, then continues with something else, humming quietly under his breath.

—I don't know, he says. Never mind.

—No, I like it, I say.

Eyes closed, melody buzzing, the night cold and quiet around us. He shrugs.

—It's your song, he says.

—Not anymore, I say.

I look up to his face again, my nose so close to his chin, it doesn't seem we can get any closer without touching. His skin is the color of sand; I want to press my tongue to it. He presses his lips softly to the top of my own, runs a hand up my thigh.

—I don't want to be your rebound, I say.

He breathes out slowly, his exhale muffled by the sound of a car rolling through a stop sign below.

—Well, I don't want to be yours, he says.

6.

Maybe there's a version of me who doesn't click on the ad at all. A version who rolls her eyes, picks up her guitar, forgets about some stupid night that happened nearly a year ago, finishes one of her own goddamn songs. A version of me that is wiser, less masochistic. Another girl—someone like Sloane or Jessika, maybe. She would shut the computer, turn off *Almost Famous*, and walk the fuck away. At least at first.

But maybe, at the end of the day, we're all the same. None of us really that noble about our pasts. Maybe we'd all click eventually.

Nick's face at the bottom of my screen:

Flirtation Device: May 12th. Saturday Night Live.

In the photo, he's wearing makeup. He's dressed in a dark green velvet suit, with Timmy and John behind him, smaller and spiraling, looking like they're circling some kind of kaleidoscopic drain. I pick up my phone to text him, then set it down again and turn it off. I didn't plan on drinking today, but now I plan on drinking today.

Some cursory research: the host that night will be a B-list actor. A bit of air releases from my lungs then. At least Nick won't be spending the evening with Justin Timberlake or Steve Martin or Emma Stone. Still. Fuck fame and all its stupid fucking layers. I pour myself a screwdriver and get in the bath.

I know that most of the bands will go nowhere, be forgotten for longer than they are remembered. I know that venues will close and be turned into condos. I know that songwriting can be cheap, formulaic, just a big machine. I know that fame and buzz will fade, even though I forget this every single night, every time I meet someone who has either. I know that a placement on a TV show or a slot on a tour can mean everything, it can mean nothing, it can mean everything before it means nothing. I know that sometimes it's not all that sexy, that sometimes it's just a job, a paycheck, a way to feed a family. And I know the saddest truth—that my job is not even really a job, not a *path* or a *career* or a *career path*. I always thought that at least I was on par with the guys—I know some of them; everybody knows some of them—who don't even get their own name in their email addresses, who are just somebody else's assistant, somebody else's tour manager, lights guy, session drummer, road photographer, stylist, backup singer, sound guy, day-to-day manager. But I don't even have an email address for my job at The Venue.

It's late and the last band is finally loaded out. I have been drinking, more or less, ever since I found out about *SNL* this morning. Rainwater shimmers off the back staircase railing, the air is a blanket of damp cement. Julien is smoking a cigarette, the tip of it burning orange, out on the back balcony. His hood up, his shoulders slightly hunched into the breeze. The city is dim and quiet above him, construction cranes elbowing each other for airspace across the river, condos going in next to car washes and body shops.

Colt's running receipts in the back. Andy's gone home. Eddie's on his fourth Mich Ultra, talking loudly with the bass player at the bar even though the guy has his coat on—he's clearly ready to go. Jessika is emailing me from work about places that have open mics next month. I'm ignoring her. I go out for a cigarette as one of Nick's songs comes on over the house music. I try to let it fade into the space, the door shutting with a satisfying, silencing click. Just like that: Nick's voice gone, Julien's face beneath the skyline, his cigarette shrinking between his fingers.

—You're still here? he asks.

—Can I bum one? I wanted to get the rest of the guys loaded out.

Julien gives me a look. Eyes wide with a joke or a judgment or a question. He knows I've been drinking during my shift, but he hasn't said anything yet.

—They're better than I thought they would be, though.

—Much, Julien says. The second half of the set had more energy than the first, but still.

—Would be cool to see them stripped down.

He laughs.

—Hear. To *hear* them stripped down. Acoustic.

But Julien's already gone, back of his hand covering his grin, laughter spilling out too quickly. Something thick in the air breaks loose, and he passes me a cigarette. In the parking lot, Colt's walking to his car now, unlocking the door to an old Bronco. The night is quiet again, mist spritzing us like we're catching spray off the ocean.

—Do you want to do something? I ask.

Julien's looking at me, his cigarette going out. His face looks briefly pained, and then—blank.

—It's almost one, he says.

—So?

—I don't know.

—Okay. Never mind.

—Haven't you already had a drink?

—Okay. I said never mind.

Downtown a streetlight flickers, casting a golden haze above the few cars left in the lot. The rain is starting to turn to ice, to snow.

—I'm not trying to be a dick, he says.

—It's fine, I say. You wanted to hang out last week, and this week you don't.

—It's not about wanting to or not wanting to, he says. I just—I don't really know if I should.

—Okay.

—I guess I just don't know what this is, he says.

—Do you want there to be a *this*? I ask.

Julien looks away.

—Al, you don't know what you want.

—That's not an answer, I say.

The only thing you can hear for a moment is the two of us breathing, Julien's long, protracted exhale before he says:

—You don't want me.

—That's not true.

The corners of my eyes, watering.

—Tonight you want me. Tonight you want me because—I don't know, for whatever reason, you want me. You're bored, or—probably you're bored. But tomorrow you won't be, and then next week you will again. So I don't know. It's more like you just don't want anyone else to have me.

Colt honks his horn at us obnoxiously as he pulls away, waving at us out of his window. Julien looks exhausted.

—I just—I don't think you want me. You just want anyone, he says.

—What the fuck is that supposed to mean?

In his black hoodie and jeans he looks like the shadow of a parenthesis, bent into the breeze, the light snow pricking the cotton of his sweatshirt.

—I mean you don't like me. You just—

—Actually I do, I say. Like you.

—And I like you, he says. But his face is horrible, grimacing, his lips dry and flaky. I wipe my nose as it starts to run in the cold.

—I just think that whatever this is—I don't know what it is, but I can't really do it.

For a moment, the air in the whole city seems sucked up. My cigarette burns into my fingertips, the pain runs from my fingers up through my palm, my wrist. A siren wails down Eighth. Traffic lights on Fifth flash yellow, like smoldering little cigarette butts tossed away on the ground.

—We're not doing anything, I say, standing up straighter. We're friends.

—You're right, he says. We're friends.

It's full-on snowing now, big dusty flakes melting on the tops of Julien's ears, dissolving on his cheekbones. He looks like he's in physical pain, his face twisted up, his pale lips tight and closed. Up above us, the moon shifting, settling behind a cloud. Another show night crossed off the calendar.

When it snows, the city is silent.

Schools close first, then small businesses and yoga studios, restaurants and hole-in-the-wall bars. Hair salons and vintage stores. Because there's a layer of ice beneath the snow, electrical lines are crippled down Eighth, all over the East Side. The Venue closes for six days. Even though I know theoretically that the days are getting longer, they still seem hopelessly short. One day I wake up and the sun is already setting. I don't speak to Julien for a week.

The cold cracks through the windows. Nobody drives anywhere for days. Streets stay a pristine, blinding white. The city is anesthetized and I am right there with it.

By day four, almost nothing has melted, but nobody cares. It is no longer cozy, now merely inconvenient. People start partying at the places that have managed to open, but the only one I can get to is the Villager. Sloane makes chili, makes chicken, makes chicken and dumplings, beef bourguignon. She pours me wine and I drink it until it tastes like nothing. Every time she sees me reach for my phone—Julien, Nick, does it even matter?—she takes it from me and insists we turn on a record instead. I tromp through the snow almost a full mile to the Villager to drink the same beer I have at home.

Pilled jersey sheets I've had since sophomore year, my sweat caked into them. A juice glass half-full of bourbon in the empty space next to me on the bed. A cotton film of ennui wrapped around my brain, the whole world echoing in lo fi. I can get myself out of bed some days, but it's late. It's closer to afternoon, the corn-yellow sun always a little too brutal. I work nights, which is a good, reasonable, *valid* excuse for sleeping late, but I'm off today, and it's still harder than it should be. I watch the Justin Wilson performance from the awards show. Once, twice, sixteen times. I read through Esther's lyrics online, then watch the video again. I listen to sad music and it makes me feel sadder before I feel better. I slip Valium under my tongue, watch the snow refuse to melt out the window, the pill starting to blunt all the raw edges of any hangover.

The only thing I write all week:

> *I hate Halloween / I just call it like I see it*
> *But I'd come to any party that you wanted me to be at*

The only reason I even decide to trek out to some bar in the suburbs, the night after the snow finally starts to melt, is that Colt texts me that Ben Folds is there. Vodka over ice, a splash of orange juice. A text from Colt: grab me a pack of American Spirits on your way? I crumble up half of one of his Valiums and dissolve it into my drink with an odd mix of hesitation and glee.

My shitty Civic is freezing. The Justin Wilson demos play from my speakers as I pull out of the driveway, palms frozen on the wheel. Black, shimmery streets. The snow has turned to rain, and it sputters down unconvincingly. The main streets are cleared, finally, but the back roads are still slush, black ice. A couple crosses the street on Gilmore, holding hands, looking into my headlights. They're both in all black, like they don't *want* people to see them—which I don't, until the very last second, my stomach sinking into my shins as I skid to a terrifying stop a few yards before I hit them. The man looks directly into my eyes and flicks me off.

I slowly let my foot off the brake as they cross to the sidewalk. All the surfaces outside the car—the road ahead and hoods of other cars, street signs and lampposts—are still reflecting glassy black light. Fogged-up windshield, puddles of gray. The road is a misty, pixelated black. Bright headlights stream toward me as I turn back behind the main four-lane road. I become very aware of my vision, of the swaths and gaps in it, the fact that it's no longer clear that I'm driving on a road at all. This, of course, is my first mistake: thinking that I'm no longer on the road.

Thinking, as I often do, that I'm already elsewhere. The second is closing my eyes. It seems obvious, of course, that you're supposed to keep your eyes open while driving. It's kind of a prerequisite.

My third mistake is not giving in when I see the animal leap across my field of vision, a rush of beige, gray, pearl, and then: crimson. The thud like a heavy instrument case landing on the curb.

There is, in any moment like this, the panic of the body. The feeling of limbs and sensations, trying to determine what is intact or harmed or broken. There is the head-to-toe scan of pain, the body's instinct to identify it and soothe it. And then there is the mind, the deluge of thoughts, the cascade of what has already happened and what could happen and what needs to be done.

A better, more sober person would have known that you're not supposed to swerve. You're not supposed to avoid the animal, you're supposed to give in, welcome the deer into the vehicle, but of course I don't, because instinct is overpowering, and I swerve off to the right, still hitting the deer, watching the blood slide across my windshield like a morbid car wash, and when the car crashes at the end of its descent, my drink is spilled and the car smells like vodka and the front of the Civic is so smashed and bloody that it looks like I've tried to massacre an animal much, much larger than a deer.

My car has landed in a rather large ditch, on a street that snakes behind a neighborhood of expensive houses and a glass-recycling center. In the ditch, though, none of that is visible. I'm under a blanket of darkness, a stage before the band comes out.

A few of the fingers on my right hand feel like they've been jammed. My cheekbone aches. And even though the airbag has deployed—delivering its own shock to my system—the rest of my body seems to be in one functional piece. The smell of the drink rushes toward me from the passenger seat, where it has spilled, and the familiar chill of nausea washes over me. I wait. The sirens, the arrest, the quick and deserved dismantling of my life in consequence for my poor choices. I am not drunk—I don't *feel* drunk—but legally I would probably qualify.

The night is quiet. Perhaps no one saw me hit the deer. Surely, though, someone must have heard. Surely beyond the ditch some Good Samaritan with a cell phone is standing out in the cold, calling an ambulance or the police or whoever it is you're supposed to call when you hit a deer.

My eyes cast around the interior of the car. In the console, I spot an ancient to-go coffee that surprisingly did not spill. It must be weeks—months?—old. I pick it up and pour it over the passenger seat. Then I toss the empty cup down onto the floor. Black coffee, blacker night.

Outside the car: putrid air, the deer out of sight. All that blood on the windshield, though—and on the bumper, the hood of the car, the headlights. The animal can't be alive. The whole scene has a gory glow to it. I gag.

I crouch behind the car, dry-heaving, waiting for the sirens, waiting for my life to change. Finally, in the quiet, I peer around the fender, up the steep ditch in front of me. No other car in sight. No one has pulled over. There is nothing. A curse or a miracle. One dark minivan drives by, and I wonder if the driver can see the ragged-looking girl on the side of the road. But the car keeps going, pulls up to the stop sign a couple hundred yards away, then heads off into the night. I am alone.

Is it sadness or relief, to have fucked up and not been seen? Is it shame or frustration, to not be found out? I go back to the car and find my phone. It, like all of my limbs, is still intact. The screen is full of missed texts from Colt: he's leaving soon, Ben Folds is gone, I shouldn't bother coming. I nearly laugh out loud. I'm tempted to call him, bitch him out or maybe ask for a ride, but he'd be too fucked up to do anything. And anyway, I know I need a real adult, not some millennial cosplaying as one. So I pull myself back over to the driver's side door, as the rain turns to sleet, and I dial Izzy's number.

I think of Julien as it rains. The pale rose of his lips as he purses them together, tearing wristbands across from me in the atrium of The Venue. His flannel that always seems to be on the arm of the couch in the office, the yellow plaid of it clashing with the chartreuse, smelling like yeast. Citrus. The sound of his sneakers squeaking on linoleum, on hardwood, on the slick tile behind the bar—the soundtrack to every night before doors open. His fingertips drumming against the vinyl stool, trickling up the denim of my jeans on my roof. His throat clearing as he unlocks doors before a show, the back of his teeth minty against my tongue.

Izzy doesn't answer the first time. I try again. The ringing is like a taunting synth note in the key of D. I hate it. I hang up and text her that I've been in a wreck—I'm okay—but is she around? Above me, at the edge of the ditch, tires rush through the rain on the street. The car must not be visible from the street; my headlights are off. Izzy's phone rings and rings.

Songs for the rain, when people aren't answering their phones:

"A Lack of Color" (Death Cab for Cutie)
"No Rain" (Blind Melon)
"Nightswimming" (R.E.M.)

"3rd Planet" (Modest Mouse)
"Champagne Supernova" (Matt Pond PA, covering Oasis)
"Look at Miss Ohio" (Gillian Welch)
"Too Stoned to Cry" (Andrew Combs)
"Daughters of the Soho Riots" (the National)
"MFEO—Pt. 1 Made for Each Other, Pt. 2: You Can Breathe" (Jack's Mannequin)
"Never Meant to Love You" (Cory Chisel and the Wandering Sons)

Julien answers on the second ring. Before I can even tell him what's happened, he asks if I'm okay. His voice is measured and quiet and calm, like maybe he's whispering in the back of a movie theater.

Less than fifteen minutes later, a pair of headlights peeks through the dark mist. In the minute it takes him to park the car and make his way into the ditch, I'm consumed by how much I hate myself, by how little I deserve this small act of grace.

He folds me into a hug, and I fight the urge to cry, though there's a nagging ache in my throat that's threatening to break.

—Are you okay? he asks.

—I'm sorry, I say.

—What? You don't have to apologize.

He thinks I'm talking about the crash, the deer, the calling him up and ruining his night, but I'm talking about all of it. Us, Nick, fucking Colt—all my flaky back-and-forth. I've been selfish. I've taken advantage of his kindness, his listening ear, his whatever—and now he's here.

—For everything, I say.

—Stop, he says.

—I've just—

—I'm calling Triple A.

I nod. Useless.

—I'm glad you're okay, he says.

—Thank you, I say. For being—for picking up.

He pulls me into another hug, and it's only then, through the moonlight, that I see the brutal truth of what has happened. The impact had been so loud, the moment had passed so quickly, that I couldn't see that it wasn't a deer at all. It was a dog.

Side Four

1.

Pale yellow light. Tension spreading across my sternum, up through my chest, landing at the back of my throat, my chin. Izzy's guest room, the windows dripping in yolky sunlight. A current of dread rushes through me. Outside, the day is blue and beckoning. So beautiful I could scream.

My phone is dead. When I emerge into the kitchen, Izzy is at the island alone, drinking coffee and eating a scone. She stands up a bit, looking up from her food, and dusts off her palms on her kimono. Coconut, salt water. Her long arms around me in a warm hug. Silk and weed and whole wheat flour.

—Coffee? she asks.

—Please.

The trickle of liquid into ceramic.

—I'm so glad you're all right, she says, touching the ends of my hair between her fingertips.

—I'm okay. Thanks for letting me stay here. I just didn't really want to go back home.

Steam escapes from the mouth of the coffee cup.

—Your friend, she says, nodding, chewing a bit.

—Julien, I say.

—Very sweet of him to come get you. I'm so sorry my phone was off. But that one must be very sweet to bring you all the way out here.

She wasn't here when I got in, but I had a key, and I texted her that Julien had dropped me off and I was going to crash in her spare room. When I search her face for more meaning, for any insinuation, I don't find it.

—Where's Clem? I ask.

—Ah, she had an early showing this morning for a property in town. Always getting a jump on the day. Much, much earlier than me.

—Anyone fun? I ask.

—She never tells me, Izzy says. All those NDAs.

—Why didn't you ever tell me about her? I ask. I mean, before this year.

The coffeepot hisses on the counter behind Izzy. She bridges her hands and cracks her knuckles.

—Oh, I guess I was waiting. Until when, I'm not totally sure. She pauses, then sighs. I should have, though, she says.

—I like her.

—Me too, she says, pressing her palm down on mine.

All morning, I think of Lou Reed.

How little attention Sloane pays him when she gets busy, as she's been these past few months. How much the fur of one animal can look like another. How hurting a dog in any way makes me feel capable of unspeakable evils. How killing a dog seems almost unimaginable. I think of how it could have happened to Lou Reed, running across the street on a cold day, a rainy day, a warm day, looking for some stupid crumb, some tiny speck of food in the grass or in the street, and colliding with a hulk of metal and rubber, his little doggy neck snapped—never able to eat ground turkey and Maldon again.

I try to imagine a world in which he will outlive me.

Mostly, I think, it's been nice to love him, even as poorly as we do. To have this small constant in my days.

I'm oblivious to so much: Izzy with a girlfriend, a personal life I've never been aware of. Other, smaller things: The restaurants off Nolensville that we never go to because we're lazy or uninterested or some naive combination of both. The openers at The Venue that go on while I'm still at the door, playing to a few dozen people, spilling their guts on the stage. A text from Jessika, trying to be friends. A look from Julien, an asinine comment from Eddie. A brush of Colt's hand across the bar. The demolition crews dotted across town, tearing down restaurants and historic homes and old studios. The gay bars over on Church Street, the drag brunches I never quite manage to get to. The messages from Sloane, from my parents. The songs I say are too boring or too formulaic or maybe both. Shows, open mics, late nights on the East Side. Julien, trying to tell me something from his stool at the door. I'm really only ever paying attention to myself. To the headliner. Except I'm the worst kind: self-absorbed and sloppy, bombing the show, again.

In the middle of my third night at Izzy's, just when I've barely drifted off, the room a quiet cocoon around me, my phone buzzes softly against the oak nightstand. I pick it up before I see who's calling.

—There she is.

And just like that, Nick is in the room, beside me, his hair falling

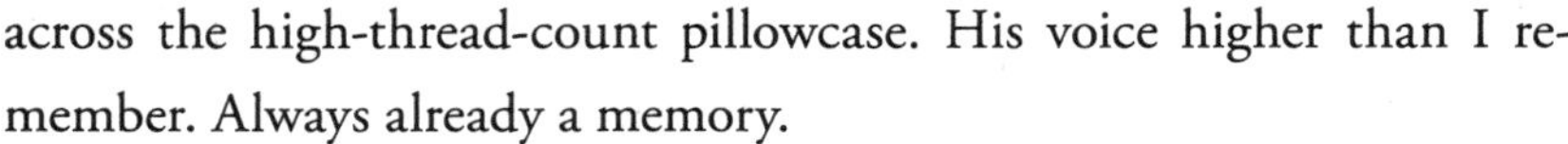

across the high-thread-count pillowcase. His voice higher than I remember. Always already a memory.

—Hello?

—Are you asleep? What time is it there? I didn't think you ever went to sleep.

I sit up, my heartbeat pressing into my abdomen, a faint pulse behind my belly button.

—Where are you? I ask.

—Just finished loading out. Waiting on Timmy to give up on some girl at the bar.

—No, what city? I ask.

—Brooklyn, he says. Just played a loft show with a few guys from Rough Trade. With Jesse? I think you met him once.

—I don't remember, I say, yawning. How was it?

—I thought I told you about it.

—Maybe that was the other Allison.

—Oh, come on.

The heat rushing through me is a surprise, and I sit up even more, my knuckles and kneecaps cracking as my body sets itself to higher alert.

—Me, come on? Please. You always do this, I say.

—Do what?

—Once there's a few months of quiet, once there's enough space between us, enough distance, enough *whatever*, you call me up or show up in town and fucking kiss me or send me a fucking demo and I just—

—You love when I send you music.

—I love—

—You love . . . ?

We breathe quietly on the line. I imagine where he is: the dark rows of Brooklyn brownstones fading into the night, hipsters walking out of dive bars and ducking into cabs, the small cluster of die-hard fans standing on the sidewalk down the way, T-shirts and records and screen-print posters tucked beneath their arms.

—Jesus, Al. Can't I just call?

—But you don't. You didn't back in Michigan, you haven't for the last year, since I've been here—

—I mean come on. I have a—

Life. He was going to say he had a life, as if I didn't factor into the one he was living at all.

Izzy's house is quiet. Somewhere from the woods, bullfrogs croak into the night.

—I can't anymore, I say. I just can't.

The line is dead quiet, like he's standing in a soundproof room instead of on some street corner in Dumbo, staring up at the bridge and the shimmering tip of lower Manhattan. Izzy's guest room is pitch-black, a cavern.

—Fine, he says. I won't call anymore.

But he acquiesces too quickly. I want to say, *No, I didn't mean it, you can still call, I changed my mind.* I want to ask if the new album is doing well, what they're going to play on *SNL*, why I had to find out about it from a pop-up ad on a streaming service.

—You don't want me, I say. You just don't want anyone else to have me.

He doesn't say anything. For a moment I want to wait him out, like if I just give him more time, I'll hear whatever it is I want to hear. But it doesn't work that way, I know this now: sitting and waiting rarely gets you any closer to what you want.

—I gotta go, Nick.

Like I have anywhere else to be.

He clicks off the line before either of us says goodbye.

A melody: cascading down some back wavelength of my brain, like the snow of an avalanche, picking up speed. The image of Nick on a street corner, me and Julien on the back balcony of The Venue. I know the window. The bursts like this are short, and I reach for Izzy's Martin in the corner, trying to capture it, grabbing at the edges of the song to shape it into something. Like trying to hold water in my hands.

You can say I don't know what I want
that you could be anyone
But baby you're not anyone

It happens like a crack in the neck of a guitar. Small bits splintering, for months and months, and then one day you pick up the instrument and play a chord and the wood cracks open, exploding in one last dying rush of sound.

Three a.m. (*I must be lonely*) and the song is finished, whole. I have to rush to catch up with it, my pen scurrying across the back of a bakery receipt as I try to get down the chords, the words, whatever bare bones of rhythm there are. But then, there it is, two hours after Nick's called, a practically tangible thing. Three minutes and twenty seconds, a rough recording on my phone. A whole song.

Songs I start to listen to again only after I've written one of my own:

"Blindsided" (Bon Iver)
"America" (Simon and Garfunkel)
"Skeleton Key" (Margot & the Nuclear So and So's)
"Maps" (Yeah Yeah Yeahs)
"Nine Crimes" (Damien Rice)

"Heaven or Las Vegas" (Cocteau Twins)
"Feel Flows" (the Beach Boys)
"Comfortable" (John Mayer)
"Cry Me a River" (Justin Timberlake)
"Swingin Party" (the Replacements)
"September Gurls" (Big Star)
"The Underdog" (Spoon)
"The End Has No End" (the Strokes)

I don't mean to, but the influence of the JwK mixes starts to slip in. I make playlists sitting on the bed in Izzy's guest room, stalking the bands Jess has put on social media. I'm deeper into the Modest Mouse catalog, listening to Counting Crows' *Across a Wire* on repeat. Her taste lives in the Venn diagram overlap between mine and Sloane's: less shiny than Sloane's favorites, more adventurous than mine. She listens to a lot more women than I do, I realize. Everything from Esther Wainwright and Gillian Welch to Taylor Swift and Paramore. Anything with a hook that gets stuck in your head like gum against a shoe on a sidewalk—anything with a three-part harmony and a tinny acoustic guitar. There's a brazenness to her taste, I think. A willingness to go for an album you might not like, to ignore an artist's weaker songs because there are others that make the hairs on your neck stand up, make you feel everything, everywhere always. You have to listen to a lot of bad shit to end up with the best shit. Worth it, I guess, in the end: most three and a half minutes of bliss are.

I call off work for the week. During the days I sit by Izzy's pool, even though it's still barely spring. Clem decides to train me as her sous chef: how to chop leeks, how to peel carrots, how to shred cabbage on a box grater, how to slice potatoes on a mandoline. How to open a bottle of

Vinho Verde correctly. I smoke Izzy's weed and take long walks. I write two more songs and don't tell anyone about them. I look at the photo of Julien and the blond girl, then log out of social media and download all of Esther's solo albums. I scour neighborhood social media boards, looking for anyone posting about a missing dog. I wonder if you can go to jail for hitting a dog with your car. I bite my nails and smoke more weed. I find nothing.

The dog didn't have a collar. Online I read that people often drop unwanted dogs in the park across the street from where I had my accident. Because they know it's a wealthy neighborhood, they know people will pick them up, take them in, maybe even keep them, love them.

Sloane texts me about the radio show. I text her back an idea for what we should call it, assuming it's all still a half joke. Julien reaches out a few times, asking how I am, mentioning that Andy might let us use the second space for real. I write another song and record it on my phone. I'm far from downtown, and at least for this week, the music is all mine. I remember what Jess said about the guys from the open mic: they're idiots. And anyway, that was all so long ago. Down here, ten miles south of the city, you can't see the desperation, the naked want in the eyes of the buskers down on Second, the washed-up men in steel-toed boots singing at Layla's. Singing at Lonnie's, singing at the Stage, singing at Robert's.

For five days, I am the only one singing.

A night I'd forgotten: Filed away somewhere slippery, my first official night working at The Venue. I arrived early, well before sound check, for a bill with three bands I hadn't heard of. Even though Andy had told me Julien would be training me, I was still surprised at the sight of him—heels up on the coffee table in Andy's office, reading *Spider-Man: Blue* on the worn chartreuse couch, dark hair falling into his eyes.

—Sorry to interrupt, I said.

He sat up straight and set his book down, then stood up and reached out to me. Beneath the graphic novel was another book, something that looked impressive—Wendell Berry or Marilynne Robinson. People whose names I knew but who I'd never read.

—Not at all. Welcome, he said. Julien.

—Al.

We stood there suspended in silence, the whole venue feeling like ours for a moment.

—Here, let me show you where to clock in and then . . .

He trailed off. Under his unzipped hoodie I could see a Springsteen tee.

—Have we met? he asked.

—I don't think so.

—Sorry, I didn't mean that to come off like—

—Like a pickup line?

—Like a pickup line.

—It didn't. But now . . .

He smiled.

—Sorry, you just look familiar.

—I've been to a few shows here?

—Yeah, he said, maybe that's it. Where are you from?

—All over, kind of. But Michigan mostly. My parents moved a lot—I don't know. Home is kind of nowhere.

Julien had a funny little smirk on his face. I was rambling. The question had been simple; a one-word answer—a city, a state, a street name—would have sufficed.

—Where in Michigan? he asked.

—I went to school in Ann Arbor, I said.

—That's right, he said. The Blind Pig.

My chest warmed.

—Yeah, I worked there.

—I saw.

—Right, sure. My illustrious résumé.

He laughed and the edges of the room quieted and softened, like the corners of paper wrapping around a gift.

—What about you? I asked.

—Minnesota.

I couldn't think of a single venue in the state of Minnesota, so I just said:

—Prince.

Julien laughed quietly again.

—Yeah. Prince.

His eyes were squinty and sleepy now.

—Minneapolis? I asked.

—The suburbs.

—Same.

—But this is home now, Julien said.

And I couldn't tell if he meant Nashville or the South or maybe Tennessee in general. Or maybe—and I didn't realize this until later—he was just talking about The Venue. And then there was a rest in the conversation, our eyes locked on each other's, trying to sort through some unspoken, imagined familiarity. A kind of conspiratorial energy buzzing between us already—as if we'd known each other for a very long time. And then our sound guy started ringing out the system in the main space and the spell was broken and there we were—just having met.

2.

I forget so much.

The beers do that, apparently. Blur the edges of the nights, mash together the fragments of memories. But this week I commit to remembering: the carpet in Izzy's living room; the bridge on the mouth of the jam jars she uses to serve wine; the saccharine yellow light splitting the shades while I thumb my way through scales. I think that I'm in the right key, that for once I'm hearing it all, understanding it: the change, him, the shift in the not-so-acute depression. But, as usual, I'm slightly out of tune. I'm too inside my own head, my own feelings, and then just like that: my own songs.

Izzy: spinning clay the color of cloudy days in the afternoons, listening to *Rumours, Déjà Vu, Pet Sounds.* Her hands working her feathery hair into braids, loose pigtails. Izzy, over at Billy Reid, thumbing through three-hundred-dollar T-shirts for a country star, picking out jeans at the designer on Twelfth, a bouquet of flowers in her hand as she presses her fingers to the denim, blue dye rubbing off on the pads of her fingertips. Izzy, picking up some Earl Grey at the Jewish deli in Midtown, buying lox (lox!), meeting Clem for a glass of wine at Giovanni's.

Sloane: saying that the negative ions in the Pacific Northwest, the

East Coast, anywhere—doesn't really matter, as long as you're near *water*—are good for recharging. The pine trees too. Leaving town for the week to go see Jamie's band in the Pacific Northwest. Standing backstage at the Crystal Ballroom, at Neumos. Wearing a rain jacket and walking down by the old canneries on the port in Astoria. Drinking beer at a dive in Capitol Hill, stuffing her purse with matchbooks. Texting Billy about the opening band, saying they should put their stuff on rotation at Lightning. Sending me videos of the best performances she hears on the road, links to the downloadable songs on SoundCloud. Texting me about the radio show, there's an open slot—nobody even died! It could be ours, we should take it. We could do it. Sloane, slurping down tequila sodas, forgetting that her phone even exists. Crushing the heart of a guy who hits on her in the coffee shop, the hotel lobby, the bar, on the street corner, at the post office, backstage—before anybody realizes she's Jamie's girlfriend.

Jessika—suddenly somebody I talk to. Somebody I text. Somebody who sprays dry shampoo into her dark curls, swipes lipstick effortlessly across her mouth. Responding to me immediately, always. Inviting me to showcases, to birthday parties. To record release parties, to happy hours and late nights. Asking me to send her my songs.

Andy: picking up his girls from volleyball practice. Colt: doing coke with the bartenders on the East Side, at the bar with the taxidermy wolf. Throwing up out a car window on Main Street. Laughing about it the next day, waiting to audition for a Jewel video that's filming in Hillsboro Village. Eddie: at Bongo Java, bitching about the neo-folk movement. Shitting on all the bands with acoustic guitars, foot-stomping, harmonies and harmonicas, bugging everyone to come to his show next week.

Somewhere, maybe, Nick: rehearsing in a studio space someone from

Rough Trade has paid for in Lower Manhattan. Getting his velvet suit tailored—he didn't like the way it fit in the *SNL* promo. On Houston, bumming a cigarette. Ordering a hoppy beer, a shot of Jameson, somewhere in Nolita. Trying to decide if he needs another haircut. Rolling a joint on a fire escape above the Bowery Electric, meeting a woman at the merch table, in the greenroom, behind Mercury Lounge, having a cigarette in front of the club. Nick, lacing up his black Vans to go onstage, tuning the high E on his Gretsch, warming up his voice on the soundstage at 30 Rock, shaking the hands of the B-list actor, the writers, Bill Hader and Kenan Thompson. Most of them haven't heard of his band. Still, Nick, pale lips around a microphone, a live crowd screaming for him.

Julien.

At his place. Reading *Spider-Man* or Michael Chabon. Turning on a Springsteen album, dicking around on his guitar on the porch. Listening to one of Jess's mixes. A bunch of songs I don't even know, wouldn't pick, might not even like or ever hear. Julien—walking down Sixteenth, thinking about stopping at Bobby's Idle Hour and then changing his mind, turning off down Edgehill, getting a black Americano. In his Explorer, down on Eighth on his way to work, trying not to think about spending the whole evening with Eddie, Vampire Weekend pouring out of his speakers as the cranes sway over the Gulch.

Julien, his hip bone pressed to mine months ago on his porch, the trees frozen fireworks, the moon an open eye above, our voices searching each other's, dipping into the cracks and crevices, climbing up scales and through chords, hovering around as we make out the harmonies and then—

Light pink lips to mine, grocery store wine, hot and tannic, a song we'd written sitting just beneath our skin.

It's a brilliantly clear evening, the moon already high above the Franklin farmlands, the expanse of former Civil War battlefields now owned by country music stars and publishing CEOs and major agents.

Tonight, Izzy's taking me to the Bluebird with Clem. A songwriter's round she swears I'll enjoy. I look up the names and don't recognize any of them, but if these past two years have taught me anything, it's not to put too much stock in name recognition.

When we arrive, Izzy squeezes both hands of the man at the door. They stand like that, holding hands, as Izzy nods and nods. We huddle into a back booth and she orders us gin and tonics, a basket of fries. The room is full, people tucked away in quiet twos and threes, twisting rings on wedding fingers, crossing and uncrossing their legs, whispering into ears, shifting wallets into back pockets, looking around the room—first for familiar faces, and then for celebrities, A-listers, B-listers, even though anybody big will be coming in from the back or is in a corner so dark already they can barely be seen by the people they're with.

I don't know who I'm looking for. When my gin and tonic is gone, I slurp at the sugary ice and glance around. A man in a very earnest cowboy hat. Two blond suburban moms. A guy in a leather jacket. Someone who could be either an eighth-grade teacher or a member of Wilco. A couple too dressed up for the occasion.

A hush comes over the crowd, but the songwriters aren't out yet. I lean over to Izzy.

—What band would you never recognize without their lead singer? I ask.

I take a sip of water, set my gin and tonic aside for a moment.

—Deep Purple, Izzy says almost immediately, as though she's given this plenty of thought before.

—Black Sabbath, Clem says.

—Damn.

—Well? Izzy asks. Tell us yours.

—Vampire Weekend?

Izzy smiles and nods her head.

When the songwriters come out, I don't recognize any of them until the lights fully flood the seats, aligned in front of each microphone. Dark hair, a familiar bright streak of gray: Esther Wainwright.

—I thought this was for up-and-comers, I say. For—

She looks at me oddly: It is.

Esther plays last, her voice huskier live than I imagined it. On her albums, and when she sings with Wilson, she stays in an almost breathy head voice. But now she sounds like Joni Mitchell after all the cigarettes, a deeper, heavier timbre. At first I'm disoriented, because I've heard the song before, but something about its contours is different. The melody is already at the back of my throat, the words to the first verse on my lips. But then a shift: the song turns in a different direction. It's not that I've never heard it before, it's just that I've never heard this version of it before: the song Wilson played at the awards ceremony, the one I've watched so many times, sung along to under my breath. Written by Esther, sung only by Esther. With her voice—and the eerie sadness that seeps in—it's a totally different song.

Izzy squeezes my leg as the crowd takes a collective breath, applauds. I blink back a few rogue tears. It's only when the lights go up that I see him: Julien, standing at the door, hands in his pockets, nodding in conversation with the door guy. Red buffalo flannel, the left sleeve rolled up. A Mazzy Star song comes on overhead, like the house music is fucking with me, and his face lights up in surprise. My mind tells me I should give him space, or something stupid like that, but instead I start walking across the room, hands in my pockets, the heat in my ears flooding. The lights are still low.

—Julien Black, I say. Didn't think I'd see you here.

For all the time Julien and I spend at The Venue, I've never run into him at another club. I have the urge to hug him, but instead I stick my arm through the air and press my fist to his shoulder in an odd platonic punch. My limbs belong to someone else. He catches my hand at his shoulder and holds it there for a moment with his. Warm, dry.

—Can I see your ID? he asks.

His hand is still on mine, pressed against his shoulder. I laugh.

—I'm on the list, I say.

—Of course you are, he says.

He drops my hand and we drop our bit.

—I didn't know you came out to these.

—Oh yeah. As much as I can.

—Really? With who?

He shrugs, takes a sip of his beer. He wipes his mouth with the back of his hand and offers me the bottle. I shake my head.

—Myself, he says. You never know who you might see.

I know he's talking about the songwriters, the people like Esther we all paid to see, but he is looking at me so intently it sounds more like—

—Thank you, I say. For picking me up the other night. For picking up the phone too.

He nods. Eyes muddy, warm.

—I'm the phone guy, he says, smiling.

—I'm sorry, I say. For sucking.

He shakes his head. He reaches out to me, and just like that I'm tucked into his chest, his neck sweaty but not at all unpleasant.

—I'm sorry, I say again.

—Stop, he says then, into my ear.

When I look up, he's looking down at me, our faces close. Steel, malt. I start to lean my chin toward his, and then: the lights go up and a bell rings for last call.

I lose track of things. A T-shirt of Sloane's I borrowed last month. I can't find it for weeks. Socks too—they seem to disappear into the dryer with every cycle of laundry. The picture of Julien with the blond girl; did he delete it? Appointment reminders, rent checks, a wedding invitation from a college friend. Gas bills, electric bills, pens, loose change. Guitar picks, packs of gum. Bobby pins, names of acquaintances, phone numbers of baristas. I try to recollect them all, but so many things slip through the cracks. I find it hard to believe that anyone is ever old enough to commit to a lifetime of anything.

In the car on the ride home, Izzy sits back and closes her eyes, her hands folded across her lap. The traffic is all gone by now, safely back in the suburbs, and the streets are quiet.

—You know, I've heard that song she played tonight about a hundred times. And I always thought it was already perfect, when he sang it. But now—

—Beautiful, wasn't it?

—Yeah. There's something different hearing it like that. Like—

—How so?

—I don't know, I say. Sang by the person who wrote it, I guess.

Izzy nods, smiling.

It's like I hadn't fully believed it, or something. He embodied so much of the song onstage that when he sang it, you could almost convince yourself that the words were his. Almost like I'd wanted them to be his all along. I was always trying to force some specific truth when the reality was something much more interesting.

I crack the window. Clem has dozed off on the opposite side of Izzy, her head on Izzy's shoulder. The driver glances straight ahead as the traffic lights flash yellow at most of the intersections, a slight breeze shaking the chestnut oak leaves outside through the tinted windows.

—I was drinking, I say out loud, when the driver turns onto Old Hickory.

—Today? Izzy asks, pulling a strand of hair off the shoulder of my shirt.

—No, I say, and my throat constricts. I try to clear it and she waits. The driver has turned on a song, but it's quiet, the reverberations echoing quietly in the car the way sound carries at The Venue when it's empty.

She's quiet.

—I wasn't—I didn't *feel* drunk or anything like that, but I had a roadie.

—A roadie?

—Oh, I'd made a drink and brought it with me. And I'd had a drink or two at the house.

—Ah, she says.

—I hit a dog, I say. It wasn't—it wasn't a deer.

Izzy's hand reaches for mine. My throat aches with the threat of tears.

—I couldn't find the owner, I say. There wasn't a collar or anything. I think—I think it was a stray.

Izzy's hand is cool and damp, tightening around my own.

—Oh, Al, she says, her voice soft.

—Something even worse could have happened. Should have.

—Should have?

—I just feel like I deserve something bad to happen to me. Especially after what happened. After what I did.

—What? Why would you say that?

—Because nothing bad ever has.

I think about Julien and his dead dad, his face in the car on the way back from the art museum. Izzy leans her head back and laughs, loud but short, like she's been caught off guard by a joke in an otherwise unfunny movie. Clem is still dozing. Or maybe she's awake, listening to all of this.

—Oh, honey.

—What?

—Don't get me wrong, she says. That was stupid. Never drive when you've been drinking—ever. But something bad still happened. You crashed your car, you hit a dog. You could have been hurt worse than you were. No need to wish for anything more than that. Be glad it wasn't. You're lucky.

—But . . .

—You are.

She puts an arm around me. I think she's about to say something else, but she just squeezes my shoulder tightly and leans into me.

Jessika is the one who ends up picking me up from Izzy's at the end of the week. Sloane is showing around a friend from Rhode Island and Izzy has to do an overnight shoot at Blackberry Farm, and I just don't have it in me to ask Julien for another favor, to make him pick up his phone again.

I leave a thank-you note in the kitchen for Izzy and Clem and slip out the front door.

—I don't know how I became your personal black car service, Jessika says, laughing loudly as I slide into the passenger seat.

—You've only given me two rides ever, I say, suddenly self-conscious.

—I'm kidding, she says, and my chest lightens. I wasn't doing shit today. This is your aunt's place?

—Yeah. Definitely not mine, I say.

Jessika throws the car into drive and sets out on the back roads of Franklin with confidence. When I ask her if I should pull up directions to get back into town, she laughs.

—No need. I'm from here.

—Wait, really? I didn't know that.

—My little secret.

—I just figured you went to Belmont, I say. You're always hanging around with that crowd.

—Berklee, she says.

—In Boston or California?

—Boston.

This explains her slightly contradictory accent—the southern drawl with the nasal-y East Coast undertones.

—I guess all I know about you is that you manage Denim. And you were . . . with Julien. And now and then you give drunk idiots like me a ride.

—I guess then about seventy-five percent of that is still accurate, she says, laughing.

I nod. She turns on the same Esther Wainwright EP we were listening to months ago, when she was my designated driver and I drunkenly stole several of her mixes. I reach to turn the volume up on the dash.

—You like him, don't you? she asks as we pull up to a stoplight. She glances over at me, a splash of freckles across the bridge of her nose, a faint smudge of mascara that somehow looks intentional.

I don't say anything for a moment.

—You know it was never really like that with us, she says.

Outside the car, birds are squawking overhead, sunlight is bursting through impossibly high trees.

—Like what? I ask.

—Serious, she says. We were both kind of the first person the other one met here. I was just back into town from Boston, and trying not to run into anyone from high school. He'd just moved here. So, you know, we kept hanging out, but I mean—we never even had sex. It was more . . . I don't know. But it's not—it's not like you guys.

—What do you mean?

The long red light finally flicks to green. Jess eases onto the gas, inching us forward.

—You know exactly what I mean, she says.

3.

This rider is absurd, Eddie says.

Sound check has just wrapped and we're in the office. Tonight will be a long night: an indie band on the rise, then an after-party DJ'd by a somewhat Big Name. I'm hours early to work, trying to distract myself from thinking about Nick's *SNL* shot tonight, his career about to break wide open while mine hovers somewhere between stagnant and nonexistent. One demo, no hook, that's it.

—What do they want? I ask, my feet up on the couch.

—Forty-eight bottles of *domestic* beer. Nothing imported. Clean socks.

—Socks? What else?

Eddie shoves a piece of paper at me.

Perrier. Glass bottles preferably. No San Pellegrino.
Wheel of Camembert, baguette, Paolo Scavino Barolo,
Thin Dunlop Tortex guitar picks, orange.
Tanqueray No. 10, no New Amsterdam plz
Tennessee whiskey, something that makes you feel like a man (or woman!) in his/her sexual peak.

The list goes on for another full page, and I pass it back to Eddie. When I glance up, Julien is in the doorway. A Fleet Foxes song has come on overhead. Julien's face has a faint shadow of scruff, making him look older than he did last week at the Bluebird. Technically, I suppose he is. I guess we both are.

—Hi, I say. You're here.

—Hey there.

I'm searching his eyes for something when he asks:

—Did you get the car fixed?

—Still in the shop, I say. Sloane dropped me off.

—What happened to your car? Eddie asks. You need some work done? I got a guy. South Nashville. Gotta pay cash, but he can fix anything.

I don't want to talk about my car. I want to get up and hug Julien. But instead I sit up, trace the outline of an Emmylou Harris record sitting on the coffee table.

—Well, welcome back, Julien says, a little awkwardly.

I hate the air between us, wishing for a fresher version of it—a breeze into the conversation, perhaps. I want to be back at the Bluebird, pulled into his chest.

—What happened to the car? Eddie asks again.

—I hit a deer, I say. The lie slips out easily.

—No shit. That's kinda cool, Eddie says.

—Not *really*, I say, a little appalled.

Julien turns to leave. Eddie looks at the empty doorway, then at me, then back to the doorway.

—What's the story there? he asks.

—Fuck off, Eddie.

Nobody tells you it's not really glamorous. Some of these places don't have greenrooms. They don't even have a backstage. The bands don't have riders. They sit in the bar, drinking their free drinks, smoking their cigarettes in the concrete courtyards of squat brick buildings, hanging out in the burger joints on Elliston until their set time. The venues are dirty, decades of debauchery etched into their walls. Whiskey soaking through the floorboards, spit and sweat, blood sprayed from the sliced fingers of the guitar players. The vans are even dirtier. The bands drive themselves; you don't realize how much a bus costs. You have to be making a fuckton, and almost none of these bands are. The food is bad; the beer is warm. You could ask for wine, but you'd be silly to try.

When bands show up at a venue, they all want something you can't give them. Sometimes it's simple, physical—primal. A shower, a hot meal that isn't from a drive-through, coffee that doesn't taste like charcoal. A Band-Aid or a roll of duct tape, a bottle of water, a parking pass, the number for a cab company.

But then there are the needs far beyond what you can give them. Adoration, worship. A fix. A drink you can't make, a song you don't like. It's transactional, even though you don't always know what you're getting. A moment or a melody in exchange for the attention or idolatry you give in return. Or maybe it's all just noise, the kind you can't live without until one day you have to—the day when you let the volume fade, let the signal fizzle out until it's all just low low static.

Three o'clock turns to four, four turns to five, I sit in the dark of the second space with Andy's guitar, singing my own songs over and over and over again, until a door creaks open and Julien appears. I stop playing.

—Figured I'd find you up here, he says. You don't have to stop.

He shoves his hands into the pockets of his jeans. They look new, nicer than usual.

—I mean, you do kind of have to stop, because doors are soon. But not, like, this exact second.

—No, I shouldn't even be up here, I say.

—Oh, you're suddenly concerned about following the rules here?

Outside, the sun peeks through the clouds and the shadows in the space shift dramatically, a beam of light crossing Julien's chest.

—By the way, Andy told you we can use this space, right? Test-drive it.

—Really?

—Not for a full-on show, but something small.

His eyes are serious. I look at him until I can't take it anymore, then look down.

—What were you playing just now?

—I finished a song, I say.

I run the guitar pick along the strings. A distorted, quiet fuzz.

—Well? Are you going to play it for me?

At the door, my phone is heavy in my hand. Doors open in five, and the hours ahead stretch out in front of us, taunting. Julien's still fielding last-minute additions to the list. Nick has sent me a picture from the soundstage at 30 Rock. For several minutes I draft and delete, draft and delete, draft and delete a response to him. In the end, I ignore the text and click out of the app.

When I look up, Julien is looking at me.

—You know, I've never been to New York, I say.

—What made you think of that? he asks.

He's got a deck of cards in his hands, shuffling them with his long fingers. He taps them against the stool, and then, the flutter of another shuffle.

—It's weird. I've been to Africa, Central America, all kinds of other places. But never New York. Have you?

—Once. In high school, he says. With my dad.

—And?

—I like it better here, he says, as if it's a simple comparison, as if Nashville has anything on New York.

My phone is still tugging at my focus. I twirl it in my palm.

—All good? Julien asks. I'm going to unlock soon.

—Do you think *Contra* is better than their debut?

I point up to the speakers, Vampire Weekend playing over the house music.

—Debut, Julien says. No question. Well, maybe a small question, but I think I prefer it to *Contra*.

—"A-Punk" is always the first song to come on when I get in my car. Alphabetical or whatever.

—I think mine's much less cool than that, he says.

—I doubt it.

Feet walking up the sidewalk, the sound of friends piling out of a cab, slamming the doors. Another text from Nick: a shot of the band doing a final sound check. Instead of responding to Nick, I look over to Julien and say:

—This song always makes me think of you.

The list is too long. Does anyone have an adapter for this? I think the amp is blown. No, no, the one on that side. I heard Jake Gyllenhaal was there. I think Bonnaroo, maybe. Coachella. No stage presence. Is Losers still open?

She got us guest passes, not artist passes. I don't know who's considered a VIP and who's not. Was it the Knitting Factory? Or Eddie's Attic? I heard he tattooed "Lobby Call" on his forearm with a line after it. Fill in the blank so he doesn't miss it. You have to go in the back door, by the alley. Dave Rawlings not Dave Matthews! At the Rabbit release party. He doesn't have a real job. Where's the TM? I don't know, somewhere in Brooklyn. He's a dick, but he's kind of the whole band. I don't care if I'm invited or not. Whiskey, neat. Do you have any earplugs? Stolen, right out of the van, in Philly.

Jess comes through early—surprising me, because for once she isn't on the list; she's actually holding a ticket, one she hands to me instead of Julien.

—I thought you were just perpetually on the list, I say. I was starting to wonder if we should just print one off every night with your name and then add everybody else below.

She laughs so loud I flinch. Julien glances over and Jess blows him a kiss.

—Well, somebody was running a tight ship tonight, she says, rolling her eyes in Julien's direction.

—Just doing my job, Julien says, and then mumbles: *Somebody fucking has to.*

But he says it with a smile, shaking his head. Jess and I both laugh and then she reaches into her bag and hands me a loose CD, the same way Sloane did the night of the flood.

—A JwK mix? I ask.

She grins and runs a hand through her hair.

—Sorry Jules, she says, but Julien doesn't even respond; he's busy checking IDs on a couple of oafish frat boys.

—Okay, I'm gonna go grab a drink, Jess says. Need anything?

—All good, I say.

She bounces up the stairs, bootheels clicking loudly on the linoleum. Julien glances over at me.

—So you guys are friends now? he asks. When did that happen?

—I don't really know, I say.

He's looking at me with that same straight gaze—I still can't suss it out.

—I mean, do you know when *we* became friends? I ask.

—Are we? he asks.

I roll my eyes and ask:

—Jealous?

I prefer the demos. The kind of songs recorded in a garage, an unfinished basement, the back of somebody's van while everybody's taking a beat outside a venue. Where the singer is hungover, hoarse, maybe even full-on sick. No production, just the bare bones of a song and a voice, a slightly out-of-tune guitar that needs a string change. I want to hear it the way it was written, in all its lo-fidelity glory, before anybody was ever meant to hear it at all.

Everyone who comes through tonight thinks they're someone. It's always the problem with secret shows that aren't secret at all. The set doesn't start till eleven, but people arrive in droves for hours beforehand. The crowd is partying. Acidheads in Dead T-shirts and Tevas, high and happy to be there. Industry tools looking to get fucked up and be seen, taking up space that real fans could be occupying. Girls being ignored by their boyfriends, standing at the bar waiting on double vodka sodas. Actual cool kids like Sloane, who slides through the crowd like she created it. Clusters of guys in loose cotton tees on Molly, running their hands through their long hair. And then there's me and Julien, too sober for this shit.

As the door finally starts to slow down, a guy in a leather jacket gives Julien a quick high five on his way up the stairs. He turns back and says: We'll see you Sunday?

—Sounds good, Julien responds.

—What's Sunday? I ask.

He's folding the list up, sliding it into his back pocket. The murmur of a quiet, judgmental crowd pulses upstairs. A bead of sweat drips down my breastbone. Neon city night glowing out the door.

—Nothing, Julien says. Band meeting.

—A band meeting, I repeat. Did So Much Man reunite? I joke. Can you put me on the list?

Julien's face flushes, peach radiating down his neck.

—I never should have told you that.

—But seriously. Are you playing with them? I ask.

My limbs feel suddenly restless, like they're trying to carry a current.

—No. They have a band. I'm not in it. They asked me about tour managing.

—I didn't know you did that.

Upstairs, the opening bar to a familiar, upbeat melody begins.

—I don't. I mean, I haven't.

The show is on now. Guitar feedback and the swell of reluctant cheering. Double bass drum, a thumping, heavy bass line.

—When is it? I ask, and he names a day that's neither soon nor far off. I ask how long the tour is.

—Which leg? Julien asks, twirling his ankle into the floor beneath the stool.

—Oh, I say, twisting at a tension throughout my neck that wasn't there before.

—There's a US leg and a European one. Europe is three months, he says.

A few meaty bros approach, smelling like cigarettes and lager, their party well underway. I stamp their wrists carelessly and they shuffle up the stairs, already bellowing.

—The US leg is only a couple of weeks. I haven't decided if I can do both.

Faces at the door again, a big, drunken group crowding the atrium, six bodies between me and Julien now. When we finally clear them out and it's just the two of us again, I say:

—That's a long time.

At the after-party, Julien disappears. Sloane and Jessika and I get silly, slap-happy drunk—a pleasant, rolling buzz, like we're skating through this disco-ball-blurry evening of LCD Soundsystem mixes and the sweaty pulse of drunk strangers. We dance until the music stops and then we dance some more. The crowd lingers longer than normal; it's two in the morning on a Saturday and no one here has anywhere important to be tomorrow.

Finally the strobe lights flicker out and the lights go up—exposing the floors strewn with confetti like carnage, the room hulking like a sunken ship we're all stranded in. I'm with Sloane's crew from the station and friends of Jess's from Red Light, and joints are lit and pills passed and bottles opened and emptied backstage and crashed into trash cans, and Andy is there, partying with us on a Saturday, because it's not every weekend that a Big Fucking Name is in town, and when Sloane and I finally stumble through the front door of our place, it's five in the morning and the sun is licking the lip of the horizon.

Up on the roof, we smoke menthols and watch the sunrise, even though it's still cold out for spring. We're still buzzed, but I think of the day stretching out empty ahead of me, until I have to be back at work, and a bit of sadness creeps back in. I try to swallow the mounting melancholy, the thought of Julien leaving for three months, as we watch people start to shuffle out of their homes and into their cars—doctors headed to rounds and teachers scurrying with messenger bags and travel mugs of coffee and baristas clipping their carabiners to their jeans, heads dipped into the six a.m. breeze as the smoke from our cigarettes curls up into the sky above, shaking off the night.

4.

I just think that if you gave *Nebraska* an actual listen—like, all the way through—you might like it. But until then you're not allowed to talk shit about Springsteen.

—I'm not talking shit about Springsteen, I say.

—You're saying you don't like Springsteen and you've never listened to *Nebraska*. Tell me an album of his that you've listened to all the way through, Julien says.

—Do you have the other mop?

—That's what I figured.

—I don't know, I say. He just never really did it for me. I get that he's important, canonically speaking.

—Canonically, Julien repeats.

—Yes, *canonically*. But I don't know, I think I'd just rather listen to—

—The Format? Taylor Swift?

—Shut up.

—Here, Julien says, handing me the mop.

Andy's agreed to let us host a couple of small, private events in the second space, but it's on us to make the place look decent. Halfway up to code, he said. So Julien and I have been up here all week, mopping the floors, dragging trash cans and barstools and cocktail tables up from downstairs, screwing light bulbs into the fixtures that still work.

Outside, the sun is starting to crest over the horizon, flooding the sky in a sickening fuchsia.

I stow the mop away in a corner and press my hands into my thighs.

—Fine, loan me your vinyl while you're gone and I'll listen, I say.

—Jess didn't put any Springsteen on your mix?

—Do you want me to listen to it or not?

I glance at Julien and he immediately looks away.

He laughs.

—Fine, he says, looking at me very intently for a moment. The room is warm, the light from the windows hitting the back of my neck, shoulders. Julien is still looking at me.

—What? I ask.

A mop handle falls to the floor, breaking the silence.

—Nothing, Julien says, looking down, digging the toe of his right foot into the floor.

—Can we get out of here? I'm starving. And it's not like we have an event tomorrow or something.

—Careful what you say, or Eddie'll be up here throwing his birthday party.

—Oh god, no, I say. Why is he always dressed like he's on his way to the saloon?

Julien laughs quietly. The Venue echoes with the sound of our sneakers against hardwood, a delivery truck idling out in the alley, the incessant dripping of an old pipe. We lock up the second space. In the parking lot, the sun is blinding, and I hold my hand over my eyes as I look at him.

—Want to get dinner? he asks.

He's tying up a trash bag, twisting the plastic around his fingers, not looking at me.

—Do *you* want to get dinner? I ask back. I was thinking about checking out the bluegrass jam tonight. At Station Inn?

He shrugs, like he didn't ask me first. His shadow stretches out behind him, infinite.

—Want to get dinner and then go to the bluegrass jam? he asks.

His face is in shadow, so I can't read his expression. But it sounds like he's asking me on a date.

A white delivery van pulls into the lot, practically dragging its muffler, beeping as it shifts into reverse. A whiff of garbage and then malt.

—You don't have to, Julien says now, and the sun shifts behind him in shards of yellow.

—No, no, I do. I mean, I know I don't have to, but I do *want* to. Yeah. Let's do it.

—Okay, he says. Okay.

—Okay.

My face is warm. Julien takes the trash bag to the dumpster and then unlocks his car. When we get into the front seats, I pull down the visor to block the sun. He leans over to pop the glove compartment open and hands me a pair of sunglasses.

—If you need them, he says.

When I put them on, the city turns to amber.

Songs for spring drives:

"My Girl to Me" (Dawes)
"The Way We Get By" (Spoon)
"As Tall as Cliffs" (Margot & the Nuclear So and So's)
"World News" (Local Natives)
"Tune Out" (the Format)
"Nothing at All" (Madi Diaz)
"West Coast" (Coconut Records)
"Breakin' Up" (Rilo Kiley)
"Walcott" (Vampire Weekend)

"That's the Way" (Led Zeppelin)
"Love Is All" (the Tallest Man on Earth)
"Coney Island" (Good Old War)
"About Today" (the National)
"Smith Hill" (Deer Tick)
"Home Is Not Places" (the Apache Relay)

The Station Inn glows gray in the shadows of the Gulch. We're both surprised there's no line at the door, where an older woman with braids checks our IDs. Will I still be doing this at her age? Will I ever actually be her age? Inside: popcorn out of paper bags, a pitcher of pale ale, four-top tables scattered beneath a low ceiling. People of all ages clustered together, talking, laughing, listening. Light denim, cowboy boots, the musicians in the round off to the right of the actual stage. Some look no older than seventeen, others are probably seventy. It's an open jam; a few folks lead, and anyone can join in. Right now there's a fiddle player, a handful of guitarists, a stand-up bass, harmonica, banjos, a pedal steel player. A preteen girl with long frizzy hair and a cardigan stands by, a fiddle on her shoulder, waiting for her opening.

The crowd is thick and space is tight. Julien orders a pitcher of beer and I find two open chairs against the back wall vacated by an older couple. We squeeze in, our legs touching. An older man in overalls plays a familiar lick in the key of G, answered by the clap of callused palms. Julien's foot is tapping next to mine, the sole of his sneaker rubbing ever so slightly against mine. He unclips his keys and sets them on the floor. Sweat builds at the base of my neck as I say quietly into his ear:

—This is my favorite thing to do in the city.

I can smell the hops from the beer on his breath as he turns to look at me, his face close, residual heat like dust in the air. He's got the pitcher on the floor in front of us, our plastic cups balanced on our knees. He's still looking at me like he did at The Venue earlier, a question somewhere in his face, but I don't know what it is. Could a look just be a look?

A round of applause, the lilt of strangers' conversations. The preteen girl pulls up a chair into the round. She's in. She looks terrified, her face tight as the bow of her instrument. But she's doing it: sitting with all these strangers, playing somebody else's song. A woman in flannel with long gray hair counts the girl in, the opening bars of "I'll Fly Away." The air beside me has cooled, and when I turn to Julien to point at the girl, he's gone. Did he say he was going to the bathroom? I look around, but all I can see are the tangled hair and bald heads of strangers. The players in the round are singing now, tapping their feet, some of them soloing, closing their eyes, losing themselves a little.

We could do this, I think, in the second space. A round of some kind, no stage or amps. Something small, just for fun. I crane my neck to look for Julien again and place my palm on the vinyl seat he's left. My hand is damp, the seat is warm. There's some instrument I can't place, that I can't see, that I'm hearing in the round now. A brassy, subtle sound, rounding out the melody and giving it some unexpected dimension. It's not until I stand up that I finally spot him, tucked behind the stand-up bass, just out of my line of sight, lips pursed against the mouthpiece of his trumpet.

It would be easy, here—in Nashville—to mock his choice of instrument. I mean, this isn't jazz night. It's not a swing session. It's a bluegrass jam. There are no other brass instruments in the round, and even the preteen girl with the fiddle is looking at Julien quizzically as she stretches her bow. I try to catch his eye, but my view is obstructed by a beam and the upright bass next to him, like I've bought a bad ticket at the Ryman.

But it's working, and now the girl with the fiddle is smiling and they do a short little back-and-forth, a call-and-response bit—playful and restrained and somehow, against all odds, sounding perfectly natural, like he's done this before, stepped into the bluegrass jam with a fucking trumpet.

Julien plays a few rounds, then steps away and comes back to me. My skin prickles. I've finished my beer and started another. He sits down like nothing has happened. I look at him and smile and shake my head. His cheeks are red, a close-mouthed grin across his face. I lean in closer, just a few inches of space between us. He tucks his trumpet back into his bag, smiling, holding my gaze, and shrugs—*What?*

Outside on the curb, the twang of banjos in the background. Our feet sticking out into the street, Julien's ankles twisting his feet back and forth like windshield wipers.

—Used to be a venue over there, he says, pointing at the dim lights of the Urban Outfitters just across the street.

Sometimes I forget he knows that kind of thing. That he's been in Nashville longer than I have, that he's seen more of the city shift and change, knows backstreets and bars and shortcuts I don't, places that opened and closed before I set foot in the city.

—Thank god we have a whole store of fake vintage tees now, though. What was that place called?

—City Hall, he says. Cool space, but the sound was always a little rocky.

—Anybody good come through?

—I only went a couple of times. A pretty good Decemberists show right after I got here.

I nod and lean back on my elbows. We soak up the quiet of the Gulch, our legs still kicked out from the curb. There isn't much pedestrian traffic, but cars pass every few minutes or so, and we pull our feet in, hugging our knees to our chests like little kids.

—When do you leave? I ask.

—Next week.

I want to say *Don't*, but instead I nod, press my lips together.

—You're really going to leave me alone with Eddie?

He laughs.

—You'll have Colt too.

The door behind us swings open, the sound of a key change spilling out onto the sidewalk. And then, quiet.

—It's not like that, I say, rolling my eyes. With Colt.

He's tracing his finger against the concrete, and he nods.

—Despite what it looked like. Or what it seemed like. I don't know—I just wanted to say that. It's not.

—I know it's not, he says.

My palms are pressed into the concrete now. A couple steps out of the Station Inn, looking around in confusion, then waving down a cab on Pine. Tourists, trying our city on for the night, discarding it in the morning with their hot chicken receipts and ticket stubs.

—If anybody can handle Eddie, Julien says, it's definitely you.

—Last week he told me he thought Eddie Vedder was *derivative*, I say. And then he read me the lyrics to a song he'd written, out loud, in their entirety. He read the chorus out loud three times. *Three times.*

Julien laughs, his body bending forward. A loud truck runs the traffic light on the corner.

—I heard him explaining the concept of a concept album to Andy earlier in the week. I thought Andy was going to light him on fire.

—And you're leaving me with him.

—I'll be back, he says. It's not like it's forever.

—Did you decide? I ask, turning my body toward him. About Europe?

—I think it's up to the band. This first leg will be a trial run to see how it goes, see how the fit is.

I nod. The traffic light changes from red to green; no cars come through. Yellow, then back to red again.

—I can't believe you joined the round with a trumpet.

—I can't believe you didn't join the round at all.

The moon is misty orange above the city.

—Sloane's trying to get us a radio show, I say. You going to listen to us while you're driving the van?

—Depends on what you play.

—It's me and Sloane. We will only play good shit.

—You mean sad shit?

—Well sad shit is the only shit, I say.

Julien laughs. The street darkens, and he leans forward next to me, his hip grazing mine. The streetlight above us flickers on and off, on and off, on and then off completely. Applause coming from inside, then the murmur of voices. The smell of gasoline, burnt popcorn, steel.

—We'll miss you, I say.

—Oh yeah?

I turn to him until our faces are so close I can feel his breath on my upper lip. He shakes his head just a bit, a smile creeping up his cheeks.

—I will, I say.

In the streetlight, with his sleeves pulled up, you can see the scars on the underside of his forearms. I almost reach out to touch them, but instead I put my hand next to his, our pinkies touching.

—It's not that I don't know what I want, I say quietly.

Julien's face is inscrutable, but his pinkie reaches for mine. My chest is pounding. Inside they're playing Lucinda Williams now.

—Nobody knows what they want, Julien says.

Our faces are still so close that I can see pinpricks of sweat around his mouth. For a moment he says nothing, just closes his eyes. Mine run over the outline of his lips, the eyelash on his cheek, the shadow from the streetlight across his jawline. Maybe I'm sick of not seeing what's right in front of me.

—I do, I say. I want—

—I'm gonna miss you too, he says, opening his eyes, suddenly all serious.

A buzz beneath my skin. Somewhere in the distance: the pop of a car backfiring.

When it happens, I can't tell who actually initiates it, who leans in more, who wants it most. But the heat rushes—from our hips to my chest, my neck, my jaw, open to his. His tongue inside my mouth, along the insides of my teeth, like he's trying to get me to come just by kissing me. Beyond us the city is muffled; the only sound I can hear is the movement of our hands against each other—fingernails to denim, cotton, wrapped around his neck. Sweat and guitar strings, a song in C fading out behind us. Julien.

My bed is unmade, which simplifies things. Julien's palms are sweaty; my chest is cool and damp. Our tongues move slowly, then frantically, his palms flat against my cheeks, my chin, the base of my skull, his tongue soft and deliberate, my hands in his hair.

It takes us a long time to remove our clothes—or no time at all. We are in that hookupblackhole of time: two minutes is twenty, an hour is thirty seconds, we don't really know. It doesn't matter. There's no music playing; our breath is heavy and melodic.

His hands inch up my shirt, my rib cage, fingertips finding the wire of my bra, like he's reached a fence and is waiting to be told he can open it. I tug off his shirt; the gate is open, all bets are off. Downstairs, Sloane has turned on music—the Postal Service or Death Cab or some Ben Gibbard solo shit, who can tell. Julien pushes my shirt up, fumbles with my bra like he's never fucking done this before.

He's hard—I can feel him, just barely, pressing against me. I run my hand along him over his jeans as he finally unhooks my bra, and we both laugh in relief, in disbelief, that something so small could cause such a fuss, that our fingers can't always do what we need them to, and then just like that they do, they can, they are—a single, long index finger slipped inside me. I'm already soaking as we fall onto my bed, my head knocking slightly against the headboard, Julien losing his footing but somehow keeping his finger inside me, curled into a comma; he is not fucking around.

Naked and tangled now, our clothes flung to the floor, Julien pressing against me, soft tease after soft tease, me biting against his lips, running my hand through his hair, softer, finer than I imagined.

I reach for a condom from my nightstand, my hand flailing as Julien keeps his cock pressed against me; if I tilt my hips he will slip right in. He giggles as my hand continues to fumble, my fingers frantic until I find what I'm looking for and pass it to him. He unwraps the plastic, keeping his mouth pressed to mine, his hands fumbling at our waists, my legs open for him as he slides it on. I bend my knees, spread my legs wider, and he watches me and laughs quietly, shaking his head a little bit, giving me a look like: *Are you sure?* And I pull him into me, hard and fast—it's too easy—and then slower, surer, the two of us moving together in a comfortable, sweaty pulse.

I never come during sex. I don't even think of it as a possibility, as an option. But already now I'm close, I'm biting my cheeks, I'm too wet, I'm going to implode, the night is going to dissolve, and I tell him so and he just pumps harder, his palms tight around my shoulders, pulling me close as I clench around him, surprised at my own climax, surprised at how long I pulse around him, how quickly he comes as well, how long he stays inside me, still hard, the two of us sweaty and ecstatic and relieved.

We laugh and the breeze rustles through my room. A car passes on the street below us, trailing the sound of a song I can't recognize.

5.

Just put the fucking headphones on and relax. We're going to sound great. We're going to sound better than great. It's all happening, baby.

Sloane is in the sound booth at Lightning 100, after midnight on a Monday. Julien's gone, off on his tour, and I don't know how we've left it. We're talking, of course, but I still don't know what it means, what will happen now that we seem to be in that hazy gray of hooking up but not necessarily *together*. Where feelings are obvious, but not quite explicit.

Sloane's boss has finally agreed to let her guest-DJ while all the other hosts are away, and she's brought me along—partially to keep my mind off Julien, partially because she needs a cohost. We're staring at each other, a little stoned, about to go on air. It's a terrible slot, a one a.m. guest spot on a weeknight, but it's still a slot. It's still an hour of unearned airtime when we can play whatever we want to play, say (almost) whatever we want to say. It's about time our year of playlist curation gets put to good use.

She barely knows how to work the boards, but we've spent the evening thumbing through demo CDs and crafting a new playlist that isn't difficult to agree on. Because it's going to be on in the middle of the night, I lean toward sleepier favorites: Sufjan and Iron & Wine, Bon Iver. Band of Horses. Mazzy Star. The Jesus and Mary Chain.

Justin Wilson. Some Esther Wainwright solo songs. I even throw in a few songs from Jess's mix. Sloane doesn't care that it's midnight; she's going upbeat with Taylor Swift and Kings of Leon. "Sun Hands" by Local Natives—a decidedly unsleepy song. The White Stripes, Steel Train, a rogue Metallica song. Prince. Kanye. A real fucking grab bag.

We end up with a playlist that's way too long, and we talk way too much, but it's still exhilarating, sitting in the booth with the headphones against our ears, the whole night's soundtrack at our fingertips.

When the studio phone rings in the middle of "The Call of Ktulu," Sloane is giddy.

—Oh my god, our first caller, she says. Look at us. We already have fans! We have a *listenership*.

She claps playfully before she picks up the line. Briefly I imagine it's Julien, listening online from across the country. As Metallica fades out, Sloane starts the next track before picking up the call.

It's her little sister.

—You're playing dead air right now, Katy tells us.

—We're playing "Manhattan" right now, Sloane says.

—No, Katy says, you're playing nothing. It's just static.

Sloane and I stare at each other. Our eyes scan madly across the board. The ON AIR button—the only button that should be lit right now—is dark. I place my hand over my mouth. For a moment, the studio is completely silent, like the second before a needle drops onto vinyl. And then we collapse into incoherent laughter. Katy is probably our only listener anyway—it's nearly two in the morning. Sloane presses the button, and just like that we're back on air.

The seeds from poplar trees float down to earth, whole notes cut from the outro of a too-long song. A memory: the indent of Julien's hip, his comforter the color of milky coffee. Julien's body pressed into mine, an LP crackling in the background. Our mouths dry, our damp palms pressed together.

The city empties out. Vanderbilt and Belmont students graduate and the city center briefly bloats with visitors. Students take their parents out to eat at the places we rarely go to: Sunset Grill and Morton's, the bar at the Palm. And then, finally, quiet. Sloane and I spend our days sending emails, making playlists. The streets of Music Row are vacant.

What we want is to host a songwriting round—like at the Bluebird, but a little more rock and roll. Something we can broadcast during our one a.m. slot—low key and late night. We email our pitches to Andy, to Sloane's boss, Billy. We reach out to several songwriters, mostly women. We start a back-and-forth with Jess, who knows everyone too—she's maybe even more into the idea than Sloane and I are.

A morning run in tangerine daylight, the neighborhood radiant before the summer heat settles. I work out four chord progressions, follow them all the way down. Place a call to Izzy, to Clem, then to Izzy again. Scribble down more lines. Listen to learn: "November Blue," Avett Brothers. "Elephant," Damien Rice. "Pictures of You," the Cure. Drive over to Marathon Music Works, then to The Venue, then to the 5 Spot, Exit/In. Send more emails. Polish the globe lights, wax the floors—slowly remaking the second space.

She wasn't even at the party. They moved so many units that first week. They're tearing it down, probably. Do you think they're sleeping together? I mean, the chemistry. Their tongues were practically touching. His voice is insane. No hers is. At Douglas Corner Cafe. But in the most random places. Stockholm. Copenhagen. Strasbourg. Marseille. Whiskey soda. Double. They're taking shots at the back bar. Never drink the water on the bus. You know they don't sell liquor there. Flirtation Device. It's a pun. I am a golden god. You can't buy wine on Sundays, remember, you can't even buy wine in grocery stores. Get there early. Nick, Alex something? The bartender, I think yeah, with Kesha. But when they sing together. They never even rehearse. Back at merch, you'll find them.

Two weeks without Julien means two weeks with Eddie. Thursday. Tonight's show is a band that had a bit of a moment in the early aughts, when their song was picked for the opening credits of a teen drama about rich kids in Southern California. People call them a one-hit wonder (nothing *wonderful* about that song, Eddie gripes), but I think that sells them a little short.

At the door, I'm staring at my phone during the lull while Eddie assaults me with a long diatribe tracing the story of modern pop country from Johnny Cash to Avril Lavigne, before taking a left turn to argue that Mark McGrath is an underappreciated rock talent. He's sitting where Julien should be, in enormous combat boots with laces so long you could jump rope with them. I miss Julien's red Chucks.

—Who's your favorite band? I ask. If we talk about music he likes, I think, maybe he'll be less insufferable.

—Unanswerable question, Eddie says.

—That's a little dramatic.

—Nobody can have a single favorite band, he says. Who's yours?

—Mazzy Star, I tell him, even though it's probably Frightened Rabbit.

—Bullshit, he says, tapping his foot like he's keeping tempo to a frantic beat.

—Okay, who's your *least* favorite? I ask.

—Probably the Stones, he says, like he's the first person who's ever dropped the *Rolling*. Overrated, he says. Keith Richards plays like a pussy.

I nod, desperately wishing I were somewhere else.

—Do you play anything besides bass and guitar? I ask.

—I dabble.

Of course he does. I shove my hands into my pockets: a small nugget of weed Colt gave me last week wrapped in foil, a loose Valium from him that I've told myself I'm not going to take. Though Eddie is making it tempting.

—Bass, mostly, and of course guitar too, he says. Piano.

Tearing wristbands at their perforated edges, I try to let the steady rip of the paper drown him out.

—Pedal steel, he continues. Mandolin. Hand saw every now and then, when the mood is right.

—Sure, I say. The mood does have to be right for the hand saw.

This place blows without you, I text Julien, attaching a picture of Eddie chattering about "Sk8er Boi." The lot outside is quiet; I have no idea what kind of crowd we're expecting tonight.

—Anyway, Eddie says. You coming to the jazz night this week?

Every night at The Venue, there are bands that no one has ever heard of, that maybe no one will ever hear of. The kind who grind along for years—writing and touring tiny clubs, writing some more and touring slightly bigger clubs, then mid-level venues, the crowds not even crowds at first, just friends, family, the bartenders and the door girls, the college interns doing lights, doing sound, doing coke—and maybe, if they're lucky, each time the band comes back to a city, the crowd grows.

At first it's barely noticeable. Negligible. Dozens, then something close to a hundred, then hun*dreds*, and if they're really lucky, maybe, someday, thousands. I'm rarely interested beyond that point. I like my bands like I like my men—that is to say: all to myself.

The set tonight is good, a bit grungy, but the lead singer is *in it*, leaving it all out there, draining himself dry for us. I send a video of it to Julien and make a joke about the TV show—we both admitted to watching quite a bit of it in high school. But he's on the East Coast right now, and it's late. He's probably in a shitty hotel bed somewhere in Long Island.

Eddie takes off early. Andy offers to help close down for Colt. Sloane's texting me about the radio show.

What do Mondays at 1 am at The Venue look like? she asks.

Closed, I say.

That's perfect, she says.

I roll my eyes. The night cleaning crew is here, trash being emptied into bins, glass crashing throughout the space. When I go to clock out, a few of Julien's comic books are on the coffee table. I slide one into my bag without thinking and when I turn around Andy's in the doorway.

—How's the space looking? he asks.

He's got a mop in his hand, a baseball hat on. He reaches up to adjust the bill. A text from Sloane: Get your ass down here ASAP! I hear TAYLOR SWIFT is on her way.

—I swept, I say to Andy. But I still need to grab a few things—

—No no, your hideaway space, he says. Where are we at?

—Julien and I cleaned before he left, and I think he got most of the lights up. Window guy is coming next week?

Andy nods.

—Shall we put it to use?

If he's not calling you he's not that into you. I think we need to bring back the key change. Celine Dion, definitely. No no no. I don't want to do karaoke. Should we do a Jägerbomb? It's not like he was throwing rocks outside my fucking window. Get in, we've got school! It's not worth your time. Don't say you're going to do it unless you're going to do it. Over on Belcourt, I think. Power outage. If I hear this song one more time. I run into that dude everywhere! No way, that shit's sketchy. He needs to get his shit together. Baby won't you change your mind?

Sloane's at the bar where the Incident took place. Normally, I'd tell her no. Suggest somewhere else and call it a night. But I resist the urge—she and Jess are right. It's been forever. Those guys don't even remember what happened last weekend, let alone last year. Plus, maybe Jess is right. Maybe fucking it up is my little *Behind the Music*.

I drive over, the moon hazy and high through my open windows, Mazzy Star's "Halah" fading out when I turn onto Division. Thursday. Most of the bars quiet, college kids home for the summer. In the back lot, remnants of wilder nights—broken glass, stubbed-out cigarettes, a single sneaker. I pull out my phone and hum a melody that's appeared in my head, like I've just recalled a dream. Two drunk girls stumble by, their phones glowing in their hands. The lyrics come next and quickly; I jot down the verse in the Notes app. A text comes through from Julien: What ya listening to tonight?

I send him the Mazzy Star song. And then, before I overthink it, the melody I just sang roughly into my phone. Want to help me finish this one? I text back. A petal from a crab apple tree floats down from a tree in the alley, a cab stalls out in the parking lot, the passenger door flung open. Inside the bar, someone's covering "Iris."

Sloane's on the porch, smoking a cig, her vintage windbreaker sliding off her shoulder. Her face lights up when she sees me. She's drinking a tequila soda, and a second one sits in front of the empty seat next to her. The air is dry, the night is lovely.

—My cohost, she says, smiling wide and taking another drag of her cigarette. I hold my hand out for one.

—Did you talk to Andy?

—Loosely, I say.

—Well?

—He did say tonight that we should put the space to use soon.

Sloane raises her eyebrows.

—I'd cheers to that, but you don't have a drink yet. Oh. By the way, this is completely unrelated but: Do you want to renew our lease?

A song of Nick's comes on overhead and I'm briefly distracted. But the voices of the bar quickly drown it out, and just like that it's gone. The band inside has moved on to an Old Crow Medicine Show song.

—Hello? Sloane asks. Are you breaking up with me?

—Who the hell else would I live with? I ask. I think I'd have to live at The Venue if I moved out. So yes, I say. Please.

The sound of cowboy boots clicking across concrete. A train roaring in the distance.

—You look fucking famous right now, Sloane says, touching my jacket.

—No I don't.

—Yes you do.

—I don't want to be famous.

—Everyone wants to be famous.

The way she says it makes it sound objectively true. I shake my head.

—I just want to be me.

—That's cute, she says, but it's total bullshit. Go get a drink. I have a tab open.

Inside, so much cigarette smoke it's like being smothered. Low, low lights, a mix of musicians and barflies and alcoholics. I get a Yuengling and take it back outside, but when I get there the seat next to her is taken by a woman with dark hair and a gray streak.

—Al, meet Esther. Esther, this is my roommate Al.

Esther turns to me and smiles, our eyes searching.

—Nice to meet—well, we've met, actually. I don't know if you—

—Oh yeah! You work at The Venue, right?

—How do you guys know each other? I ask. I'm trying to catch Sloane's eye, but she's busy fending off a drunk guy in a flannel behind her.

—Sloane's dad used to manage me, Esther says. Years ago.

I try not to show my surprise, but it *does* feel like someone should have mentioned this. Doesn't Sloane know about Esther's connection to Justin Wilson? This album, this person I've been talking about for months?

Sloane turns back around.

—Esther's an absolutely *insane* songwriter, she says.

I almost say: *I know.*

—Here, you can sit, Esther says.

—Oh no, I'm fine, really.

—Al writes songs too.

—Really?

—Sloane, no—

—Yes, you do.

—Barely.

—What kind of stuff? Esther asks.

Sloane's grinning idiotically. I take a sip of my beer and when I look down it's nearly half gone.

—It's, uh—

—Oh my god! Sloane says. You guys need to write together. And Esther—you need to come on our radio show. We've got a prime-time slot.

Sloane winks at me and laughs.

This is how it happens: Sloane, pushing, prodding, not shutting the fuck up. Asking me to play my songs for her, then play them again. Waking me up in the middle of the night to tell me an idea she has. Making calls to Billy and Andy and Billy again. Jess doing the same. They really are both so fucking annoying. Pulling strings and dropping names, but mostly just being Sloane, being Jess. Being friends, I guess.

I wonder, sometimes, about who gets the credit, who deserves the recognition for all the songs that float around this town and into my life. Was it Wilson's voice that made that performance or Esther's lyrics, her high harmony? Does it matter that he didn't write the hook if he can sing the hell out of it? Probably not. Elvis didn't write his own songs. Elton doesn't write his own lyrics. Rihanna, Frank Sinatra. Celine Dion, Britney Spears. They could all kill you with a performance, though. But me: I want to see the scraps of paper, hear the melodies the moment they took form and sprang to life. I want to be in the room, want to feel the magic that happens that moment you turn nothing into something.

Clear azure spring sky. The neighbor walking a Jack Russell past the corner store on Tenth. Colt's weed stinking up the whole living room.

Movers lifting a piano into the second-story window of the house down the street. A Kurt Vile song, a Vampire Weekend song. I don't want to miss anything else. I'm memorizing the chorus.

Julien, probably at the Southgate House in Cincinnati, looking at a clipboard, a checklist, answering a call from the drummer. Not responding to my text but answering the band's. Does he want anything from Panera? Julien, checking his bank account on his laptop, wondering how much longer he can afford to make so little money. A show in Austin, Lawrence, Denver. Selling merch at the State Room in Salt Lake City, even though they have someone along with them to do that. The glow of the gas station on Colfax, across from the Ogden Theatre, a brutally cold Colorado spring day. Julien smoking a cigarette in Boise, a cigar in Spokane, a joint in Olympia. A missed call from outside the Fillmore.

Colt, trying to kiss me outside FooBar. Me, too sober to let him. By the time we stumble down Gallatin, closer to downtown, at the bar with the taxidermy fox, I'm buzzed, but still I push him away. A text message in my pocket.

In the end, it's Sloane and Jess who really help tie up the loose ends for the live show. Billy and Andy already know each other, so they have no problem working out a deal to hold the round at The Venue after hours. But Julien knows nothing about all this. He's driving down I-5 in Seattle, Nirvana's *Unplugged* blaring out of the speakers, the sky stretched out before him as gray as Nashville. He's on a stool at the Knitting Factory, drinking a Yuengling. The rocking chair on his porch empty. On a Tuesday I stop by his place and sit in it, the spring air still a touch too cold to be outside after dark. Singing under my breath while Sloane orders a martini at the bar at the Hutton, waiting for me. She wants to celebrate—Andy's officially given us the go-ahead—I tell her I don't know why.

If I called you blacked out in the suburbs, would you come out
or just say I fucked up?
If I ran into you at the grocery, would you walk past and not
even notice me?
I'll pay attention, I swear I'll listen

I'm almost there, but it's the bridge of the song that I'm stuck on. Trying to connect the last verse back to the chorus, I can't get it to open up. Across the street, an older couple looks at the magnolia tree in their yard, pointing up at it. The neighbor to the left is blasting Feist like it's heavy metal. The day is warm but we'll still turn the heat on tonight.

6.

When I first understood how it worked, I couldn't fathom the idea of giving your song away for somebody else to sing. But isn't that why these people get onstage every night?

Maybe, I thought, writing a song for someone else was less about giving it away than about sharing it. After all, sometimes a song barely feels like a song until you're singing it with someone else. Sure, you can play your guitar alone in an unfinished space, listen to the radio by yourself in your car, or with your headphones on. But something different happens when you hear a song with other people. The music transforms. That's why we want a crowd: enough people to remind us that we're not alone, no matter how low the lights dim, no matter how quiet the band gets. That collective comfort.

Late afternoon, then, at The Venue: Julien, stepping out of an unfamiliar car, a girl's dark hair flapping out the driver's-side window. He's just gotten back into town today. Cornflower-blue sky, sun bursting through high, feathery clouds. I'm waiting for him on the balcony, an unlit cigarette in my hand as he shuts the car door, messenger bag slung over his shoulder. That fucking trumpet poking out.

Inside, at the entryway, he hugs me and I smell the distance on him. The hotels he's stayed in, the floors he's crashed on, the cigarettes he's smoked, the Yuenglings he's finished, the faces he's flirted with.

—Welcome home, I say. How long do we get? Forty-eight hours?

—Not even, he says, his arms still wrapped around me.

For just a moment I remember walking into the office months ago, finding Julien and Jessika wrapped in a hug. Their arms swung around each other just like this, their bodies close. And then the memory is gone—a verse cut from a song—and it's just Julien's hand against my hips, his fingertips grazing my skin as I lean against his chest.

When he pulls away, the sun shifts and the entryway is dark.

—Who's that? I ask, pointing to the parking lot.

—Who?

—Your friend who dropped you off.

—Oh. Lila.

—Lila, I repeat, like I'm swallowing the syllables.

The car in the parking lot is gone, but that glimpse of dark hair is still in my head.

—What? he asks.

—Never mind.

—She's on the tour, he says.

—Cool, I say. What does she do *on the tour*?

—Merch, he says.

—Cute.

A look passes between us. At least she's not in one of the bands. Merch, I can handle.

Maybe.

—What? he asks.

—Nothing.

—Al, come on.

He's already sitting down, tearing off sheets of neon-green wristbands. He's barely been here five minutes, and already he's doing more than I am.

—I just didn't expect you to find a tour girlfriend so quickly, I say.

He exhales.

—Al.

—Julien.

—She's not my tour girlfriend, he says. She's my—she just dropped me off.

—That was very sweet of her.

He laughs, sharp and lovely, mouth open wider than it needs to be. A glimpse of his tongue; I imagine it on mine. Upstairs someone's playing "Cape Cod Kwassa Kwassa."

—You're jealous, Julien says, glancing up at me, eyebrows lifted, eyelashes delicate.

—No I'm not.

He smiles and I look at my phone.

He's trying to get my attention, holding The Venue stamp and looking from my eyes to my forearm.

—You are, he says, and then: I didn't take you for jealous.

His hand is warm. I feel his heartbeat in the crevices of his palm. He starts to press the stamp into my forearm and then stops. I lace my fingers together with his and we stand suspended in time for a moment, a measure of rest.

Songs I listened to on repeat while Julien was gone, that will probably always make me think of him:

"Atlantic City" (Bruce Springsteen)
"Bring on the Ending" (Matt Pond PA)
"Go Your Own Way" (Fleetwood Mac)
"Call Your Girlfriend" (Robyn)
"The Gambler" (fun.)
"Thirteen" (Big Star)

"Ambling Alp" (Yeasayer)
"Mr. November" (the National)
"The Modern Leper" (Frightened Rabbit)
"For You" (Springsteen)
"Enchanted" (Taylor Swift)
"Written in Reverse" (Spoon)
"Airplanes" (Local Natives)
"See You Soon" (Coldplay [yes])
"Talking in Code" (Margot & the Nuclear So and So's)
"3 Rounds and a Sound" (Blind Pilot)

I listen to them in the car while I'm driving down Music Row, down Eighth, past the new restaurants in our neighborhood, the taproom that I hope never closes, no matter how much the city changes. Am I home now? Is this it? Driving around, not looking up the directions before I snake through the back roads of bungalows and backyard studios? Or is it the Tennessee license, tucked into my wallet, my face slightly younger than on the old Michigan one tossed in a drawer—does that make me official?

Or maybe it's something else entirely: the way I answer when someone asks where I'm from. Not Missouri not Ohio not Michigan, no.

Maybe I've forgotten I was ever anywhere else.

All things considered, it's surprising that I don't run into Esther again sooner. I'm at a coffee shop in East Nashville, the only part of town that seems to be safe from the victims of my somewhat slutty winter. I've just ordered a gourmet Popsicle and a latte when the barista calls her name.

Other things I've missed: a light rouge lipstick she had on every time I saw her. Usually overdressed for wherever she was—or maybe *overdressed* isn't the word. More like incongruously dressed. Today: a lacy black shawl down to her ankles, combat boots with neon laces. She has a guitar in a hard case, leaning against her hip. We've met more than once, we have a mutual friend, but when she notices me now, I still can't shake the sensation of being a voyeur. I give her a small smile, and she raises a hand in a tentative wave.

—Al, right? she asks when I approach.

—That's me.

My Popsicle starts to melt, a drip of lime juice down my inner wrist.

—Do you live in the neighborhood? she asks.

—No no no, I say. To be honest, the baristas in this city have become a bit of a minefield for me. So I crossed the river.

She laughs, surprisingly loud and rich. She licks the tip of a coffee stirrer.

—Are you playing somewhere tonight? I ask, nodding at her guitar.

—Oh, I was just getting this gal set up at Fanny's. She taps the case, her smoke-colored fingernails drumming along the neck.

I don't know what comes over me exactly, but I say:

—Hey, you don't ever write with anybody besides Justin, do you?

She cocks her head.

—'Cause if you do—or if you would—and you're free . . .

Things I don't say to her yet: Is he okay? Are you sure? I'm not sure I would have finished my own songs if not for his, for yours. Are *you* okay?

The door to the shop opens, a man in a denim jacket with long black hair walks in, sunglasses still on. The day outside is bright—lemon honey sky. The sun shifts between the doors and then disappears again. The Popsicle drips.

—Here, she says, handing her phone to me. Put your number in.

I stop trying to learn other people's songs. I stop looking up the tabs online, trying to match the rhythm of the strumming. I stop trying to imitate a song so perfectly that it loses all meaning, all spark—so that suddenly it's just a chord progression and some words and a metronome clicking. I was never very good at it anyway; I could never get the rhythm down perfectly enough to sound like the original song, could never transform it enough to make it my own.

Plus, there's something about covering someone else's song that always made me feel like I was crawling backward.

Somehow, word about our show spreads. We planned for it to be small, especially this first one. We lined up a few songwriters, regulars at The Venue, people from the radio station. Jess got one of her up-and-comers, and Sloane insisted I follow through on my invite to Esther. I almost begged off—*Esther is too intimidating*, I told her—but she simply said *No, she's just the right amount of intimidating*. What choice did I have?

We were supposed to be keeping it under the radar, relying on word of mouth, but Sloane's been putting up flyers and Jess can't shut the fuck up about anything. No wonder Denim's been on the rise. I see flyers for our night on telephone poles down Twenty-First, at coffee shops all over the neighborhood. And when I walk upstairs, as the main show is wrapping up, she's setting up a card table with Lightning 100 stickers, T-shirts, and more posters.

DEAD AIR @ THE SECOND SPACE:
A SONGWRITING JAM
MONDAY, MAY 20TH–1 A.M. (FREE)

Seeing the date written out that way, I suddenly realize: it's been almost exactly a year since Nick first showed up at The Venue the night of the flood. I don't know what city he's in tonight: Lincoln or San Diego, Seattle or Birmingham. It doesn't matter. Whatever was between us is no more, even if I still stop when one of his songs comes on at the grocery store.

I fell for Nick—and all those boys in all those bands—the same way I fell in love with music: some combination of melody and chemistry, all of it crystallizing into sharp little memories over the course of days or months or years. The bands don't ever love you back, of course. They say they do, but what they really love, mostly, is just that you love them.

Most of the bands will split up. In the moment, of course, it doesn't feel that way—even though we know better, even though all the evidence points that way. No one does this shit until they die. The lead singers sometimes disappear completely; the guitar players join other bands, become session musicians, backup guitarists, producers. Others will thread themselves into a different fabric of the city, settle down as baristas or bartenders or graphic designers or stay-at-home dads.

But here, right now, it's hard to imagine any of us ever doing anything but this.

Sloane's applying lipstick behind the card table, straightening out her posters and stickers.

—I told you not to put these up around town, and you've definitely been putting these up around town.

—Well, did you want people to show up or not? Sloane asks. She looks to Jess, who's going over some lists. You should be *thanking* us, Sloane says.

—She's right, Jess says.

I roll my eyes.

—Are you sure about "the Second Space"? I say. Did Andy approve?

—I got that from you! Plus, it's a play on *The Second Sex*, right? Because, you know, we're feminists or whatever. That's probably what you meant all along.

Not really, but she's right—it's good. Sloane is savvy like that.

—I just don't know that anybody is going to pay ten bucks for a promo poster, I say, nodding at her merch.

—Well, they're coming for free. You know that's how bands make all of their money at first: merch, baby. Come on, Al—with all your BIBs, you should know that.

—BIBs? Jess asks.

—Boys in a band, Sloane says.

—I don't have any BIBs anymore. Maybe BIB-adjacent.

—Julien's not a BIB? she asks, winking at me.

I laugh and grab one of the posters, rolling it into a cylinder and tucking it under my arm. When I turn around, the space looks dreamy, I have to admit. The lights are strung haphazardly, but it works, dotting the space with a low, caramel-hued glow. Through the windows, the moon is full and bright. Izzy and Clem show up with a case of wine and start pouring it into plastic cups, handing it out. Andy's talking to Esther and the other two songwriters in the back, before he starts shifting some of the small tables around the space. Our sound guy, Danny, is there, a loopy grin across his face, a case of beer tucked under his arm like a football. He's passing out beers to strangers, greeting people like they're family.

Eddie's there, wearing a Suicide T-shirt, talking loudly at a goth-looking pixie girl on his arm. Colt is out of town—a nice coincidence we didn't even plan for. A few dozen other people trickle in and the space is bustling and warm. Some of the songwriters start playing in the corner, just quiet little background riffs for now. The lights are low, only one mic, like they do at the Station Inn. No amps, pretty lo fi.

And then, finally, Julien. He's just finishing up a late load-out downstairs, and now he's looking around the space with a sheepish smile, like he's just waking up from a good dream. He catches my eye from across the room and I smile. My heart is in my throat, my jaw, my temples. Julien's lips on mine, his fingertips tracing the skin of my forearm.

Laughter in the corner from a group of Izzy's friends. Mouths open, wine-stained teeth. The cracking open of a beer, the dribble of liquid into plastic. Jess, hyena-laughing in a corner and sucking down wine through a cocktail straw. The taut sound of a Martin being tuned up in the corner.

Julien weaves through the space, his eyes focused, taking it all in. I never told him what we were working on while he was gone. I wanted tonight to be a surprise.

There are still things I miss. Even when I'm sure I'm catching everything, when I'm certain I'm paying attention. The brewery by Sloane's office, now moving to a new location on Division, a stone's throw from The Venue. A photo flash: Julien reaching high into the air to snap a picture with a disposable camera. Driving down Twenty-First with Sloane, screaming along to the Strokes, our voices carrying out the windows as we pass all the recording studios. Julien's porch, radiant spring light, a green Dunlop pick in my fingers, the back of his hand brushing mine. Broadway by daylight. Gibsons, Taylors, Martins pushed into the backs of trunks. Neon honky-tonks confused by the sun.

It's quarter to one. Sloane grabs me by the hand, squeezing it in hers.

—I'm going to fire up the boards in a second and do my best to, you know, *not* broadcast dead air. Did you get a drink? Here, have mine. I think I've already had, like, a dozen, but they're so tiny I don't think it counts. You good?

—I'm fucking great, I say.

She laughs.

—That's what I like to hear.

I take her wine and throw it back in one hot swallow.

Is there a bartender or is this BYOB? She got promoted at Vector. I don't know anything about his sobriety. Malibu, recording I think. My feet were on a pile of soda cans. It's pretty much the most self-indulgent thing you can do. Oh I've got the demos. They fired him. I think he's going solo. Yes they are absolutely fucking. In Rolling Stone*! Did you see it? It was at City Hall. Maybe in 2006. Do you want to go on Monday? Motown night or whatever? Yes, Ezra Koenig. Of course she knows him. Of course.*

Julien doesn't realize what's happening until it's happening. I don't know how we've managed to keep it under wraps this long, but when he puts the pieces together, the evening is pitch-black, and the only lights in the Second Space are the globe lights he and I strung together.

I don't know what will happen when he leaves again tomorrow—but maybe I don't need to. Maybe, for once, I can just keep living the life I have here rather than trying to constantly be somewhere else—wherever Nick is, wherever Julien is, whatever party is happening or bar is open that I'm not at. Even though it's still a bit like sinking when I'm standing in one place, it's good to have a place to stand.

There are the things I have to put here, to make sure I don't lose them:

Julien, his leg against mine on my roof, rubbing his fingers across his forearm, a tiny bruise on his pinkie nail. Sitting on the hardwood with Sloane in our living room, trying to harmonize to a song we loved in high school. Sloane stubbing out the end of a joint on our porch. An unlit cigarette left on a sink in the men's room. A Black Keys, Justin Wilson, LCD Soundsystem, Dead Weather poster, taped to the door of the bathroom stall. Yuengling, Four Roses, High Life. The Villager—lights up after close. Laced-up red Chucks, white rubber fading to black. Julien, a silhouette in a black T-shirt, a little smile on his lips as if a song he loves has just come on.

It's too hot. Sweat is starting to form between my shoulder blades, in the crooks of my elbows. People move about the space quietly, huddled in clusters holding plastic cups and rolled-up posters and stickers. A hollow, nagging nausea lurks in the back of my throat. I walk quickly through the crowd toward the songwriters. At the card table I see Julien, holding one of our posters. His green eyes follow me as I walk over to my guitar, holding up my wrist with the cat on it. A look on his face like he wants to ask me a question. Izzy, hair glowing golden beneath the low lights, Clem's arm in hers. Andy, smiling and talking in animated bursts with Danny. Sloane, headphones on, hair tied back in a short, blunt ponytail. In the corner, I pick up my own guitar; it finally seems to fit.

Andy lets out a shrill, deafening whistle and then cedes the floor to Sloane. She pulls her headphones down, the foam resting against her shoulders. I let her introduce the evening, because really it was her idea. She's annoying, persistent, demanding, but of course I love it, because here we are. Dead Air, live. She talks briefly about the night—with a blistering amount of profanity—while I wait in the corner with the others. Esther's next to me—she'll sing harmony on my set, including a song we finished together—and with us are two other songwriters, recent acquaintances, maybe new friends. My whole body is numb. My wine is gone. I'm on my own.

Somewhere down the road, after the bands move on or give up or grow up, perhaps, they'll do reunion tours or one-off shows, or maybe those four or five or eight people will never appear onstage together again. They'll go gray and their voices will grow gravelly. Lots of them will die young. And when their songs come on years later, it won't be them I think of, but—

Julien's trumpet sticking out of his messenger bag, eyes flicking green and then brown and then hazel and then back to green. Sloane, her mascara on the kitchen island, her glance across a dinner table to let me know that she Does Not Have the Patience for This Person, her hair band left on a vinyl sleeve, her ponytail bouncing as she dances in the back row of a show. Sloane, again, blasting Owen, going fifteen over down Sixteenth Avenue, well after midnight, the stars stupid bright, the moon hovering like a ghost over the gleam of downtown, of The Venue, its sticky floors and constant scent of stale beer, menthols, whiskey, whiskey, whiskey, a little more whiskey. Of Julien again, his silhouette set against the skyline—the city small but bright, unassuming but scrappy. The kind of place you could fall in love with. The kind of place where you could fall in love.

Beneath shadows and celestial yellow light, Sloane puts us on air without another word. I sit down.

The Second Space is quiet. I am sure I can hear Julien's breath from across the room. And then: applause, the vibration of dozens of high-pitched cheers and *woos*. He's looking at me now, more questions scattered across his face. For once I know how to answer him. I dry my palms on my jeans and slide the capo onto my guitar.

—Hi. I'm Al. Thanks again for coming out tonight. I wrote this first song about somebody who's in the room now. I hope you like it.

ACKNOWLEDGMENTS

Cal Morgan, I feel lucky every day that you fell in love with this book, that you found Al so "unabashedly thirsty" but also "gimlet-eyed." Riverhead was a publishing dream I never let myself have, and I am so grateful for your generous, kind, empathetic, *sharp* editing, for reassuring me so much along the way. For changing my life. Please keep posting bunny content forever and ever and ever.

Catalina Trigo—you have held so much together over the last year and I'm so grateful you've been along for this ride since day one. For the many astute, detailed notes, joyful responses, and, of course, the many conversations and back-and-forths about Taylor Swift. What an absolute thrill.

To the broader team at Riverhead: Most days, I cannot believe I ended up here and am certain there has been a clerical error. Kitanna Hiromasa, Viviann Do, Nora Alice Demick, Glory Anne Plata, Lavina Lee, Alexis Farabaugh, Kym Surridge, thank you. And Emily Mahon, your cover is perfect.

Andrianna deLone. Everything about my writing felt so hypothetical until we found each other. You are my toughest editor and biggest champion, through all the ups and downs so far. I'm so glad you're so much smarter than me *and* so much fun. Please, let's work together forever. In the meantime, see you at Long Island Bar.

Avery Carpenter—you have been so integral to every moment of my writing life since July 8, 2018 (*Les Éditeurs, c'est parti!*). For the *incessant* rapid-fire texts I've sent you over the last six years; for your early reads, thoughtful notes, and unwavering belief in *Lo Fi*; and for the friendship I didn't even know was missing in my life—thank you.

Caitlin Stubner, you are in so much of this book; you are in so much of my Nashville. What a gift to stumble through nearly half of my life with you. To all the shows, nights at Mercy Lounge and the Villager, to So Much Man and Apache Relay—thank you for keeping me cool, for giving so much of your cool to Sloane.

To my professors at NYU: Nathan Englander, Katie Kitamura, Hari Kunzru, John Freeman—I owe you immensely for your wisdom and generosity. To the provost's Global Research Initiative, as well as Deborah Landau and Lisa Gerard for running the incredible Writers in Paris program.

To the many talented writers who read so much of my early work with such kindness and honesty—Jessica Anya Blau, Daisy Alpert Florin, Louise Kennedy, Andrew Porter, Stephen Fishbach, Shanteka Sigers, Hayley Phelan. Extra special thanks to Jenni Zellner—in my mind, we always live at Suze's. And Ellen Wright: they'll never be used to such loud women on Mondays. Erin Connal, for all the phone calls and sharp reads, among other things.

Sheila Yasmin Marikar, Colleen McKeegan, Brittany Kerfoot—for your early and ongoing encouragement and feedback. Lina Patton, for reading an early draft of this book and venting with me on the phone *many* times about *many* things. I can't wait for *The Summer Club.*

Heather Karpas and Cat Shook, for making connections and responding to panic texts.

Several books helped build out Al's world and musical knowledge in *Lo Fi*, in particular Oliver Sacks's *Musicophilia: Tales of Music and the*

Brain and Daniel Levitin's *This Is Your Brain on Music.* There is also an homage in this book to Sleeping at Last's "Seven"—a song that got me through the pandemic.

So many friends over the years have saved me from my own music taste, from listening to the same songs over and over and over. Some of you even co-hosted the Real Life Dead Air. Maggie Effler, Chelsea Doyle, Hampton Howerton, Theo Beidler, Em Miller, Krista Schmitt, Sam Sosey, Shuhei Yamamoto, Sam Hughes, Emma Supica, Chelsea Johnson. An extra special thanks to Bo Brannen for opening the door to the entire Nashville scene.

Chris Youngblood, the Buzards, Ryan Scott, The Masons.

Court Bailey and Judson Collier: my *Lo Fi* Braintrust, among other things.

Alyce Youngblood, thank you for listening to every possible detail of this process, for laughing at screenshots of copyedits, for reading this book on a screen. For making all my recent Nashville memories a little brighter.

Jess Tantisook—so many songs, so many shows, so many memories. You're everywhere in *Lo Fi.*

Campbell Moore: Thank you for bringing me onto the fabulous lou team as a Personality Hire with no experience. For making me laugh, especially in the midst of rejections and endless waiting. For so many memories in Nashville and Paris. To many more tinis.

Victoria Quirk and Ellen Pelletier for the badass photos. Nicole Mendoza, Emma Morrison, Hugh Trimble, Chris Housman, Julia Knight, Mailea Wegner, for so many lovely memories at and around lou. Alex Pepel, for being one of *Lo Fi*'s earliest readers in book form and bringing so much joy into my nights at lou. All of you, there is no *Lo*(u) *Fi* without you.

Garret Koehler, Ben Majoy, thank you for being creative forces and beautiful friends in my life and encouraging my writing always. Andrew Koehler, thank you for reading this book as a PDF and showering me with compliments, among other things.

To the team at Instruction Partners: many of my "day jobs" supported me over the last fifteen years as I figured out just what kind of writer I wanted to be, but none quite as ardently as you. Extra special thanks to Elizabeth Ramsey, Kelsey Hendricks, Bonnie Williamson-Zerwic, Camesha Jones.

Joelle Herr and The Bookshop—thank you for cheering me on, for opening one of my favorite sanctuaries in Nashville. Another big thank-you to Jessica Pearson and Neta Harris.

Alison Taylor, thank you for your early reads, endless enthusiasm, and friendship. Stephanie Smith, for your guidance while I was applying to NYU.

Steven Bauer, Don Daiker, and Miami University, thank you. Tim Clutter, who unfortunately will not see this—it was in your class where I first thought: *This* is what I want to do.

David Supica and Mike Harris for answering many questions about venues, tour buses, and riders, among other things.

Rebecca Walker—for knowing just the right way to push me forward and keep me sane.

My Paris crew, especially Aurelie and Alessio Zenaro (& ZoZo!).

My family—Emily, Patrick, Ellen, Neal, Austin, Andrea. Austin: extra special thanks for all the music we listened to driving to AHS. And of course my parents, for encouraging me to pursue this dream and supporting it in so many ways. You have given me everything.

This book was written in many places, most of which are in my home, but Café Roze, Living Waters, and Mokonuts deserve special thanks.

Willie and Ozzie, my gremlins!

Tyler, Tyler, Tyler: Without you, none of this would be worth it. My first reader, first editor. It has always made sense that we fell in love with each other's words first. I can't wait to hold your own novel in my hands someday soon. I love you so much. You, my dear, are home.